Slocum held his pistol ~~~~~~~~ ~~~ ~~~~~ ~~~~~~~ toward the pair. The men didn't see him until he was twenty
feet away.

One turned and said, "That you, Al? You're back mighty
quick."

Slocum raised his six-shooter and fired. The bullet
caught the man in the head. As he fell, the other outlaw realized his mistake. He went for his six-gun, only to discover he had taken off his gun belt when he had started
raping the woman. He spun and dived for it.

Slocum didn't cotton much to shooting a man in the
back. This time he made an exception. The man died as he
pried his six-shooter from its holster. He twitched, and
Slocum shot him again . . .

JAKE LOGAN

SLOCUM
AND THE
TOWN KILLERS

JOVE BOOKS, NEW YORK

THE BERKLEY PUBLISHING GROUP
Published by the Penguin Group
Penguin Group (USA) Inc.
375 Hudson Street, New York, New York 10014, USA
Penguin Group (Canada), 90 Eglinton Avenue East, Suite 700, Toronto, Ontario M4P 2Y3, Canada
(a division of Pearson Penguin Canada Inc.)
Penguin Books Ltd., 80 Strand, London WC2R 0RL, England
Penguin Group Ireland, 25 St. Stephen's Green, Dublin 2, Ireland (a division of Penguin Books Ltd.)
Penguin Group (Australia), 250 Camberwell Road, Camberwell, Victoria 3124, Australia
(a division of Pearson Australia Group Pty. Ltd.)
Penguin Books India Pvt. Ltd., 11 Community Centre, Panchsheel Park, New Delhi—110 017, India
Penguin Group (NZ), 67 Apollo Drive, Rosedale, North Shore 0632, New Zealand
(a division of Pearson New Zealand Ltd.)
Penguin Books (South Africa) (Pty.) Ltd., 24 Sturdee Avenue, Rosebank, Johannesburg 2196,
South Africa

Penguin Books Ltd., Registered Offices: 80 Strand, London WC2R 0RL, England

SLOCUM AND THE TOWN KILLERS

A Jove Book / published by arrangement with the author

PRINTING HISTORY
Jove edition / December 2008

Copyright © 2008 by Penguin Group (USA) Inc.
Cover illustration by Sergio Giovine.

ISBN: 978-0-515-14550-2

JOVE®
Jove Books are published by The Berkley Publishing Group,
a division of Penguin Group (USA) Inc.
375 Hudson Street, New York, New York 10014.
JOVE® is a registered trademark of Penguin Group (USA) Inc.
The "J" design is a trademark belonging to Penguin Group (USA) Inc.

PRINTED IN THE UNITED STATES OF AMERICA

10 9 8 7 6 5 4 3 2 1

1

"Kill them. Kill them all!"

A cheer went up from the thirty gathered men, who waved pistols in the air, anxious to get on with the slaughter.

Clayton Magee sat a little straighter on his nervous black stallion. The horse was as eager to get into the fray as the men arrayed in front of him. Magee straightened his Union uniform with its faded gold braid and numerous rips, and bent forward so that the morning sun glinted off his major's insignia to give more authority to his words.

"You know the standing orders," Major Magee said. "There will be no killing."

"Until we've made sure *they're* not among the combatants," Albert Kimbrell said, some of the crazy fire dying in his dark eyes.

"Find them. If they are there, find them and take them into custody. They must not be harmed in any way." His fingers tapped on the butt of the pistol slung at his right hip.

"Then kill everyone else?" The insane fury returned to the smaller man's eyes. He watched closely until Magee nodded the slightest amount. "Can I give the word, Major?" Kimbrell asked, keyed up and breathing more harshly than before.

Magee looked at his second in command. If Kimbrell

was eager to get on with the attack, Magee felt only a hollowness inside. He sought. How he sought. And always he failed to find those he sought so tenaciously. One day, though, he would find. Until then . . .

"Attack," Magee said.

"Get 'em, boys, get 'em all!" Kimbrell fired his six-shooter into the air as a signal, as if the small army needed such an order. More than half had already jumped the gun. The thunder of hooves pounding against the dry Oklahoma road leading into Cherokee Springs brought the early stirring residents out, eager to see if storm clouds building on the horizon had finally delivered much-needed relief from a monthlong drought.

This thunder brought only leaden death.

Major Magee sat astride his stallion, eyes closed as he listened to the sharp reports of dozens of Colts firing until their hammers landed on spent chambers. He had trained his men well. During the war, a handful of guerrillas, riding with multiple six-shooters slung around hips and in shoulder rigs, had sported more firepower than an entire company of soldiers carrying only muskets. His small army carried not only half a dozen six-guns each, but also two rifles. A single pass through Cherokee Springs would send over a thousand rounds through buildings—and people.

Screams reached his ears, but Magee did not open his eyes. He had seen the carnage many times before. What he longed to hear was Kimbrell or another of his men sing out with the joyful cry that his search was at an end.

"Major!"

Magee's eyes shot open. Albert Kimbrell rode back. His face was streaked with half-burnt gunpowder from firing all his pistols. A rifle rested in the crook of his arm. From the way he lifted it off his sleeve, the barrel was hot from half a dozen rounds being fired as fast as he could cock and pull the trigger.

"You've found them?" Even as he asked, he knew the answer. Major Magee slumped in resignation. Cherokee Springs had been a long shot. Information had reached him from unreliable sources, but he was too desperate not to ride here and see for himself.

"Sorry, Major. Not a trace," Kimbrell said. He was almost gasping for breath. Through the soot on his face showed a flush that faded slowly. "What're your orders?"

"I'll reconnoiter personally." Magee put his heels to his black stallion's flanks and rode forward slowly. Earlier in his quest, he had ridden at the head of his men with every incursion. Over the past few weeks, the killing had come to wear down his spirit and cast him into a great, dark depression.

By the time Major Magee trotted into town, most of the killing had been done. It wasn't the smell of blood or the sight of so many dead that caused his melancholy, but the growing awareness that he might never find those he sought so diligently.

His horse tried to rear when it smelled fresh blood. Magee held it down until its fright passed. Men and women lay sprawled in the street where they had been gunned down without quarter. A few had been shot in the back as they tried to flee to safety. There was no way for them to realize that nothing in Cherokee Springs would have afforded them safety. Magee's men were too efficient and bloodthirsty.

The wanton killings didn't matter to Magee. The townspeople were guilty of hiding what he wanted most in the world. If not the citizens of Cherokee Springs, then the next town along this road. Oklahoma was a big territory, but he would not stop until he succeeded. He rode about for a while, and finally circled back to where Kimbrell knelt beside a man who had been shot down trying to take refuge behind a water barrel. The barrel staves had been riddled with bullets, causing water to pour out onto dry ground where it mixed with the man's blood and begot a gory mud.

Kimbrell had the man's hand in his, holding it up to examine the ring on the man's right hand. He drew a knife from a sheath in his boot top and applied it to the bone just under the ring. Kimbrell sawed back and forth a couple times before the finger, with the ring still on it, popped free. He worked the ring around and around, but it would not come off the severed digit. He held up ring and finger to the morning sun and smiled.

"None of them, Albert?" Magee's question startled Kimbrell. The man hastily shoved the finger with the ring still in place into his vest pocket and stood to face his commander.

"No, sir, none even look like 'em." The flush had gone from Kimbrell's face and a tic under his left eye caused it to almost close with every spasm. "I checked 'em all myself."

"Yes, of course," Magee said. At one time he had done this himself, but they had found towns, much like Cherokee Springs, where there had been too many residents for one man to roll over every likely body and look it square in the face. He gave strict orders about the killing, but always it seemed that his men got out of hand. With his increasing pessimism went a rage that often filled the void within his soul and gave some purpose to his life.

"You checked before the killing began?"

"Oh, yes, sir," Kimbrell said. He bobbed his head up and down. "'Fore we fired a single shot, we looked the place over. Uh, is it all right for the men to get on with it?"

"Loot the town. Be sure to take enough supplies to get us to the next possible sighting."

Magee did not wait to see the fierce grin on his lieutenant's face. He dismounted and began walking about, looking at the bodies. A booted toe poked into the side of a man lying facedown in the street. The man moaned and stirred.

"Help me. Murderin' savages. Yer a soldier. Help me—"

Magee drew his pistol, cocked, and fired in a smooth motion. The slug blew off the side of the man's head, killing him outright. Magee's right arm turned to lead and fell to his side, the six-shooter dangling from almost nerveless fingers as he began walking about, looking at the dead and shooting the few his men had carelessly left alive. When his pistol came up empty, he returned it to his holster and walked a little faster.

They got what they deserved, harboring the two he

sought. If they had not hidden them, he would have found them by now. It was all a vast cabal to keep the two from being found, and he would have none of it.

He went into the dry-goods store. This was always the first building he searched. Bolts of cloth had been knocked from shelves. A few had unrolled in a red and green carpet under his boots. Magee walked over the cloth without so much as an instant's hesitation. None of this was useful. And none of the several dead in the store, draped over counters and sprawled on the floor, were those he sought.

The major stopped and pictured the ones who had slipped through his fingers. His hands clenched into fists. Then he spun about and stormed from the store.

Kimbrell had finished robbing the bank. The money from the vault would be divided equally among the men. Magee was more interested in what was taken from the general store and a gunsmith nearby. Their supply wagon had rattled along the rocky Oklahoma roads, increasingly empty over the past week. They needed supplies desperately. More than one of his men's weapons had become damaged through overuse and lack of cleaning and oiling. No matter how he issued the orders—sometimes forcefully, at other times as a father might chide a son—they refused to maintain their six-shooters properly. They needed replacements.

"Got two crates of brand-spankin'-new rifles, Major!" One of the newer men in his company, one with knife scars crisscrossing his face and attesting to a violent trail through the West, waved to him. "I got half a dozen six-guns, too."

"Distribute them judiciously," Magee ordered.

"How's that?"

"Make sure the damned men who need the damned guns get 'em, shit-for-brains," snapped Kimbrell.

"Enough," Magee said, seeing how the scar-faced man bristled at the insult. "See to it. I want a word with you, Mr. Kimbrell."

Kimbrell looked around like a fox standing outside the henhouse.

"I'll be brief," Magee promised.

"What is it, Major?"

"They weren't here?"

"Told you that already. We got to move on."

"Yes," Magee said tiredly. "We must move on. Never slow, never stay our hunt. We may find the spoor in the next town."

"We 'bout got this town gutted." Kimbrell shifted nervously.

"What is it?" Magee saw that Kimbrell wanted something more.

"The saloon. Saloons, actually, since there are several of 'em. Can I throw a few cases of booze into the wagons for the men? For the celebration?"

"They got knee-walking drunk the last time," Magee said. Then old lessons returned. Morale. The men remained with him because they chose to do so of their own free will. This was not the army where deserters could be executed. "Yes, do it. What else?"

Kimbrell licked his lips. "Well, sir, there might be a woman or two left in town."

"You mean left alive?"

"Don't much matter since they'd still be warm."

Magee let the momentary dizziness pass over him. He had long ago realized it was not useful to inquire too deeply about Kimbrell's and the others' personal tastes.

"Burn the town when you're done," Magee said.

"Yes, *sir*!"

Clayton Magee mounted and rode through Cherokee Springs looking at the dead until the crackling of burning buildings forced him to ride to the far side of town. He never looked back at the fire devouring the stores. His thoughts were fixed on the next town and, for a while, hope flared. Maybe in the next town he would find those he hunted.

He trotted off, letting Kimbrell muster the men behind him and follow. It was only fitting for a leader to be at the head of the column.

2

John Slocum wiped sweat from his forehead, trying to keep ahead of the muggy Oklahoma day but failing. He pushed his floppy-brimmed hat back on his forehead and looked around. The sun beat down out of a clear blue sky, and the distance vanished in a gray haze promising more stifling heat without any relief from a rainstorm. He patted his horse on the neck and got an aggrieved whinny in response.

"We should find some shelter, I know," Slocum told the sturdy paint. "These sweet gum trees aren't going to give us enough shade. Let's get on into the next town and rest a day or two there."

The horse showed approval with a toss and shake of its head. Slocum settled down again for the rest of the ride. From his recollection, there was a town not too far away. He couldn't remember the name, but what did it matter? He was on his way out of St. Louis heading down into Texas. What he expected to find in Texas he could not say, only that it wasn't St. Louis or Missouri or any of the unlucky poker games and unwilling women he had found there.

Unwilling except for one with a jealous husband Slocum had not known existed. Shotguns, too much liquor, and lying women made a mix Slocum chose to avoid.

The road came on him suddenly. Slocum turned left and right before deciding on the route westward. He urged his horse to a trot, then slowed and finally halted entirely. He dismounted and studied the road. A frown crept onto his face as he tried to count the number of horsemen that had preceded him this way. The horses were shod, so he doubted they were Indians. The disorganized way the horses had milled about, cutting up sere grass on either side of the road before finding the double-rutted dirt path, made him wonder if a cavalry troop was ahead of him. The number was about right.

"One way to find out," he said to his horse. This time he got no answer since the paint was too busy cropping at the trampled grass. Letting the horse eat a few minutes longer, Slocum continued to explore the trampled area. A few dropped cartridges, all for a .44, made him reconsider his guess that this was a company of cavalry. Soldiers were not usually so careless with their ammo. Every round meant life or death in a fierce fight. He tried to get an idea of the lay of the land. Any soldiers would come from Fort Gibson, although that was some miles away eastward.

Slocum shrugged it off as he mounted. The paint reluctantly allowed him to follow the hoofprints until he came to a badly painted sign promising him that he was almost inside the town limits of Cherokee Springs.

Slocum did not remember the name from any map he had seen, but it hardly mattered what the town was called. Towns came and went fast, sometimes not even being boomtowns that had a reason for existing and then dying. He wanted a meal that wasn't half burned over an open fire, and his horse could use a good currying and a bag of oats. He had enough money for all that, and then some. The poker in St. Louis hadn't been *too* bad.

The road went directly up the side of a low hill, but Slocum stopped and stared before he reached the ridge. A tiny curl of smoke appeared, then was carried away on a fitful breeze. Slocum sniffed hard and caught the stench of burned wood—and meat. His stomach churned at the all-too-familiar smell. He had gone through more than one battle during the war with this peculiar, gut-twisting smell lingering in his nostrils and on his uniform. No amount of washing or nightmares ever entirely removed the memories.

If he had the sense God gave a goose, he would have reversed his course and ridden east. That was as good a direction as any and promised less misery. Or he could have ridden south. Eventually, he would cross the Red River and find himself in Texas. Any of those options was still open to him.

Slocum rode to the top of the rise and looked down at Cherokee Springs. The source of most of the smoke was obvious. Half the town was still enveloped in flames eating away at what remained of walls. Even as he watched, one roof fell into a building amid a tower of sparks that cascaded down onto other buildings and ignited more fires.

The smell of burned human flesh was not hidden by the new fires.

Hating every instant of it and fighting to keep his more sensible horse from bolting and running away, Slocum made his way slowly into Cherokee Springs. Everywhere he looked he saw dead bodies. In the streets, hanging out of windows in smoldering buildings, in the fires. He started breathing in short, quick gasps through his mouth, then gave up and pulled his bandanna up over his nose and mouth. The cloth ought to be wet to keep out the worst of the odors.

Slocum dismounted and made sure his horse was securely tied to a post before going to a rain barrel. It had so many holes in it, there was hardly any water left. He dipped his bandanna in it, then wrung it out and tied it tightly around his nose. This made it almost bearable to breathe.

Almost.

He began a careful search of the town for survivors. The bank had been looted before being set ablaze. Slocum found three men inside, all charred. From what remained of one's clothing, Slocum guessed he was the bank president. The other two might have been tellers. All three were laid out side by side. In his mind, he pictured what had happened. They had been forced from behind the tellers' cages and ordered to lie down beside the bank officer. All three had been shot in the back more times than he cared to count. One shot would have been callous. So many needless shots after the men were long dead was sadistic.

He bent and picked up a dozen brass cartridges. All were .44s. The owlhoots doing the killing had reloaded so they could keep firing into dead bodies. Slocum tossed the brass from him angrily. He had seen savagery during the war. He had ridden with William Quantrill and had taken part in the Lawrence, Kansas, raid. Kill every man above the age of eight had been the order. Burn the town to the ground. There had been more than the killing of young boys that had sickened Slocum then. He had protested, and been shot in the gut and left for dead.

He had recovered slowly, but the hatred for such brutalities had never faded. Slocum picked up a few greenbacks that had survived the fire and tucked them into his pocket. These pieces of paper might be the only survivors of the vicious raid.

Store by store, building by building, he searched for anyone still alive. When he came to the only saloon in town that had not burned, he wished he had found some other place. Three of the Cyprians who had worked in the bar were stripped naked and laid out, one on a green felt-covered poker table and the other two across the billiards table. They had been raped. Slocum couldn't tell if it had been before or after their throats had been slit with such power that their heads were almost separated from their bodies.

He had toyed with the idea of burying the dead, but the sheer numbers dissuaded him. Getting everyone decently planted, even in a mass grave, would take more effort than he was willing to expend. It might be a week to gather all the bodies, and Slocum was increasingly anxious to leave Cherokee Springs.

He found a bottle of liquor behind the bar and pulled the

cork out with his teeth. He spat it in the direction of the three raped whores and raised the bottle in salute.

"You deserved better," he said. "Might be I can find who did this to you and settle accounts." He took a long pull of the whiskey and almost gagged. It was trade whiskey that had not cured long enough. The rusty-nail taste lingered, and the hydrochloric acid the barkeep had added for kick burned at his lips and tongue. Even though it blistered his mouth, Slocum took another swig, letting it sear all the way down to his belly.

He flung the bottle away and left the saloon without a backward glance at the three women.

There were too many more dead in Cherokee Springs for him to mourn just a trio of soiled doves he had never met.

He began hunting for supplies he would need to keep him on the trail of the men who had done this massacre. Even if he had not seen the evidence of shod horses riding into town, he would not have believed any of the Oklahoma Indians were capable of such violence. They weren't called the Five Civilized Tribes for nothing. Chickasaw, Choctaw, and Seminole, along with the Creek and Cherokee, had fought fiercely in the past, but since the war those days had been over. They had settled down in Indian Territory and had been peaceful, as such things went. Part of this was the iron hand of Judge Parker over in Fort Smith, but mostly the tribes wanted to be left alone and to govern themselves.

Slocum saw not a single hint amid the killing and pillage to show that Indians had been responsible.

"Looks like guerrillas who can't believe the war is over," he said aloud. He had no idea if the gang rampaging through had ridden with the Union or cleaved to Southern ways, nor did it matter. Missouri and Kansas had bred a particularly vicious variety of war and warrior. It was too bad for the people of Cherokee Springs that their killers had never forgotten the old days.

Slocum lugged an armful of airtights from the general store and dumped them near his still-nervous horse. The smell of burnt wood and human blood would keep the horse jittery until they were long gone.

Although he knew what he would find, he turned back to make a quick run through the rest of Cherokee Springs. The hotel had been burned to the ground with most of the customers still inside. The schoolhouse had been partially destroyed, but the attack had come too early for any children to be inside. Slocum doubted that would have mattered to any of the gang raping the entire town. Incongruously, the church at the edge of town remained unscathed.

He went inside and stood for a moment, looking at the altar. Soot had blown in through the open doors. Otherwise, nothing in the church looked out of place. There was an eerie silence, though, that ate away at Slocum's soul— or what remained of it. He felt only coldness and the desire to do to the killers what they had done to this town. Such unbridled ferocity could only be met with equal ferocity.

Then he sagged down and sat in the back pew, head bowed. He was not the one to bring the killers to justice. There were too many of them and the murders had been committed on such a large scale that even the entire cavalry in all of Indian Territory might have trouble stopping them.

Slocum knew that, having gotten away with destroying so thoroughly an entire town, they would repeat the atrocities. Even simple murder and rape would not be enough. For all he knew, Cherokee Springs was not the first town they had delivered such vengeance upon. But in his gut he knew it was not going to be the last. Such hatred could only be snuffed out with a noose or a bullet.

Looking up, he stared at the altar and wondered what fate the minister had suffered. Slocum hoped the man of the cloth had truly believed in Heaven because that was where he was bound.

Slocum put his hands on the back of the pew in front and heaved to his feet. He was done here and had found no peace in the house of the Lord. As he stepped out into the noonday sun beating down so harshly, he rested his hand on the ebony butt of his Colt Navy slung in its cross-draw holster. He was as ready as he could be to move on. After the butchers who had destroyed Cherokee Springs.

Slocum froze when he heard a slight sound behind him in the church. He turned slowly, drawing his six-gun. Moving deliberately, he went back into the church, but stopped just inside the door this time. He pulled down his bandanna and took a deep whiff, trying to identify the odor that had not been here even a few seconds earlier. Nose working like a rabbit's, he homed in on the flowery scent. He went to the side of the church and looked around. He heard nothing and the faint rose odor—it had to be roses—disappeared amid a strong gust of wind blowing from the direction of the town. Whatever respite the flower scent had given, it was gone now, once more buried under the ugly stench of burned buildings and charred human flesh.

He shoved his pistol back into his holster, backed away, still alert, then left the church. His stride long, he walked back to his horse. Somewhere along the way, his bandanna had finally dried out. For a few yards, Slocum thought he would not need the filter of a water-soaked rag across his nose, but when he began gagging so hard his stomach felt as if it would empty, he turned toward another water barrel. Like the first one, this had been filled with more lead than he could imagine being fired at an inanimate object. He yanked off the bandanna and thrust it into the water remaining in the barrel. As he stood and wrung it out, he froze.

The soft moan was almost too low to hear. Slocum finished his chore and tied the bandanna around his face, then turned slowly, hand moving to his holstered six-shooter. When he homed in on the sound, he drew, cocked, and aimed in one smooth motion.

"Who's there?" Slocum wanted to take no chances. If a resident had survived, the man was likely to shoot first and keep firing until his pistol came up empty. Slocum wouldn't have faulted him for that either, not after the carnage he had seen already.

"Help me," said the weak voice.

Slocum saw a body mostly buried in mud formed by the draining water barrel and a goodly amount of blood. If he had not called out, the man would have gone unseen, part of the ground rather than a human being. This was probably how he had survived the slaughter.

Cautiously circling, Slocum made sure he wasn't walking into a trap, then shoved his six-gun back into his holster as he knelt. His hand pressed down into mud and dried blood to find a quaking arm.

"Help me," sobbed the man, still facedown. Slocum took hold of the man's shirt and tugged, trying to figure out how badly he had been hurt. As the man's body came off the muddy ground, Slocum saw. He sucked in his breath and then heaved once to roll the man onto his back. A shriek of pain escaped the man's lips.

"Thanks," he said to Slocum in a voice hardly above a hoarse whisper. "I couldn't roll over. I wanted to see the sky again 'fore I died."

"Nickson? Are you Jerome Nickson?" Slocum used his fingertips to remove the mud and gore from the man's face. It was racked with pain, but it was a face that Slocum recognized.

Nickson coughed up some blood and turned toward Slocum, fighting to focus his eyes.

"As I live and breathe, it's John Slocum." He coughed again and smiled wanly. "Reckon I'm not gonna be doin' either livin' or breathin' much longer." A coughing fit lifted his shoulders off the ground. Slocum tried to hold him down. A man could do himself a powerful lot of harm by coughing so hard. Slocum wanted to make things as easy as he could for Nickson before the man died.

Slocum wiped more blood from the face of the man he had ridden with for almost six months when they had both worked for the Cross T ranch. Those had been good times, and they always had full bellies and earned reasonable wages, thanks to the Cross T owner, Ben Charteris. Charteris has been killed in a stampede. Nickson had tried to save their boss and had failed in the attempt, getting thrown when his horse stepped in a prairie-dog hole. Slocum had saved his life then, but there was nothing he could do now.

"The whole town's been shot up and burned," Slocum said. "Who did it? I can tell the federal marshal or maybe ride back to Fort Gibson and let the army know."

"The army," said Nickson in a voice as natural as if he was bellied up to a bar, cold beer in his hand. "I was in the army."

"Yeah, I know," said Slocum. "You were a Federal."

"That never came 'tween us did it, Slocum?"

"Never did. The war's over."

"You know I was a captain?"

"Reckon you mentioned it," Slocum said. He had seen the West Point ring Nickson always wore, in spite of being surrounded by former Rebels at every turn down in Texas. Most of the cowboys they worked with had not cared and seldom spoke of their own backgrounds. They certainly never pried. Even in as friendly an outfit as the Cross T, poking around asking questions about another man's history was a good way to end up dead.

"You know I had a son?"

"That you never mentioned," Slocum said, not too surprised. One subject Nickson had always steered clear of was his personal life. Slocum figured it was a sore spot, just as his own was. After the war Slocum had returned home to Calhoun county, Georgia, to recuperate from wounds, only to find a carpetbagger judge had taken a fancy to the farm that had been in the Slocum family for generations. Bogus tax claims had been filed, and Slocum had found himself on the wrong end of an eviction notice.

The judge and his hired gunman had come out to seize the farm. They got more than they had bargained for. Slocum buried both of them near the springhouse, then rode West, never looking back. The wanted posters had followed him like a bloodhound on the scent, but he had kept ahead of the law and arrest on charges of judge killing. He doubted Nickson had such a sordid past, but he figured a woman played a more prominent role in the man's reluctance not to talk much about himself.

"Never did right by him," Nickson said. "I wasn't that good a husband and was a damn sight worse as a father. Slocum"—Nickson reached out and clutched Slocum's sleeve—"I don't have anything to give Patrick. Nothing but my West Point ring. See that he gets it."

"I will," Slocum said.

"You were always a man of your word, Slocum. You've promised. You've promised. Take it off my finger and give to Patrick and tell him not to think too poorly of me."

Nickson's fingers tightened on Slocum's arm, then relaxed a little as he died. Slocum reached over and pried the fingers loose. For a moment, Slocum couldn't figure out what wasn't right.

Then he saw. Jerome Nickson's ring finger and the ring that had been on it were both gone.

3

"Faster, Mama, we have to go faster." Sarah Beth Magee craned her neck and looked back down the road. The dust cloud kicked up by their buggy wheels obscured the road, but she felt in her gut that they were not going fast enough to get away.

"The horse is tiring, dear," her mother said. Louisa Magee snapped the reins to get their swayback mare moving faster. The horse balked, bringing the buggy to a sudden halt. "What am I going to do? The horse just won't keep up the pace." Louisa pushed a strand of blond hair back under her wide-brimmed hat. The unconscious gesture caused the flower-decorated hat to go flying. "Oh!" she cried as it sailed away on the sudden wind.

"I'll get it, Mama."

"But we have to keep moving," Louisa protested.

"The mare's not budging. I can convince her to move." With that, Sarah Beth jumped to the ground and wobbled a bit. Her long legs had been cramped in the buggy all day long, but there had been no way to stretch them—not if they wanted to continue traveling to stay ahead of her pa.

She hurried back to grab her mother's Sunday-go-to-meeting hat before the fitful wind blew it into the ditch alongside the road. Sarah Beth snared it and tucked the hat under her arm as she rushed back. Her mother snapped the reins, but the horse refused to do more than twitch her tail about to keep off buzzing deer flies.

"There's nothing we can do," Louisa moaned. She sank down in the buggy seat, slumped forward in defeat. She began to sob.

"There, there, Mama, we'll reach town before Pa catches us."

"He's so close. What he did to that town!"

"Cherokee Springs," Sarah Beth said. Her lips thinned to a determined line, and she lifted her chin defiantly. "We'll get to safety, Mama. I know it, but we can't give up. He'll get us for sure if we quit." She handed her mother the hat, now dirty and all the worse for the wear and tear. Louisa took it, brushed off the dirt, and smiled wanly.

"Where do you get that optimism? Not from me." Louisa smiled a little, then turned grim again. "Certainly not from your father."

"I'll talk to the horse," Sarah Beth said. She went to look the mare squarely in the eye. She pressed her corn-flower blue eye within an inch of the horse's big brown eye. For a long minute, she and the horse had a stare-down. Then the horse neighed and tossed her head about.

"She'll go now," Sarah Beth said, backing away. Barely had she gotten out of the way when the horse rushed past. Sarah Beth jumped and caught the side of the buggy, pulling herself up to land hard beside her mother.

"I don't know what you did, but it's a miracle," Louisa Magee said. She put her head down a little and stared ahead. Now and then she snapped the reins, but the horse was trotting along on its own, taking the two women for the ride.

A half hour later, Sarah Beth rose in the buggy and pointed.

"There, Mama, there's a town. Charity! How can we go wrong in a town called Charity? They'll have to help us."

"It had better be a big town. Remember what your father

did to Cherokee Springs. There must have been a hundred people there."

Sarah Beth's heart sank when she saw a sign proclaiming Charity to have safe water—and a population of only seventy-eight. It was smaller than Cherokee Springs. There was no way such a small town could stand against Clayton Magee and his men, unless . . .

"Find the marshal, Mama," Sarah Beth said as they neared the tight knot of houses at the edge of town. "If they're waiting, lying in ambush, the townspeople can stop them. Give those bastards some of their own medicine!"

"Watch your language, young lady."

"Mama, I'm nineteen years old. I've heard worse. I've said worse."

"You shouldn't."

"This isn't the time or place to discuss my manner of speech, Mama," Sarah Beth said. "There! There's the marshal's office. Stop now."

Louisa Magee braced her feet against the front of the buggy and leaned back, tugging hard on the reins. The mare stopped so fast both women were thrown forward. Sarah Beth tumbled from the buggy into the dusty street. Aware of the attention she was getting, she got to her feet, but did not bother brushing herself off. She walked around the buggy, only to be stopped by her mother.

"Don't, Sarah Beth. Think what you're doing to them."

"What?" Sarah Beth stared at her mother. "What *I'm* doing to *them*? Think what Papa and his butchers will do to everyone in Charity!"

"He won't hurt them, not if we keep going. Please, Sarah Beth, don't tell them."

"Why are you sticking your head in the sand like one of those African ostriches, Mama? Cherokee Springs was completely destroyed because of him. He'll do it again and again." Sarah Beth closed her eyes and wobbled a mite. Then her eyes opened and she finished in a cold tone. "Until he catches us. I don't know what he will do to me, but I can guess what he'll do to you."

"I'm his wife," Louisa said in a tiny, trapped-animal voice.

"A man who slaughters dozens—hundreds!—of people is not going to kiss and make up. Even if he wanted to, do you think those cutthroats riding in his gang would let him?"

"Kimbrell is an animal," Louisa said weakly.

"An animal isn't cruel like Kimbrell. Even a cat playing with a mouse isn't cruel like Albert Kimbrell." Sarah Beth pushed past her mother and opened the door to the marshal's office. The musty smell hit her like a club, but she went in anyway.

The marshal looked up from his desk where a newspaper was spread out. He puffed away at a dirty pipe that released clouds of noxious smoke that partially hid his face. All Sarah Beth could tell was that he had a goatee and a bushy brown mustache. As her mother came in, leaving the door open, a gust of humid air pushed the blue smoke away from the marshal's face. He was younger than Sarah Beth had thought on first look.

"What kin I do fer you ladies?"

"You the town marshal?"

"Lester Vannover," he said, putting his pipe down carefully on the desk at his elbow. Then he meticulously folded the paper and placed it on the far edge of his desk, as if it were some sort of peace offering to his visitors. "What brings you here?"

Sarah Beth and her mother exchanged a quick glance. Sarah Beth saw that her mother was not going to say a word. So she let her concerns come tumbling out before she lost her nerve.

"Whoa, little lady, draw rein and let me git this straight. You're sayin' Cherokee Springs got burned to the ground?"

"Every last man, woman, and child was murdered," Sarah Beth said.

"You saw this?"

"We did," Louisa said. "We were only a few minutes ahead. He killed them all, hoping to find my daughter and me."

"A man would kill a couple hunnerd folks jist to take you two prisoner? Now, excuse me when I say this, you're both lovely women, bein' blondes and all, but I can't believe no man would commit such a terrible crime jist because of you."

"He's crazy," Sarah Beth said. "There's no stopping him and his men. He's crazy but his men are even crazier."

"Albert Kimbrell is the worst of the lot."

"Kimbrell, you say?" Marshal Vannover dug around in his top desk drawer and pulled out a stack of wanted posters. Carefully removing the top one and looking at it, he went to the next, and the next. The fourth wanted poster he held up for Sarah Beth and Louisa. "This the outlaw?"

"Yes!" Sarah Beth blurted. Her mother covered her mouth with her hand. Kimbrell had a five-hundred-dollar reward on his head for more crimes than she could read in the small print.

"Yes, ma'am, a real desperado. You say him and this Clayton Magee are on their way to Charity?"

"With an army!"

"An army?" Marshal Vannover chuckled. "Kimbrell was in the Union Army. That what you mean?"

"My papa was a major before he was mustered out," Sarah Beth said, "but that's not what we meant."

Vannover grinned.

"You don't understand, Marshal. They wiped out Cherokee Springs. There's nothing—and no one—still alive there. They'll repeat that destruction in Charity, unless you get ready for them."

"How, Miss Magee, do I do that?"

"Ambush them when they ride into town," Sarah Beth said. "Don't give them the chance to shoot up everyone."

"I suppose it's not too hard to git a few of the fellas together."

"A few? You mean dozens. It'll take that many to stop them," Sarah Beth said. The marshal looked at her in amusement. "Please, Marshal Vannover, we're not making this up. It's serious." Sarah Beth turned to her mother for support.

Louisa Magee backed away and stood in the door, nervously looking out into the street as if her husband and his horde would come galloping up at any instant.

Sarah Beth knew that they would soon enough.

"Why don't you two go on over to the hotel and get settled?" Vannover suggested. "I'll round up a little posse and take care of your problem." Vannover tapped Kimbrell's wanted poster. "If this pans out, there might be a few dollars in it for you."

"We don't want money, we want my pa stopped," Sarah Beth said. Her voice rose to a shrill pitch. "Don't underestimate him or Kimbrell or any of the others."

"You jist run on now and let me do my job." Vannover stood and settled his gun at his side.

Sarah Beth started to say something more, then spun and pushed her mother out of the marshal's office. They were assaulted by the sultry day. Sarah Beth felt her clothing gluing to her body, but she realized it was less from the humid air than from the way she was suddenly sweating from fear.

"They'll all be killed like the others. The entire town," Louisa Magee said, looking at the citizens of Charity going about their business, unaware of how close destruction was for them and their town.

"We did what we could," Sarah Beth said. "The marshal thinks this is a joke. No, not a joke. He looked like he could use that hogleg strapped to his hip. He just has no idea what he's facing."

"There's no way to convince him," Louisa said. "Come on, Sarah Beth. Let's keep going."

"Mama, we can't. The horse is exhausted, and we don't have money to buy another. Even if we swapped, we wouldn't get a horse as good." The swayback mare turned her head and glared at Sarah Beth as if in reaction to the combination of insult and compliment.

"What are we going to do?"

"Get supplies for the road, let the horse rest, then pray that Papa doesn't get here before we can leave."

"How far is Cherokee Springs from here? I was so intent on driving, it's all a blur."

"Not far enough," Sarah Beth said. "Let's get something to eat and be on our way."

"The Christianson's Café is 'bout the best place in town, ladies," Marshal Vannover said, coming from his office. He carried a shotgun in the crook of his left arm.

"Thank you," Louisa said before her daughter could utter a word. She took Sarah Beth's arm and pulled her along down the street toward the Café. The sign above the door was freshly painted, and the interior looked inviting.

"I . . . I've lost my appetite, Mama," Sarah Beth said. "Let's leave now. We don't have to have the horse pull the buggy too fast."

"We have to stop running sometime, dear," Louisa said. "The marshal looks like he might—"

"Might nothing!" flared Sarah Beth. "He doesn't understand."

Her mother broke out crying. Sarah Beth threw her arms around the woman and hugged her close.

"You're right, Mama. We can't run forever."

They went into the restaurant and sat at a table by the only window. Sarah Beth watched anxiously as the marshal stopped one man after another in the street and talked to them. Her heart beat a tad faster when she saw that he'd recruited almost a dozen men. Then she held back a sob of disbelief as half the men shook their heads and left. The marshal had only six others to defend the town.

"They won't be able to stop them," Sarah Beth said in despair. Her mother had ordered for them, and the waiter dropped a plate of roast beef and gravy in front of her. She looked at it, then back to the marshal as he positioned men on either side of the main street, then back at the food. Sarah Beth began eating with real hunger. How she could be starving one instant and wanting nothing the next was a mystery, but the beef went down well. She gulped at a glass of water and finished before her mother did, who only picked at her meal.

"What are we going to do?"

"Get ready to leave," Louisa Magee said. "Maybe Marshal Vannover will hold them back long enough."

"What are you saying?" asked the waiter. "Who's the marshal supposed to go after?"

A bullet sang through the window above Sarah Beth's head and hit the waiter in the middle of his chest. He looked stupidly at the blossoming red flower on his chest and reached for it. Then he sank to the floor as if all his bones had turned to rubber.

"Down!" Sarah Beth jumped across the table, wrapped her arms around her mother, and bore her to the floor as more bullets broke out what remained of the window glass.

Out in the street came sporadic firing; then all hell broke loose. Sarah Beth scrambled to protect her mother and see what was going on at the same time.

"Stay down," Louisa ordered, but she was in no position to do anything about her daughter. Sarah Beth upended the table and used it as a shield to peer out from behind.

Her eyes went wide as she watched the carnage being wrought. She didn't see her father, but recognized Albert Kimbrell right away. The man had six-shooters in his hands, and fired until both were empty. In a smooth movement, he put the six-guns back into his holsters and went to the pistols shoved into his belt. Firing both guns, he galloped ahead of the rest shooting at anyone or anything that moved. Sarah Beth saw a man go down, his face a ruin from Kimbrell's bullets. Seconds later, Kimbrell shot a dog.

"What are we going to do?"

"We can't get to the buggy," Sarah Beth said. "When Papa sees it, he'll know we're in town." Sarah Beth looked toward the rear of the café. "There's got to be a way out."

"Then what? Our horse and buggy are out in the street."

"Our bags!"

"Sarah Beth, no!" Louisa grabbed for her daughter and missed by inches.

Sarah Beth crawled to the door, opened it a few inches, and peered out. Marshal Vannover had finally realized the extent of the opposition. His six deputies were fighting the best they could, but they had prepared for only a skirmish, not a major battle.

Even as she watched, two of the deputies went down under the gang's withering fire. As the men crashed to the ground, Vannover stepped out and fired both barrels of his shotgun. He took out one outlaw and caused another to yelp in pain as a pellet tore across the man's face. This drew the attention of most of the gang, giving Sarah Beth the chance to scramble outside to the buggy and grab her and her mother's bags.

"Sorry to leave you, but there's no other way," she said to the nervous horse. Sarah Beth was loath to leave the horse behind, but had no choice. The mare had carried them to safety more than once in the past three weeks since they had been on the run.

A new fusillade from her father's killers brought down another of the marshal's deputies. She cried out when she saw Vannover spin away as blood sprayed from his arm. The lawman dropped the shotgun and drew his six-shooter. He turned back and started firing.

"Shoot 'em all!" Sarah Beth cried. Her words were drowned out in the roar of rifle fire. The outlaws had exhausted their pistols and were beginning to use their rifles to devastating effect.

Sarah Beth scuttled like a crab, dragging the bags behind her. She got into the café and dropped her burden behind the table where her mother cowered.

"You shouldn't have gone out there. He's found us, oh, I knew he would find us." Louisa put her arms around herself and drew up her knees. She shivered as if she had a chill.

"Mama, come on. We've got to go. Now!"

Sarah Beth grabbed her mother's arm and tugged insistently. Louisa tried to curl up even tighter.

"He *will* kill us," Sarah Beth said brutally, "but not until after he's made you pay. Made us pay. Both of us."

"We should never have left. I could have stayed. That would have appeased him. You would have been safe."

Diminishing gunfire outside showed that the resistance to Clayton Magee and his small army was decreasing. More of the people of Charity died with every passing instant.

"Come *on*," Sarah Beth said insistently. She got her mother crawling on her hands and knees to the back of the café and then into the small kitchen. The back door stood open. The cook had already fled. Sarah Beth wasted no time in pushing her mother outside and shoving both of their bags into her hands to keep her occupied.

"I've got to get horses. We can't stay."

"He'll find us," Louisa Magee said dully.

"He might, but he'll damn well have to work hard to do it."

It took Sarah Beth only a few minutes to catch a couple of horses running loose. From the blood on the saddles, she guessed two of her father's men had been killed. She felt a small bit of pride in Marshal Vannover and the valiant fight he had put up. But he was dead now. The smell of gunpowder hung in the air, but there was no more shooting.

Sarah Beth lashed down their bags and helped her mother into the saddle, then clumsily mounted her own horse and galloped from town, hanging on to the horse for dear life. It was hard fleeing like this, leaving behind Charity and anyone still alive, but Sarah Beth had no choice. Her pa cared nothing for the others. He sought her and her mother.

Sarah Beth vowed anew that she would kill him before allowing him to touch either her or her mother again.

4

It had happened again. Slocum rode slowly toward Charity and saw Cherokee Springs instead. Fire leaped high into the sky as flames devoured buildings by twos and threes. Men and women lay dead everywhere he looked, but this time there were survivors who worked furiously to put out the fires.

"Who're you?" demanded a man with clothing so blood-soaked Slocum could not even determine the original color of the man's coat. He held a six-gun at his right side and his left arm was oozing blood.

"Not one of the men responsible for this," Slocum said.

"What do you know about them?" The man struggled to lift his six-shooter and aim it at Slocum.

"I came across Cherokee Springs just after they had left. There was one survivor." Slocum paused, wondering how much he should tell this man fighting to aim his gun. The man's hand trembled so much, Slocum began to worry about getting shot accidentally.

"Who did this? Kimbrell?"

"That's not a name I know," Slocum said.

"Who was the survivor?"

"He's dead now. He was shot up pretty bad. I have no

27

idea how he lived long enough for me to find him. Everyone else—everyone—was shot to hell and gone," Slocum said.

"So you don't have any idea who was responsible?"

"For Cherokee Springs or for here?" Slocum looked around and saw stacks of bodies piled like cordwood. The largest of the fires was under control thanks to bucket brigades and what looked like a pump and hose working out of a large water tank.

"Reckon I mean both."

"Who are you?" Slocum dismissed the threat from the man's pistol now since the harder the man tried to lift the six-gun, the more the muzzle bobbed about. Slocum had seen men at the end of their rope before, and he saw another one now.

"I'm the marshal of this here town."

"Then you have an interest in tracking the men responsible," Slocum said. He wondered if he ought to mention the promise he had made to Jerome Nickson, and finally decided against it. The marshal wasn't likely to care.

"As soon as I can git things in order, I'll be settin' out after the sons of bitches."

"How many of them did you kill, Marshal?"

"Enough. Not many. They lit out when we started shooting at them. If it hadn't been for two women what came in with the tale of what happened in Cherokee Springs, I wouldn't have had anybody ready to fight."

"Two women?"

"Right good-lookin' women, they were."

"Where are they?"

"Don't know. Things are still a mite confused around here."

"Where are the dead outlaws? You have any objection if I look them over?"

"You lookin' to rob the corpses? I don't hold with that, mister."

Slocum said nothing until the marshal jerked his gun around and pointed to a pile of about half a dozen bodies. "That's them, the ones we shot out of the saddle."

"Why'd the rest up and leave before everyone was dead?" Slocum asked.

The marshal shook his head, then turned to answer questions from two men more intent on putting out the fires that threatened their town. The lawman ignored Slocum now, leaving him to his searching of the bodies.

After ten minutes of turning out pockets and hunting for anything that might identify the outlaws, Slocum gave up. They all had money on them—upward of a hundred dollars between five men. Slocum left it in plain sight for the marshal to find. The money would go a ways toward rebuilding Charity. Not far maybe, but it seemed fitting that the men responsible for such wanton death and destruction would have their money used to remedy their crimes.

The one thing Slocum hunted for and did not find was Jerome Nickson's West Point ring. It had been too much to expect that one of the dead outlaws carried it in a pocket, or even wore it on a finger. From the number of hoofprints, Slocum reckoned there might be thirty or forty killers left in the small army rampaging across Oklahoma. One of them must have Nickson's ring. But even when—if—Slocum found the ring, he still had to track down Nickson's son.

He abandoned his search and left the already decaying pile of bodies so that he could wash his face and hands in a rain barrel, only to find it empty. The water had been used to put out a fire. Slocum used his bandanna to wipe away what gore he had accumulated, and then walked back into the middle of the main street. Charity was coming alive, like a prairie-dog town after the coyote had left. Heads popped out of windows and doors swung open until most of the survivors had gathered to listen to the marshal.

"Folks, I ain't the best talker in the world," the marshal said. "I'm about all that's left in the way of a town official. Mayor Gladstone's dead and so's all the town council."

"You're not takin' over, are you, Lester Vannover? I want a vote. We elect our leaders in Charity!"

"Shut up, Ferguson," said a man in the crowd behind the

speaker. "You're still all twisted up 'cuz you weren't elected mayor."

"I wish he had been," said a woman near Slocum. "Maybe then he'd be dead." Her eyes went wide when she realized what she had said. She looked around at the destruction and the bodies and went pale. The man with her steadied her, and then helped her to sit on the edge of an unburned boardwalk.

Slocum had seen reactions like this before. The survivors were glad others had died, and then felt guilty for it. Worse, some might feel they should have died instead of those that had. Guilt might wreck their lives or turn them into something they had never been before. Some men became stone killers and others became preachers. Slocum had no desire to stay in Charity long enough to see how this tragedy would affect those remaining.

"I'm 'bout all you got till you have an election," Marshal Vannover went on. "Hurry up and git a new mayor. I got my job to do, and I want to track the sons of bitches who did this. They got to be brought to justice."

"They killed damn near half of us, Marshal," protested another man. Ferguson had slunk off, tail between his legs. Slocum knew men like Ferguson would not stop kicking up dust for long, though.

"Don't matter. They got to be arrested, tried, and hanged for what they've done here today," Lester Vannover said. Slocum heard more in the marshal's words. The lawman was pissed that he had not taken the warning given by the two women more seriously. He blamed himself for not stopping the onslaught, and maybe thought he was responsible for not only the deaths but the burning of his hometown. Slocum saw that as a dangerous way to think. The men who thought nothing of destroying entire towns so thoroughly would not be stopped by a jerkwater town marshal, no matter how big his posse.

"I want a posse to trail them. Where'd Ferguson git off to? He's a good tracker."

A murmur passed through the crowd. Ferguson had

hightailed it. Slocum looked around and saw a few men volunteering, but not enough to matter. If they found the owlhoots responsible for hurrahing the town, they wouldn't be able to do anything about it—except die like their neighbors.

"You! You, mister," the marshal said, pushing through the crowd. Slocum froze. He knew the marshal had singled him out. "You got a dog in this fight, don't you?"

Slocum cursed Nickson and the promise made to the dying man.

"I'm looking to get back some stolen property," he said.

"Then you can ride with us. You're hereby deputized."

"Don't like that much," Slocum said. More often than not, he found himself on the wrong side of the law. He wasn't above a little bank robbing or holding up stagecoaches if the need arose. Mostly, he preferred a legitimate game of poker or faro or punching cattle. He was good at that. He had even worked as a miner, but being a deputy struck him as a whale of a lot more dangerous. Especially when he knew the type of men the marshal was likely to find at the end of the trail.

"Then you ride along without a badge. Don't have enough to go around anyway," Vannover said, a small smile curling his lips. Then he sobered. "You can track. You have the look of a man who's spent his life either running or running after."

"Done both," Slocum admitted.

"You do a good job of going after 'em and I won't pry into what you've been runnin' from," the marshal promised.

Slocum reluctantly agreed. Then he asked, "What about those two women who warned you? Are they anywhere to be seen?"

"Their buggy's still in front of the café, but their luggage's gone. I would like to ask them some more questions about this here Clayton Magee. And Kimbrell. I got a wanted poster on him. That's what made me take what they said the least bit seriously."

The marshal fumbled in his shirt pocket, pulled out a

blood-soaked wanted poster, and handed it to Slocum. "You know him?"

Slocum shook his head. Likenesses on wanted posters were seldom good, and this was probably no exception. He scanned the crimes Albert Kimbrell was wanted for, and tried to remember if he'd ever crossed paths with him. The West was wide open, and the patch around Slocum was always small. He had never set eyes on Albert Kimbrell before.

"The women were running from the leader of this gang? Clayton Magee?"

"One looked old enough to be the young one's mother, so I took 'em to be his wife and daughter. They mentioned how he was a major in the Union army. Don't reckon you ever served under him then?"

Slocum laughed ruefully. There was no chance in hell he had served under a Federal officer.

"I need to tend to my horse," Slocum said. "When are you setting out on their trail?"

"As soon as I can," the marshal said. "Poke 'round in the general store. If there's anything you can use, take it. No need to square it with the owner. He's dead." Marshal Vannover's voice took on a hollow quality. He started to say something more, then turned and went to the small knot of men who had volunteered for the posse. Slocum gave them a quick once-over, dismissing the lot as sodbusters and clerks. Not a one of them would be worth his weight in shit if they got into a fight with Magee and Kimbrell and the brutal killers riding behind them.

Slocum wondered about the women who had warned Vannover. Wife and daughter of Clayton Magee. On the run and fearful of what the man could do. Slocum wanted to talk to them. While the marshal was whipping his posse into shape, Slocum explored the area in and behind the café, eventually finding small footprints. It was the work of a few minutes to figure what had happened. The women had been eating in the café when the shooting started. The waiter was killed and the two women grabbed their bags from the buggy and ran out back. By then, stray horses were running everywhere, and they took a pair of them.

Slocum wanted to track them down, but the marshal had other ideas. Once they were on the trail of the outlaws, it might not be difficult for Slocum to slip away and find the two Magee women to get real answers. Slocum doubted it was possible, but he might get some useful information about Nickson's ring from them, too. More likely, they had already been on the run when whoever took the ring by severing Nickson's finger committed the deed.

As Slocum went back through the café, he stopped and took a deep whiff. The same scent of roses that he had scented back in the Cherokee Springs church lingered here. Slocum frowned when it occurred to him that the odor had not been present when he had first entered the café.

He stepped out into the street and looked around. He saw nothing other than what he expected. The marshal waved at Slocum to join the group of unhappy-looking men. Slocum saw how they fingered their rifles and shifted uneasily. Riding with them might be worse than trying to tackle Magee's renegade army all by himself. At least he would be certain where the bullets would come from. These men were so on edge, they would shoot at their own shadows.

"We got ourselves one of the finest trackers in all of Indian Territory," Vannover said by way of introducing Slocum to the others. They gave him a quick look and then retreated to their own worries.

"What you expecting to do, Marshal?" Slocum asked. "We can't arrest forty or more men, not when we're only a handful." He left unsaid that Magee's men would likely murder anyone they saw on their trail. There would be no palaver before lead flew.

"Find them. We'll track them and see what we might tell the cavalry 'bout them," the marshal said. "If we're lucky, we might catch a couple of them off scoutin'. We can find out more 'bout them that way."

Slocum's mind rested a little easier hearing that the marshal hadn't any highfalutin notions of what to do if they caught up with the rampaging army of killers. He was still worried that the marshal would try to be a hero to avenge what had been done to his town. The marshal's speech earlier had warned Slocum he dealt with a man whose ideals might get in the way of his common sense.

"There's not a whole lot of guesswork needed to know they rode that way," Slocum said, pointing toward the west end of town. The fires had begun on the easternmost part of Charity, and had been snuffed out before a quarter of the town had been consumed. However, men and women lay dead all the way out past the city limits to the west. Magee's gang had left town shooting as they went. "What scared them off?"

"Can't rightly say," Vannover admitted, "but if I was a gamblin' man, I'd say Magee saw his wife or daughter and lit out after them."

Slocum did not contradict the marshal, but he knew that wasn't true. Mother and daughter had gone due south and Magee's small army had gone west. Whatever had sparked the retreat on Magee's part was something other than the two women.

"I want to find out fer myself," the marshal said.

Slocum looked hard at the man. Somehow, Lester Vannover had read his mind. Slocum was a good enough poker player not to let his thoughts run all over his face. The marshal was more than he appeared, but that didn't make him any less a fool wanting to tangle with a force ten times the size of his posse.

Slocum left the marshal and the nervous posse members to fetch his horse. The paint had been ridden hard, but did not protest as Slocum climbed into the saddle. He patted the horse's neck, then gently urged the animal forward to join the marshal and his deputies. Slocum took the lead, following the trail without any effort. He thought hard as he rode on the trail of Magee, Kimbrell, and the others.

He thought, but found no answers. Nickson's ring had to be on the finger of an outlaw, but winnowing them down to find the thief would take more than a few men in a posse. Slocum couldn't keep his promise by brute force; he had to find a way to sneak up and steal the ring back so he could deliver it to Patrick Nickson, wherever he might be.

"Stop!" Slocum barked. He held up his hand, then pointed along the road toward a grove of trees.

"What is it, Slocum?" The marshal was keyed up and his hands shook as he clung to his reins. "You spot 'em?"

"Take a deep breath," Slocum said. The marshal did, then shook his head.

"Don't smell nuthin'."

"It's your clothing," Slocum decided. "You still reek of smoke from having your town burned down around your ears. That masks the campfires." He watched the horizon carefully for even a single wisp of rising smoke, but saw nothing. Only his keen nose warned that the outlaws were ahead.

"What do you think we oughta do, Marshal?" asked one of the nervous posse. "If we found 'em, we ought to fetch the army to arrest 'em. Right?"

"Right," Slocum said. "Send them back, Marshal."

"But—" The marshal bowed his head in defeat, then gave the order. The men who had ridden from Charity all turned tail and galloped away into the twilight. Slocum hoped the pounding hooves wouldn't alert Magee's sentries. He put his index finger against his lips to keep the marshal silent, then waited until the dusk turned into inky darkness. The stars gave the only illumination, but the moon would rise within the hour. Slocum had to reconnoiter and get out of the outlaw camp before that. Otherwise, the bright lunar light of a waxing three-quarter moon would give him away.

Slocum dismounted and made sure his Colt Navy slipped easily from his holster. He looked at the marshal and said, "Time to earn my pay."

"Deputies in a posse don't get paid," the marshal said.

"I know." Slocum turned and set out to scout Magee's encampment. At least he didn't have to worry about who should get his salary if he didn't come back.

5

"Go on, kill the bastard!"

The cry went up around the circle of men as the two faced off. Clayton Magee stood back and watched dispassionately. To maintain discipline, sometimes a good leader had to let the men blow off steam. Bare-knuckles fighting was unlikely to see either man kill the other, but the major would have still let them have their pointless battle even if they had armed themselves with knives or guns. One look at his second in command would have told him that would be the right thing. Albert Kimbrell was bloodthirsty, but the best lieutenant a leader could have in the field. He kept the men fed, with munitions and weapons—and in line.

Magee wanted to keep Kimbrell happy, and seeing one man fight another made Kimbrell the happiest.

"Go on, you stinkin' cowards. Fight!"

The cheer went up around the circle until Magee looked away. He had to keep the men's spirits up—along with their courage. Without those traits, he would never find his wife and daughter. Magee sucked in a chestful of air and held it until the buttons on his uniform jacket almost popped free. Someone had taken his wife and daughter and moved them constantly to stay just ahead of his rescuing them.

That was the only explanation for not finding them right away.

Whoever it was that had kidnapped Louisa and Sarah Beth had to be powerful. To counter such mightiness, he needed his small army. Magee let out his breath slowly. They were killers, each and every one over there watching one man bludgeon another with his bare hands, but they were *his* killers. They were loyal to him and would fight without asking needless questions.

"Mix it up. Fight!" Kimbrell stepped forward and grabbed each of the men by the collar and shook them like a terrier would a rat. He shoved them forward until their heads banged before he released them. They took the hint and squared off.

One took a wild swing that would have felled an elephant. He missed by a country mile, but his opponent's short, sharp jab to the ribs connected. The man staggered back, stunned by the blow. He recovered fast and the fight was on. One fought wildly, and the other took his licks while waiting for better-chosen jabs and hooks.

"To the death," Kimbrell called out. "I want to see some real blood spilled."

"Albert, a word with you," the major said.

"But the fight. I don't want to miss it."

"Albert." When Magee spoke now, cold steel edged his tone. This brought Kimbrell around, the wildness in his eyes dying.

"What, Major?"

"We need the men. We need them all. It's all right to goad them to fight harder. It is another matter to urge them to kill one another. No one in my company is the enemy."

"'Whoever stole away my family is your enemy,'" Kimbrell said, repeating words he had learned by rote.

"He's our enemy, Albert. Never forget that."

"We got a new town to hurrah?"

"I was sure I saw Louisa and Sarah Beth," Magee said. "I had hoped they'd escaped their captor, but I was wrong." He heaved a deep sigh. He had been so sure he had seen one of them leaving Charity that he had called off the attack to go after them, but he had not found them or the one responsible for kidnapping them. "This is new territory for me. They would be taken to the next town, whatever it is. We must catch up with their captors and deal with them."

"In the next city," Kimbrell said, grinning like a hungry wolf spying a lamb.

"I hope so. I miss them," Magee said. Then he stood straighter. It did not pay to show any sentimentality in front of subordinates, even ones as loyal as Kimbrell.

He turned and watched intently as the two men continued their bout of fisticuffs. Both were bloody from the fight and staggered even when not hit, but the cries from those watching spurred them on to swing weakly. Kimbrell knew neither of the men would pull their weight in the next day or two, but this was for the morale of the entire unit. Magee jerked around at the sound of an approaching rider.

"See who it is," he ordered Kimbrell. His lieutenant was already running toward the perimeter of their camp, where two lookouts came forward, rifles aimed at the rider.

"Stand down. It's Lasker," called Kimbrell.

Magee walked more sedately, trying to keep his rampaging emotions under control. Lasker was the best scout in the unit.

"Report, trooper," Magee said, although Lasker and Kimbrell already spoke in guarded tones. "What have you found out?"

"Major, I think I got a line on them two women you want," the scout said. "There's another town, not fifteen miles down the road. I talked to a couple men in a bar there and they was goin' on about a woman they spotted ridin' all alone."

"One? Only one? Not two?" Magee's heart almost exploded in his chest. There had to be both of them. He would not let one slip through his fingers. There *had* to be both of them in the town.

"Only one, but he thought there might be somebody else. This one was a young woman."

"Blond?"

"Couldn't say for certain sure," Lasker said. He grinned. "Seems all he was lookin' at was the woman's tits. Besides, she had her hair all pushed up under a hat, so he couldn't get a good look."

"Major, her hair would've been dirty. Hard to tell one way or the other," Kimbrell said. Magee ignored him.

"Well? Go on. What else was there?"

"Not much else. Just that they seen a solitary woman. In these parts, the men know all the women, and they had never seen this one before. She's a newcomer."

"Very well, Lasker. Thank you. Get some grub and rest. You'll lead the troop tomorrow at daybreak."

"Yes, sir," Lasker said, but he looked at Kimbrell, who nodded. Lasker hurried off.

"Sir, what are your orders?" Kimbrell asked.

"We need to avoid the errors that allowed them to slip through our fingers at the last town."

"Charity," Kimbrell said. "Not much Charity in that place."

"I don't give a damn what they call their towns. I want my family."

"Why's that, Major? We been shootin' up towns and then burnin' 'em to the ground for more 'n a month now. What's so all-fired important about these two women?"

"You wouldn't understand, would you. They are *family*," Magee said with so much fire that Kimbrell took an involuntary step back. "All that is required of you is that we find them. Kill anyone with them. Kill everyone around them."

"That sounds mighty fine, Major," Kimbrell said.

"We must hone our skills and become more efficient. I leave those details to you. Carry on." Magee put his hands behind his back and walked off, thinking hard on what the next day would bring. Fifteen miles away, the scout had said. That was a hard ride and would push his men to their limit when they arrived. He had complete faith that they would be up for the fight, but he was worried that they might be so tired that they would accidentally hurt Louisa or Sarah Beth.

Magee almost turned back to voice his concern to Kimbrell, then stopped. Kimbrell would obey orders. He was a good soldier, even if he had no concept about how a man could love his wife and daughter. Kimbrell would just obey. Magee lowered his head, looked hard at the ground without seeing it, and walked to where he had spread his bedroll. He lay down, but his mind refused to allow him to sleep. Over and over, he thought of once more being reunited with his wife and daughter and killing everyone responsible for taking them from him.

Albert Kimbrell watched Magee walk off, lost in his own thoughts. Kimbrell held down the cry of triumph welling up from within. Magee had just given the order to raid another town. To hell with the women the major chased after. The killing was fun and the burning was an added bonus, but looting the towns was best of all. Kimbrell had more than ten thousand dollars stashed along the Oklahoma road they followed. When the major got tired of chasing after the will-o'-the-wisps or was gunned down in a fight, Kimbrell would retrieve his loot and head south. He could live like a king the rest of his life in Mexico.

The lure of those willing, lovely señoritas and of gallons of tequila and pulque was almost more than Kimbrell could fight. He could leave the major any time he wanted. Magee would never send anyone to track him down or even to find what had happened to the best lieutenant he ever had because he was too focused on finding the two blond bitches. Still, those women were the reason Kimbrell stayed with the major and his murderous gang.

More towns, more killing, more money from banks and businesses. Kimbrell grinned broadly, then yelled, "What's the matter? Go on, finish him off!"

The men roared as one of the fighters reared back and punched his opponent. They both went down in a pile, exhausted from their fight. The men crowded close, but Kimbrell did not join them. He wanted to savor the idea of another town.

Ride like the wind, shoot until the gun smoke from his six pistols and two rifles filled the air, and then snuff out the buildings with purifying fire. That was the icing on the cake, after he had taken as much money as he could carry.

Kimbrell flopped down on his bedroll and looked up at the sky. Wisps of clouds moved across the stars, promising rain later. But that was later and didn't much matter right now. Kimbrell lived for the present. He fished around in his saddlebags, pulled out a small oilskin package, and carefully unwrapped it.

The severed finger had begun to wither, but the bulky gold West Point ring was still firmly attached. Somehow, Kimbrell liked it this way. He had never risen above private in rank during the war. Whenever he would get promoted, once to sergeant, the officers would always find fault with him and bust him to the ranks. He was better than any of those officers. He could never get a ring like this by graduating from West Point. Now he didn't have to.

Kimbrell stroked over the stiff, bloodless finger, and stopped only when he touched the cool metal ring. A thrill passed through him that was more than sexual. No whore he had ever had made him feel this good. He had taken this from some Federal officer. It made him feel superior. The man had been a weakling and had died as Kimbrell pumped bullets into him and had given up his ring so easily.

Kimbrell might never have been promoted to the officer ranks, but he could have all the trappings. He carefully wrapped the finger and ring in the oilcloth and tucked it into his vest pocket where he could touch it whenever he liked. Then he put his hands behind his head and watched the clouds dancing about until they obscured the moon. He had the ring. When Major Magee finally died, he would have command. If he wanted it, he would be an officer.

Or he might just collect all his money and go to Mexico. It was nice to have choices. Kimbrell fell asleep thinking about the men he would kill and the towns he would burn.

6

"I can't go on," Louisa Magee said. "Every bone in my body aches so! Please, Sarah Beth, let's rest."

"The town's not too far ahead, Mama. We can make it. Hot food."

"Can't eat," her mother said. "Too tired."

"There'll be a hotel with a nice feather bed. You can sleep."

Louisa broke out crying. The more she tried to control her outburst, the worse she sobbed and shook. Sarah Beth rode closer until their legs brushed so she could reach out and put a hand on her mother's shoulder.

"We'll get away from him. He won't catch us."

"He won't stop until he either catches us or he's dead. You go on. I . . . I'll wait for him. One of us ought to get away."

"We both can," Sarah Beth said firmly. "We can get far, far away from him, but we can't give up."

"So tired," Louisa repeated. "How much farther?"

Sarah Beth squeezed her mother's arm reassuringly. She wished she was as confident as she tried to appear. They had ridden into the night, and once they had found a road, had ridden parallel to it. Sarah Beth had worried that her father might have lookouts posted along it. Or scouts. Or someone would see them and tell Clayton Magee. Sarah Beth had seen how persuasive her father could be. And how crazy.

"It's not much farther. I saw a sign somewhere when I rode back to see if anyone was on our trail. Foreman was the name. Does that mean anything to you, Mama?"

Louisa shook her head. "I'd never heard of Charity or Cherokee Springs either. We can't run forever, Sarah Beth. When do we stop? *How* do we stop?"

Sarah Beth didn't have an answer for that. Her father had to die for their nightmare to end. Or they had to find somewhere where he could never find them, not in a million years. Getting away long enough to set up a new life was the problem because Magee was so close. A month, even a week. There had to be something they could do to win the time to get away from the juggernaut trailing along behind them, destroying everything and everyone.

"There's the edge of town," Sarah Beth said. "We got here, Mama. We can rest."

"I don't have any money. What are we going to do for money?"

"You worry so. We're smart. We'll find something."

Louisa Magee chewed at her lower lip and shook her head, as if saying it wasn't going to happen, but Sarah Beth wouldn't let her get down on herself.

"Think of all the things you do well. You're a fine seamstress. Nobody makes a better quilt or man's shirt." Seeing how her mother tensed at this memory of repairing all the holes in Clayton Magee's uniform, Sarah Beth rushed on. "You can cook better than anyone else I know. There are ways to make a living in any frontier town."

"But this one? Shouldn't we keep riding? To get away?" Louisa looked over her shoulder, as if she expected to see her husband watching her, his disapproving glare ready to wilt anything she might do.

"We need to rest for a spell. You said so, Mama. And I'm sore from so much riding, too."

"These horses are stolen. The law . . ."

"Mama," Sarah Beth said sharply. "You can't steal from a dead man. Think of them as gifts from Papa so we could get away from him. Unintentional, yes, but gifts. He owes us so much. It's the least he could do."

"All right, daughter," Louisa Magee said, finally giving in. "The town's called Foreman? You don't think he will find us here?"

"Yes, it is, and no, I don't. Now come on. I smell baking bread. We should find whoever's responsible and ask for some."

Sarah Beth rode ahead, letting her mother trail her. It was just as well. Sarah Beth spoke more confidently than she felt. They had ridden all over Oklahoma, and she really had no idea where they had ended up. For all she knew, her pa and his killers had already found their trail. If so, riding into Foreman meant another town would die.

It was either that or the two of them would die from hunger and exhaustion. Sarah Beth had already made up her mind. Let the town defend itself. Eventually, one would present such a challenge that her father would fail amid a fusillade of bullets. It might just be this one. If Clayton Magee was still on their trail at all.

"Good morning," Sarah Beth called, standing just outside the bakery door. A woman used the edge of her apron to wipe sweat off her face as she turned from her oven to look at Sarah Beth.

"Don't open for another hour. Come on back then and I'll sell you the finest bread in all of Foreman."

"It's got to be," Sarah Beth said. "It surely does smell delicious." She hesitated, then her hunger forced her on. "I need a job. My mother and I both need jobs. We're on our way . . . west. Just passing through unless we find a hospitable spot to call home."

"Foreman's hospitable enough," the woman said. She wiped her hands on the apron to get flour off. "You ever do any baking?"

"My ma has."

The woman looked Louisa Magee over and nodded slowly.

"You're not some flighty young thing. You look like you know how to work."

"I . . . I do," Louisa said. "Like my daughter said, we both need jobs."

"My assistant upped and left me," the woman said with a touch of bitterness. "Truth is, he was my husband. We'd been married more than a year before he decided a dance-hall floozy was more his style. He left with her almost a month back, and I've been killing myself to furnish every-one in town their bread." She thrust out her hand. "Name's Maggie Almquist."

"Pleased to meet you," Sarah Beth said. She had intro-duced herself and her mother using their real names before it occurred to her to hide their identities. Then her resolve stiffened. As she had told her ma, if Clayton Magee found them the town would have to fight. However her father did his scouting, just lying about their names wouldn't slow him down one whit.

"Louisa, get on over there and pop the loaves into the oven. Then get to kneading the bread we'll let rise for to-morrow's batch." Maggie Almquist critically eyed Sarah Beth, thought for a moment, then said, "Mrs. Post just down the road needs a housekeeper. She's getting up in years and can be cantankerous, but you don't look like the type to take any guff off her. That doesn't mean you can slack off the work or sass her."

"I won't."

"Didn't think so. You might get a room for you and your ma there, too. Mrs. Post has a big house ever since her hus-band and three sons died of diphtheria."

"There's disease in the town?" Louisa sounded uneasy at the prospect.

"There's sickness everywhere. Wasn't worse here than in other places. Just hit the Post household hardest last year. Can't hold that against her none."

"Mama, I'll go see about us sharing a room. How do we ever thank you, Mrs. Almquist?"

"Work hard and call me Maggie. Otherwise, no need to go out of your way."

Sarah Beth left her mother shoving a dozen loaves of bread into the oven and went to find the Post house. She led their horses rather than riding since her hindquarters were so stiff and sore from the all-night ride. She tried to remember how many times they had cut across the countryside, gone up rises and through woods, along streams and down roads hardly bigger than a pair of ruts, in their attempt to elude Clayton Magee. It all blurred together in her head.

She was staggering a little by the time she found the house, a small, slightly dilapidated dwelling not a quarter mile from the bakery. Sarah Beth fancied she could still smell the baking bread, although the wind worked against that notion.

Going up the walk, she worried it might be too early to inquire after the job, but she saw a small woman bent over like a question mark, working at sweeping the front porch.

"Mrs. Post? Maggie Almquist said you might need a housekeeper." She hastily explained her plight and hoped the old woman would take pity on her.

"Can't hire the both of you. Just one," Mrs. Post said. Her body might be old and tired, but she was sharp as a tack. Sarah Beth guessed her tongue was, too.

"We'd share a room. I'm sure Ma could pay a little bit from her wages at the bakery, and I would clean and cook and do whatever else you needed me to do for my share."

They dickered a little more, and finally Mrs. Post handed her the broom.

"Porch," she said simply. "Then you can take out the rugs from the front room and beat them. Got a line out back to hang the rugs. Dust. When you finish that—" The woman stopped and squinted. She pushed her glasses up on her nose, then turned a little to look past Sarah Beth.

"What is it?"

"Might be you shouldn't do any dusting today."

Sarah Beth turned and saw a brown cloud of dust miles off along the road she and her mother had taken to reach Foreman.

"That's one mighty big dust storm coming," the woman said.

"Or riders," Sarah Beth said in a choked voice. "It might be riders."

"There'd have to be a powerful lot of them. And they'd have to be riding hard to stir up that much dust. Nope, it's one of those darned dust storms we get here."

Frozen to the spot, Sarah Beth clutched the broom handle hard and stared at the approaching dust.

7

Slocum paused and looked through the darkness at Marshal Vannover. The man walked like he had one foot in a bucket. Slocum had heard drunks make less noise as they staggered along on their way home from a bender.

"What's wrong?" The lawman turned to Slocum and peered at him through the darkness.

"Don't step on every damned twig, and keep from scuffling your feet through the leaves," Slocum said. He tried to keep his voice low, but his anger was growing. The marshal meant well, but had no idea what he faced. It might have been better if Slocum had taken the man to Cherokee Springs and shown him what Clayton Magee and his horde could really do. Charity had been almost destroyed. Almost. That small difference had led Vannover astray into thinking he could personally do something about the plague that had descended on his town and then left.

"I'm not as good as you, Slocum," the marshal said. His ire was growing, too, but from a different source. Slocum knew the lawman had to be scared out of his wits by the notion of sneaking up on the campsite. The pungent smell of burning oak from the campfires reached them now, and more than a little of the smoke carried coffee odors, too.

The outlaws were awakening, although it was still an hour or two until dawn.

"You stay," said Slocum. "Let me scout the camp."

"I have to see with my own eyes. If I got to report to the army, I need to be sure."

"You calling me a liar?"

"Stop it, Slocum, stop it right now. We got a job to do. Let's do it without fighting."

"Watch where you step," Slocum said. He moved through the trees like a ghost. Vannover did better, but still made a racket loud enough to waken the dead. Slocum only hoped those dead wouldn't be *them* if one of Magee's sentries heard them.

Slocum stopped suddenly as the trees thinned and a grassy meadow stretched into the darkness. He saw more than one fire sputtering and several being stoked. He counted the men who were awake and getting ready for breakfast. He had silently hoped to take out a guard or two, killing them if necessary, but capturing someone to interrogate. With so many outlaws already awake, that hope vanished. All he could do now was observe. If he got lucky, he might get a count on the number in this large outlaw gang, and even catch sight of their leader. Those were more important for any army pursuit than anything he could do personally to Magee.

"Wha—?"

Slocum spun and clamped his hand over the marshal's mouth to silence him. For a moment, he thought he had been successful. Then he heard the metallic click of a rifle cocking.

"Who's out there? That you, Kimbrell?"

Marshal Vannover tensed at the name. Slocum recognized it as the name belonging to the wanted poster Sarah Beth Magee had identified.

"Naw, Kimbrell's still sacked out," Slocum said in a low whisper. "I was just takin' a leak."

"Who is that? Come on out, and you better have your hand on your dick or I'll shoot it off!"

Slocum moved fast. He shoved the marshal in one direction as a diversion and went in the other, getting around to the guard's flank. The sentry saw movement as the lawman thrashed about to regain his balance. Then came the blur of Slocum coming at him like an avenging angel. The man let out a tiny gasp and then sank to the ground with Slocum's knife in his side.

Grabbing the rifle to keep it from hitting the ground and possibly discharging, Slocum stood over the man and turned his back on the camp as another guard called out, "Lemuel, what's the fuss?"

"Nuthin'," Slocum replied, keeping his voice low and gruff like the dead guard's.

"You sure?"

"Go to hell."

"You first, you silly son of a bitch. You still pissed how I cleaned you out in the poker game?"

"Yeah." Slocum knew the longer they traded words, the guard asking questions and him fielding with only single-word answers, the more dangerous it got.

"Kimbrell will divvy up the take from that last town soon enough. Then I kin clean you out again!" Laughing at this, the other guard strolled off. Slocum stayed stock-still until he no longer heard the man's steps. He dropped to his knees and pulled out the blade from the guard's ribs, wiped the metal off on the dead man's shirt, and then returned the knife to the top of his own right boot. He hastily searched the man's pockets and found a single dollar bill all wadded up. This had to be the sole survivor of that poker game. He tucked it into his own pocket and then stood, keeping his back to the camp.

No West Point ring. He had to keep looking.

"You out there, Vannover?" He spoke in a low voice that carried but would not alert anyone in camp. Over the years, he had found that whispering drew more attention than simply speaking in subdued tones. Something about a whisper carried, and everyone immediately wondered what was being kept secret.

"Damned near busted my arm. You shoved me into—"

"Never mind," Slocum said. "Get over here. Now!"

The marshal jumped like he had been stuck with a pin.

"Stand here with the rifle. Don't talk unless you have to and don't face camp so they can catch a glimpse of your face. There's a lot of them to remember, but it's a tight-knit outfit. They're going to know anyone who doesn't belong."

Slocum did not add that Vannover lacked the killer look that most of the gang had. There was a coldness in their stares that the marshal could not fake.

Without another word, Slocum set off to explore the perimeter of the camp. He disliked leaving the lawman behind like that, but if anyone made a casual inspection, they would see a man where a guard was supposed to be stationed. Putting Vannover out in plain sight was less risky than leaving a hole in the outlaw perimeter.

Every step silent, Slocum moved about, counting the outlaws and seeing the kind of equipment they carried. He went cold in the gut when he recognized it as what he had carried when he had ridden with Quantrill's Raiders. Back then, they had bristled with six-shooters and rifles. Going up against a company of men three times their size had been easy enough, especially if the Federal soldiers had been armed with single-shot muskets. A decent soldier could get off three shots a minute. Any one of Quantrill's men could empty his six-gun accurately in half that time and be reaching for a second loaded pistol before his target had hit the ground. They depended on speed and sheer quantity of lead aimed at their target.

More than once that target had been an entire town. Slocum still had nightmares of what they had done to Lawrence, Kansas. Clayton Magee and his band of cutthroats had brought similar carnage down on at least two towns. Slocum figured the coordination and ease of the attack, especially on Cherokee Springs, meant those had not been their first towns. Magee led an experienced, brutal gang.

There had to be something Slocum was missing,

though. Magee might be hunting for his wife and daughter, but the rest were intent on robbing and killing. And raping. The saloon girls sprawled naked on the pool table reminded him that these men took their pleasure in all things brutal and bloody.

He found the ammo dump covered with a tarp. He would have considered blowing it up if it hadn't been guarded by no fewer than four men. Magee took no chances. The two women had said he had been a major in the Union army. His expertise showed in the way the camp was laid out and the supplies guarded.

Knowing there was little else he could do, Slocum made his way back around the slowly stirring men. Dawn was still an hour away, but they rose early. He guessed they cleaned their six-guns and other gear like any good military unit before reporting for their day's duty.

Where that would take them, he had no clue. He had not found where Magee pitched his tent, though even if Slocum had, there would have been nothing he could do. Cutting the head off a rattlesnake worked real good to stop its venomous attacks. Killing the leader of a gang this size only meant someone else would take his place.

Slocum hurried now to get out of the camp before everyone was awake. He made his way back toward the spot where he had left Marshal Vannover on guard duty, but got clumsy. The toe of his boot caught on a rock around a fire pit and sent it rattling into a coffeepot. Several men looked up.

"Sorry," Slocum said, moving his hand over his face to hide his identity. The men grumbled and went back to their chores, most of them cleaning their six-shooters. But one man watched him with cold intensity.

Slocum walked on, trying not to hurry. He felt the man's eyes boring into his back. Not turning to confront the outlaw took all of Slocum's willpower. It was then that Slocum made his second mistake. He went directly to where the marshal kept guard.

As he approached, Vannover turned toward Slocum, showing his face to anyone behind Slocum.

"Who the hell are you?" came the shouted question.

Slocum thought about bulling his way through. He had learned to bluff well playing poker, but Vannover did not allow him to even attempt it. The marshal gasped and lifted the rifle taken off the dead guard.

"Kimbrell!" the lawman shouted as he raised the rifle and fired. The slug tore past Slocum's head, causing him to flinch. From the commotion, Slocum knew the marshal was no better as a shooter than he was at keeping a low profile. He had missed Kimbrell by a country mile.

"Git 'em, boys," cried the outlaw. "We got spies in our camp."

Slocum swung around, slapped leather, and drew. He fanned off three quick shots. He didn't care how accurate they were. He wanted to sow confusion all around. If he did, it was not apparent. Three outlaws were hastily loading their six-guns and Kimbrell had his out and firing.

Two bullets ripped past Slocum. One might have found Vannover from the way the lawman grunted. Looking to see how badly injured the man was would have meant Slocum's death. He fired with more accuracy now, straight at Kimbrell.

They faced each other at a distance of twenty feet. In the dim light of almost dawn, Slocum had a difficult target to hit. The only saving grace was that Kimbrell had the same handicap. As the outlaw moved, Slocum saw how Vannover had identified him. Fires blazed high to either side and sometimes lit up the outlaw's face as if he was on a theater stage with a spotlight trained on him.

Slocum aimed carefully with his final shot and squeezed the trigger—just as Kimbrell jerked to one side. The outlaw had stepped into one of the cooking fires and danced out of it at the same instant Slocum sent a slug in his direction. Kimbrell yelped, but Slocum knew the shot had barely scratched the man's skin, if it had hit him at all. The outlaw might have reacted to his pants leg being on fire, or the notion that anyone had sneaked into his camp undetected.

"Come on," Slocum said, spinning and reaching down

to grab the marshal's shirt. He pulled the man to his feet. "You hit?"

"I stumbled," Vannover said. "I twisted my knee, but I can walk."

"Don't walk, run," Slocum said. He kept the marshal ahead of him and moving. They had barely reached the thicket before the outlaws finished loading their six-guns and opened fire. The tree trunks and limbs exploded in a sticky mass of sap and splinter. Leaves fluttered down all around. Then came a second volley, as deadly as the first.

"I can't—"

"You'd better," Slocum said, shoving the marshal again to get him deeper into the woods. He yanked the rifle from the lawman's hands and turned, took a deep breath, and waited. He saw Kimbrell leading the charge coming after them. Slocum squeezed off a round, and knew he'd hit the outlaw this time. Kimbrell dropped his six-shooter and grabbed his right forearm with his left hand. Slocum was not as lucky with his next shot. He missed Kimbrell but hit another outlaw. Slocum cursed his bad luck in missing what should have been an easy shot. He wanted Kimbrell brought down. From everything he had read on the man's wanted poster, Kimbrell had to be second in command.

This wasn't as good as cutting off the snake's head— killing Magee—but it was better than randomly taking pot-shots at the men riding behind the major. That was too much like dipping water from a well using a sieve.

"My ankle's startin' to swell up," Vannover said. He gasped for breath and limped more with every step. "You go on. I'll hold them off."

"You'd be dead in ten seconds. Five, if they see your badge."

"What are we goin' to do?"

Slocum had no idea. He heard the outlaws gathering just at the edge of the clearing. By now all thirty or forty outlaws would be awake. Magee might take over. Slocum was not discounting the man's tactical skills, even if he might be crazy as a bedbug.

"That way," Slocum said, herding the marshal in a direction parallel to the clearing. They stayed in the woods, but no longer tried to plunge deeper. He remembered his brief scouting of the camp, and knew they had to create a diversion or they were goners. Too many killers on their trail with limitless ammo spelled only shallow graves—or simply being left out for the coyotes and buzzards.

"What are you going to do?"

"Keep them confused," Slocum said. "It's our only chance." As he walked, he reloaded. The rifle he had taken from the marshal was useless now. The .36-caliber ammo for his Colt Navy wouldn't fit the .44 Winchester. Slocum cut back toward the camp and chanced a quick look.

Luck was turning in his direction again. Most of the outlaws were clustered behind Kimbrell at the edge of the woods where the guard lay dead. Nobody even glanced in their direction because they thought anyone running away from them would run fast and hard in a straight line.

"They're not huntin' for us," the marshal said. "What do you make of that?"

"Kimbrell will get a few of them organized and those will be the only ones after us. Following our trail's not going to be hard once the sun comes up." Slocum estimated they had less than a half hour before it got light enough for a decent tracker to find their spoor and realize they had not run directly away. Before then he had to have come up with another plan.

"There're the horses. In a rope corral," the marshal said. "We can steal their horses."

"That's good, as far as it goes," Slocum said. "How good a shot are you?"

"Fair to middlin'," the marshal said with enough confidence that Slocum believed him.

"Here." Slocum shoved his six-shooter into the lawman's hand. "See that pile over yonder? The one covered with the tarp?"

"Supplies?" The marshal thought for a second, then

said, "That's their ammo dump. My God, they have enough for an army!"

"They *are* an army," Slocum said. "Walk over there, get close enough to be sure you are putting every last round into that pile, and don't stop until both six-shooters are empty."

"They'll kill me!"

"They just might, even if my plan does work. If it doesn't, you'll have the satisfaction of blowing some of them to hell and gone and making it damned inconvenient to keep killing towns."

"What are you going to do?"

Slocum slid his knife from its sheath and thrust the tip in the direction of the ammunition. He didn't wait to see if Vannover followed his orders. A pair of guards wandered along the rope holding a dozen horses. If they spotted Slocum before he got to them . . .

Slocum walked quickly, but did not run. The men were arguing, and only noticed Slocum when he was a few yards away. Then it was too late. Slocum closed the distance with three quick strides. His knife slashed furiously and caught the closer guard across the eyes. As the man screamed in pain, Slocum spun about and kicked the other guard in the kneecap, taking him to the ground fast. He used the knife to kill that guard before returning to the first one. In seconds they were both dead.

Panting harshly, Slocum took their rifles and six-shooters and went to the string of horses. He slashed the rope holding the horses, then began firing. When he did, he heard answering fire. He smiled. The distinctive sound of his Colt Navy told him that Vannover was going after the ammunition dump.

Slocum exchanged rifle fire with another guard, then finally winged him severely enough to make him go scuttling off for shelter. Using his knife, Slocum freed three more strings of horses, only holding onto a pair. He'd gotten a bridle onto the first one when Vannover finally struck pay dirt.

The explosion from the ammo drove him to his knees. Hot lead sang all around him as box after box of ammunition discharged. There wasn't time to get a bridle on the second horse. Slocum swung onto its back and clung to its neck for dear life. He lost the second rifle he had, but managed to draw one of the captured six-guns and empty it at a few outlaws coming to stop their horses from stampeding.

He threw that pistol away and tugged on the bridle of his first stolen horse to get it trotting in the direction of the ammo dump.

"Get on," Slocum said. "No time to saddle up."

Marshal Vannover didn't have to be told twice. He jumped awkwardly, almost slid off the far side of the first horse, then found his seat. Bending low, reins in hand, he galloped off. Slocum followed, not caring what direction they went. The outlaws had to run down their escaped horses—and with the sizzle and explosion of cartridges still filling the air with noise and death, it might take longer than any of the outlaws expected.

That gave Slocum and Marshal Vannover that much more time to get the hell out of the outlaw camp.

They rode without speaking into the sunrise, each lost in his own thoughts. Slocum had no idea what went through Vannover's head, but he could not keep from wondering if it would be Kimbrell or Magee himself who finally came after them.

8

"Settle down, child. It's only an Oklahoma dust storm," Mrs. Post said. "Now get on with the cleaning. However, save the dusting for last."

"I . . . I need to fetch my belongings and tell my ma. I'll get right to work when I come back."

"Oh, very well." Mrs. Post sniffed and shook her head. Sarah Beth heard her say under her breath, "Young people. Lazy bunch. Lazy!"

Sarah Beth almost blurted out what she feared would happen to Foreman when the dust cloud arrived. It was a storm, all right, but not blown by the wind and driven by nature. She was sure her pa had found her again and no one in Foreman would be alive by the time the sun set. Running hard, she got back to the bakery. The delicious odor of baking bread no longer thrilled her. Instead of making her mouth water, the scent turned her stomach. Her mouth was as dry as cotton and not quite as tasty.

"Ma, he's coming. Please, ma, we got to—" She looked up and saw Maggie Almquist looking at her as if she had grown three heads.

"What are you going on about, dear?" Louisa Magee came from the rear of the bakery, struggling with a large sack of flour. Her face was a spolotchy white, and her hands and arms were completely covered in the flour. She was actually smiling for the first time in ages.

"Mama, th-there's a cloud of dust. Coming toward town," Sarah Beth stammered.

"We'll shut the door. Dust storms aren't uncommon in the Territory," Maggie said. "You ought to know that if you've traveled much here. Get over into red clay country and you'll end up redder 'n an Indian after a storm. Try to wash it off and your skin gets dyed bright red."

"Sarah Beth, please. I have to work."

"Come look, Mama. Please." Sarah Beth grabbed her mother's arm and pulled her to the door and pointed at the dust cloud. It was visibly closer to town now.

"How about that," said Maggie, peering around the other two women. "Looks like we got visitors. Riders and a passel of 'em by the look."

"It's not a dust storm?"

"Naw. Why'd you ever think that?" Maggie looked hard, and Sarah Beth felt the woman's piercing gaze go to her soul. Maggie knew she had never thought it was a dust storm.

"We . . . we have to go, Mama."

Louisa pulled free and shook her head.

"We're staying, daughter. We're staying. No matter what."

Maggie Almquist watched the two of them closely, but said nothing.

Sarah Beth sagged and began to cry. She had worked so hard and taken so many risks to get them away from her father. Now they had been run to ground. Clayton Magee would take them prisoners again, and his bloodthirsty men would rape and kill and destroy everything and everyone in Foreman.

"There's the scout comin' in now," Maggie said. "Louisa, get back to work. We got a lot of bread to sell to those fine gentlemen, if you can call 'em that. Last time they rode through, they shot up the saloon when a couple of 'em got drunk."

"They've been here before?" Sarah Beth looked up and swiped at the tears welling in her eyes. She blinked hard and then laughed. She fought to keep the laughter from becoming hysterical. "That's a soldier."

"Not just any soldier," Maggie said. "That's Roop Benedict."

"You know him?"

"I do, and in the Biblical sense, too, just last week. He's my beau. Someday I'll make an honest man of him." Maggie waved, and the sergeant waved back and grinned from ear to ear.

"We got a squad of hungry fellas comin' in, Miz Almquist," he called. "You baked enough to take care of their appetites?"

"Yours maybe." Maggie wiped her hands on her apron as she went into the street to stand beside the cavalry sergeant. She reached up and put her hand on his thigh. Even though she had tried to clean her hand, she left a white handprint. Sergeant Benedict did not seem to mind.

Sarah Beth swallowed hard as Maggie finished talking to the sergeant and came back.

"Said Captain Langmuir's not ten minutes out. Only got the one squad with him this time, and he left the drunkards back at the post."

"Post?"

"Fort Supply, out on the Canadian River to the west of here."

"West? But they came in from the east, from where we'd been traveling," Sarah Beth said weakly. She was not sure she wanted to believe these were real soldiers and not renegades riding with her father.

"They patrol all over central Oklahoma. They'd gone north of here, then swept south, and are on the way back to Fort Supply. Surely is good seeing Roop again." Maggie looked hard at mother and daughter. "Anything you want to tell me? Before you get back to work?"

"No, nothing," Louisa said, looking sharply at her daughter. "We have a lot of work to do, and I ought to get to it."

"That's the spirit," Maggie said, following her. She stopped in the door of the bakery and waved to the sergeant, who waved back.

Then Maggie Almquist ducked inside and began barking out orders like a drill sergeant. So many hungry troopers would leave nothing for the townspeople and more bread had to be baked, and there was no time for the yeast to rise, much less bake it and—

Sarah Beth shut out the litany of problems the bakery suddenly faced. She leaned weakly against the wall and stared at Roop Benedict, hoping that he was exactly as he appeared—a soldier from a commissioned army post.

The sergeant sauntered over, leading his horse.

"Ma'am, I saw you with Miz Almquist. You know her?"

"My mother works for her."

"Do tell. Ever since that no-account husband of hers left, Maggie's been workin' her fingers to the bone. Glad to see she's got dependable help. Miz Almquist, I mean."

"She said you were stationed at Fort Supply."

"Yes, ma'am, under the command of Captain Isaiah Langmuir, the best damned horse soldier in the Territory."

"You know Major Magee? Clayton Magee?" She watched the man's reaction closely. Unless he was a better actor than she thought, he had never heard of her pa.

"Can't say that I have, though I heard tell of a new officer at Fort Gibson. He stationed there?"

"No, just asking."

"Is Maggie—Miz Almquist—at a spot where she could take a few minutes from her work? I hate to ask, but the captain's gonna be here 'fore we know it."

"I think that's Captain Langmuir now," Sarah Beth said. She saw a ramrod-straight officer sporting captain's bars at the head of a column. The guidon carried the designation of a company she was not familiar with, which made her all the happier. She knew every single unit her pa had ever been in or commanded. This was not one of his.

"Yup, surely is. Thank you, ma'am, for not lettin' me go astray."

"I need to talk to the captain. Could you ask for me?"

"What about, ma'am?"

"He . . . it's of great importance, but I want to speak only with an officer."

"Yes, ma'am, I'll put that in my report."

Sergeant Benedict hurried to where the captain had halted the column, saluted, and began his report. Sarah Beth knew the instant the sergeant got to mentioning her because the officer's eyes snapped over to her and did not leave. His expression was neutral, but she got the feeling he looked at her just a trifle longer than was polite before turning back to his scout's report.

Sergeant Benedict saluted again, turned, and bellowed orders to the column of troopers. They dismounted amid a new cloud of dust. In spite of the early hour, they had ridden for a spell to accumulate so much road dust on them. The captain dismounted and brushed dust off his own uniform. Sarah Beth hurried over to him.

"Captain Langmuir, did the sergeant mention I wanted a word with you?"

"He did, but he failed to say who you were or the nature of your request." He fought to keep from smiling. The corners of his mouth turned up the smallest amount. Sarah Beth could not keep herself from returning the smile as she introduced herself.

"Pleased to make your acquaintance, Miss Magee. I knew there was a reason I headed for Foreman."

"Oh, my mother and I only arrived . . . recently," she finished. Giving out information to anyone, even this handsome, charming young captain, did not come easily for her. She had learned to distrust anyone wearing a uniform—but those had all been in her father's command.

"Some other town's loss then. What is it I can do for you, Miss Magee?"

She turned her back to the nearest troopers and lowered her voice before speaking.

"Have you ever heard of Major Clayton Magee? Or Albert Kimbrell?"

"Can't rightly say I have. A major? Is he new to the Territory? A relative of yours, since you share the same last name?" The man's tone turned a little more brittle.

"My father," she explained.

"I see. You and your mother are looking for him. Well, if I come across him, I will tell him you're here."

"No!" The word escaped her throat like a horse from the starting gate. She felt all the blood drain from her face and she wobbled. Captain Langmuir grabbed her elbow to steady her.

"Are you well?"

"You must *not* let him know where we are. He . . . he destroys entire towns hunting for my mother and me."

"I'm sorry. He destroys towns? He gets drunk and—"

"No, he has his men kill everyone, every last living soul. Then he burns the town to the ground and moves on."

"The sun is fierce in Oklahoma," the captain said. "Come along. Sit in the shade a spell and—"

"I am not suffering from sunstroke, and I am not crazy," Sarah Beth said hotly. "He beat my mother terribly, and he kept me a prisoner. He locked me in the cellar to keep me 'pure,' he claimed. He is a monster. We got away and he's come after us, him and his gang of bloody-handed killers."

"I see," the captain said, obviously not believing a word of what Sarah Beth said. "Which towns has he burned?"

"Cherokee Springs and Charity. Three others farther east along the same road. There might be others I don't know about."

"Those are out of my patrol area," he said dubiously. Langmuir took off his broad-brimmed hat and ran his gloved hand across his forehead to get the blond locks back from his eyes. He carefully removed his gloves when he noticed he still wore them and tucked them under his belt. The officer sought words and found them elusive.

"He's after us," Sarah Beth went on. "He'll find us, too, and destroy Foreman looking for us. He threatened to put me in shackles until he finds a man worthy of marriage."

She felt light-headed again. "I'm afraid he might marry me off to his second in command."

"This Kimbrell fellow?"

"He's worse than my father, in his way. My pa's crazy. Albert Kimbrell just loves the smell of blood, seeing his victims die. He enjoys others' suffering. I can't imagine what he would do to me if we were married. It would be worse than what Pa does to my mother, I'm certain of that."

"I heard of men in the war like that," Captain Langmuir said, still hunting for words and not finding them.

"You served?"

"I did not have that privilege. I graduated from West Point in '66."

"There aren't many commands available, so you must be quite good at soldiering." Sarah Beth saw him puff up at the praise. He did not believe her father and Kimbrell were a threat, so she had to work her wiles on him to make him aware of the danger.

"I do what I can," he said. "General Sherman is a fine example, and I try to emulate him."

"Then you are aware of what he did to Atlanta. Major Magee is doing the same thing to every town he finds."

"I've had no report," the captain said.

Sarah Beth tired of trying to win him over by wiles or threat. She grabbed the sleeve of his blue wool jacket and pulled on it insistently.

"You have to believe me. Foreman is in danger. You and your men are, too. Major Magee's men are killers, each and every one, and there are three or four dozen of them."

"Miss Magee, I need to see to my men. I'll make inquiries."

"Of whom? The towns are dead. Except, except possibly Charity. We barely escaped him there, and he might have left the town to come after us."

"He cannot be too efficient if you escaped."

Sarah Beth bristled at the implied insult. "Our lives are

in peril. Are you saying that two women couldn't possibly elude an army officer?"

"Not exactly, but if he is as determined as you say . . ."

"He is."

"Then I find it difficult to believe you have outlegged him."

Sarah Beth tried to find new words, but could not. She slumped and shook her head. When she looked up, Captain Langmuir was staring at her with pity in his gray eyes. He thought she was the crazy one, not her father.

"Be careful, Captain. Be very careful. If you meet up with my pa, he will kill you and your entire company outright."

"I am always cautious. Indian Territory is rife with brigands and outlaws of all stripes."

He nodded once to her, put his hat back on, and hurried away. The set of his shoulders showed how eager he was to leave her and her wild claims behind. Sarah Beth had done her best and had failed. All she could do was hope that her father did not get on her and her mother's trail because Foreman would die. Her mother had reached the end of the road, and no argument would get her to run any more.

Sarah Beth saw the captain mustering his men. The sergeant saw that all the horses were watered, and then they mounted and rode from town. The captain glanced back in her direction once, then sat a mite straighter and looked ahead, leading his men.

Away from the direction from which Clayton Magee would approach the town.

The only thought rattling in Sarah Beth's brain was that the captain and his men would be safe, even if she wasn't.

9

Slocum glanced to his side to see how the marshal was faring. Vannover clung to the horse with grim determination. If Slocum had not been able to put on the bridle before giving the horse to the lawman, Vannover would have fallen off. Behind them came random shots and angry cries. Kimbrell and his cronies would recover their horses in jig time and be on the trail quick.

"Circle," Slocum said, pointing. "If we circle around, we can get back to where we left our horses."

"I can hang on," the marshal protested.

"That's not the point. They're coming after us. We can shoot it out with them, but it's like stepping on ants. No matter how fast you stomp, a few more always boil up until you're swamped."

"We ride these horses till they drop, then go to ours because they're rested. Think that'll work?"

Slocum didn't answer. It had to work. The sun was poking up over the horizon, promising to silhouette them if they kept riding eastward. Even with the outlaws' ammo dump being blown up, each man carried enough spare rounds to fight a small war. Getting rid of two snoops wouldn't take anywhere near that much.

They rode steadily, varying the pace to get the most distance and speed from their stolen horses as possible. As Slocum led them up a slope, he heard a thud. He looked back and saw Vannover flat on his back, gasping for breath. Cursing, Slocum wheeled about and trotted to the lawman.

"You still in one piece?"

Vannover tried to sit up, but the wind had been knocked from his lungs. He gasped and finally got to breathing again.

"Sorry, Slocum. My ankle's botherin' me something fierce. I tried to reach down to rub it. Not used to ridin' bareback, not like when I was a kid."

Vannover's horse had not stayed to see the fate of its rider. It had galloped away into the grove of bois d'arc and cedar and was nowhere to be seen. Slocum held out his hand. Vannover took it and swung up behind. The horse staggered under their combined weight.

"Don't know how good I can ride like this," the marshal admitted. "No saddle and no bridle." He favored his ankle, but Slocum saw his left arm, injured back in Charity, was hurting him, too.

"We don't have much farther to go," Slocum said. He thought they were only a mile or so from where they had left their horses. It would be good to feel the saddle under him again, but it would be even better to get the boxes of ammunition from his saddlebags. Try as he might, Slocum could not remember how many rounds he had left with him.

"You're what the town needs for a deputy, Slocum. You think you'd consider stayin' on full time?"

Slocum snorted and shook his head. This produced a laugh from Vannover.

"Didn't think so, but had to ask. If I get back to Charity in one piece, I'm not sure the town fathers'll want to keep me around. Not done a whole lot to keep the peace there."

"If Magee and his killers go back, there's nothing anyone can do," Slocum said. "Unless you've got an artillery battery and about a hundred trained soldiers to back you up."

"A mite short on those, though we do have some army

troopers what move through the countryside from time to time. No way to let 'em know what's going on, short of sending a courier. Charity's not near big enough to warrant a telegraph station, and we're miles from a railroad."

Slocum wondered if the two women had a better chance at getting away from Clayton Magee by staying in the bigger towns. If thirty or forty cowboys shot up Wichita, even using guerrilla tactics, there'd be plenty of firepower to slow them down. Eventually, a force big enough to deal with Magee would be rounded up. As it was, he destroyed the small towns completely and nobody noticed.

Nobody but the people who had lived in them—and they were all pushing up daisies.

Slocum topped a rise and started down into a hollow where he thought their horses were tethered. He was so intent on getting back to his paint and getting the marshal astride a saddled horse that he got careless. The bullet took off his hat and missed his scalp by only inches.

He reacted by jerking to the left. This carried Vannover off the horse with him. They both slammed hard into the ground. Again, the marshal had the wind knocked out of him, but Slocum was in better shape. He drew his six-shooter and rolled away until he came to a shallow, weed-overrun ditch. Without moving a muscle, Slocum lay surrounded by the weeds, watching and waiting. There were several spots in the woods where the shot might have come from, but he dared not risk exposing himself until he knew exactly where the sniper hid.

Slocum sucked in a deep breath and let it out slowly. He might face more than a single gunman, too. Kimbrell would have rousted the entire camp after their horses had been shooed off and the ammunition had been blown up.

A fitful wind kicked up, further camouflaging any hidden sniper. Leaves sighed and the tree limbs began to bend in the wind. Worse, Vannover groaned and started to thrash about on the ground.

"Stay still. For your life, don't move. They think you're dead."

"Feel past dead," the marshal said. He flopped back and lay still. In a lower voice, he called to Slocum. "You spot the sons o' bitches?"

Slocum was more intent on sorting out sounds mingling with the wind through the trees. He rolled onto his back and fired twice. An outlaw had been sneaking up behind him, coming from a totally unexpected direction. Slocum's first slug hit the man in the jaw and twisted his head about. The second ended his life. Slocum rolled back onto his belly and peered through the weeds.

He saw two more outlaws coming from a spot affording a good shot at any rider. One of them had taken the earlier potshot. Slocum braced his pistol, aimed, and fired. The first man grunted and clutched his belly. The second was used to gunfights, though, and did not freeze when his partner got hit. His six-gun came up and homed in on Slocum like it was a compass finding north.

He blazed away as he ran for cover.

"Get into the ditch," Slocum ordered Vannover. The marshal wasted no time obeying. Dirt and plants kicked up in tiny fountains as more bullets came their way.

"I shot a man behind me. Grab his six-shooter. I'm about out of ammunition."

"Got it," Vannover said. Slocum was pleased that the marshal had already been scuttling for the fallen gun without being told. In spite of their sorry position, they might just get away yet.

Slocum took the pistol from him when the Colt Navy came up empty.

"Our horses are—were—in that grove yonder," Slocum said. "They might have found them or they might just have gotten lucky and spotted us riding along the ridge."

"Jist the three varmints?"

Slocum shook his head. He hoped so. Two down, one to go presented easy odds. If there were more, they would be in for the fight of their lives. Without saying a word, he began wiggling down the ditch. Vannover lay so that the crown of his hat poked up over the edge of the ditch, offering a decent target. Slocum hoped the outlaw would be too intent on filling the hat with holes to notice him.

When he got close enough to a sweet gum tree, Slocum clambered to his feet and slipped through the grove, thinking to flank the remaining outlaw. After only a few yards, he realized what they faced. He saw two more men crouched, clutching rifles, waiting for their chance at a killing shot.

He had not checked the six-gun in his hand to see how many rounds remained. It might carry a full load or it might be empty.

"Here goes nothing," Slocum said, stepping from behind the tree. He leveled the six-shooter and fired twice into the first man. As the second outlaw turned in surprise, Slocum shot him twice also. A fifth shot caused the hammer to fall on an empty chamber.

He dropped the empty six-gun and took both rifles. Already exposed, he knew only audacity would keep him alive. Striding purposefully through the trees, he came out a few yards away from the man who had Marshal Vannover pinned down. A rifle came easily to Slocum's shoulder. He squeezed off the shot and ended the man's life.

Then he held out his hand to keep Vannover in place. Slocum strained all his senses. All he heard was wind through the trees. He sniffed hard, and then sneezed from the noseful of pollen. Nothing moved that shouldn't. Only when he had waited a decent length of time that would have caused a nervous outlaw to bolt and run or attack did he signal the marshal to join him.

As Vannover came hobbling over, he scooped up the dead outlaw's pistol.

"Can't have too much firepower."

"Here," Slocum said, tossing him the second rifle. "I think we got rid of all of them."

"We? You're a one-man army all by your lonesome," Vannover said in admiration. "Do we find their horses and take whatever we can?"

"They must have come straight here from their camp. We'd better ride like we mean it. Any more of them who show up aren't going to be as pleasant."

"Pleasant? That what you call having your hat shot off your head?"

"My hat," Slocum said, frowning. He went back to one of the outlaws he had killed in the woods and snatched up the man's hat. It had a snakeskin band around it and a small white feather. Slocum plucked out the feather and dropped it on the dead man's chest, then settled the hat on his head.

"Seems like a fair trade," Vannover said. "One of them ventilates your hat, you get this one. Why didn't you keep the feather?"

"Don't want to be mistaken for an Indian," Slocum said. For a moment, Vannover stared at him, then laughed.

"You got a weird sense of humor, Slocum."

They took what they could from the bodies in the way of pistols and ammunition, then found their horses where they had left them tethered. A quick search failed to find the horses ridden by Magee's killers. It didn't matter, although more ammo would have made Slocum feel a tad more secure. He swung onto the paint, and then reached back to find his spare box of ammunition in the saddlebags. The balance and accuracy of his Colt Navy were unparalleled. He kept the weapon well oiled and in good repair so it would not fail him when he needed it most. Like now.

"You look like you're openin' a gunsmith's store," Vannover said. "You're positively bristlin' with guns."

Slocum remembered what it had felt like riding with Quantrill. He didn't like it one bit.

"Whatever gets us back to Charity is fine with me," Slocum said, shoving a pair of six-shooters into his belt and making sure his Colt rode easy. He still had his Winchester, but left the other rifles behind.

"Do we head straight on back or try to lay a false trail?"

Slocum considered the marshal's question carefully. They had exchanged a considerable amount of gunfire killing the outlaws. If that alerted others, trying to gallop back to town would be foolish. Before they had ridden a couple miles, the entire gang would be on their necks. However, the longer they stayed in the area, taking their time to cover their tracks, the more likely an outlaw would blunder onto them. The hills were teeming with Magee's killers.

"Straight back, fast, hard," Slocum decided.

"I'm up for it. Reckon my horse is, too, havin' done nuthin' but rest while we were getting shot at."

The marshal swung around and trotted off in the direction of Charity. Slocum followed a dozen yards back, alert for any sign of trouble. It took only minutes to find it.

"Vannover, hold on! Up ahead!"

The marshal drew rein and saw the riders working along a ridge, moving in and out of the thick growth of trees.

"I don't know this terrain too well, but if we follow the stream, it's got to lead us somewhere that we can find a road," Vannover said.

Slocum nodded and let the lawman slosh about in the shallow stream. The running water would cover both their tracks and the sound of their horses, but he didn't like the way they had to travel. The stream might have been the one near the outlaw camp. If they went too far in this direction, chances were good they would find themselves in Magee's gunsights.

"They're on either side of us," Slocum said, "but they haven't spotted us. Keep moving but do it quietly."

Vannover craned about in the saddle and looked at Slocum, then nodded. Slocum saw how the man winced as he moved. His ankle might be so swollen they'd have to cut his boot off to examine it. Right now, though, Slocum and Vannover had other problems.

Slocum heard loud splashing in the stream behind them. They were boxed in and being herded forward. He started hunting for a place to make a stand, but the forest provided nothing in the way of shelter. He urged his horse to a faster gait, caught up with Vannover, and said in a low voice, "We're going to have to fight it out."

"Behind us?"

Slocum's opinion of the marshal went up a notch. He had noticed the outlaws on their back trail, too.

"We might have a slim chance," Slocum said, looking up. He pushed back the hat he had taken from the fallen outlaw to peer through the canopy of leaves at the sky. The day had begun bright and sunny, but leaden clouds had drifted in. He caught the scent of rain on the air. If the sky opened up with a typical Oklahoma frog strangler, they might snake past their hunters.

"Don't count on it being in our favor," the marshal said. He jerked his thumb upward. "If 'n it rains, we're likely to get washed away."

Slocum saw that the streambed was broad with steep, cut banks. He had not considered this might turn into a raging river, if only for a short time after a summer cloudburst. Still, he would rather be washed away than be caught by Magee and his bravos.

"The trees are thinning out. They're sure to spot us from one side or the other," Slocum said. He turned and looked behind. The stream was straight, but no one had come into sight yet. The sounds of horses in the stream were distinct, however. Their time was running out. "We've got to get under cover."

As he spoke, a fat raindrop spatted against his gun hand. Then came another, colder, bigger. Soon enough, the rain against his hat sounded like someone hammering tin.

"What do you think? It's not much, but it'll have to do us." The marshal pointed to a lightning-struck tree lying along the bank. It had partially rotted and would give almost no protection against a bullet.

"It's all we've got."

Slocum got his paint up the steep bank and went to the fallen log. Close by, it gave even less protection than promised from the middle of the stream. Termites had hollowed out the tree and rot had done the rest. If they intended to hide, it provided small cover. Shooting it out gave them no hope at all. Every last bullet aimed at the wood would rip through into anyone hiding behind.

"We can try to run." He found himself raising his voice to be heard over the rain. Leaves above hummed with drops hitting hard. Thunder in the distance told of an even greater storm moving in their direction. Slocum had long since given up trying to imagine what his dying day would be like. Violent? That was most likely. He wasn't the kind who died of old age or in bed, unless it was with a filly who had a jealous boyfriend with a fast, accurate gun. Still, he had never imagined his last minutes being in a gunfight in the rain.

He hit the ground and swung his horse's reins around a low limb before pulling his rifle from the saddle sheath and diving behind the log. Vannover was slower to join him, hobbling so much that he dragged his leg behind him as if it had turned into lead.

"Three rifles," the man said. "I got two, you got one. And our six-guns."

Slocum drew both the pistols he had taken from the dead outlaws and laid them where the rain wouldn't hit them directly. He had a pocket full of ammunition for his rechambered Colt Navy and a desire to get the fight over with.

Through a curtain of frothy white rain he saw a rider coming up the stream. He sighted along his rifle barrel and got a good sight picture as he prepared to start what would likely be the last fight of his life.

10

"Somewhere ahead," said the scout, Lasker. "Not too damn far either."

"Get the boys ready," Albert Kimbrell said, the cold hatred in his gut beginning to warm. He tapped the butt of a six-shooter shoved into his belt and imagined what it was going to be like when he drew and fired six rounds into the belly of the son of a bitch who blew up all their ammunition. His hand moved to another pistol. That one was reserved for the other son of a bitch who had cut the ropes and scattered the horses. It had taken more than a half hour to round up the frightened animals and get them back into camp.

He wanted to kill both men, but would settle for either one.

"How you want to do this? Both flanks move in, squeeze 'em back downstream so we can take potshots at 'em? Or maybe all sides close in and crush 'em that way?" Lasker spoke in a low, matter-of-fact voice. He didn't get the pleasure out of killing that Kimbrell did.

Kimbrell thought a moment. He had found tracks going into the stream and had guessed the two riders were going upstream, since that was in the direction of a town Magee's gang had already destroyed. One rider had sported a badge. It might be the town marshal out to get some revenge. Kimbrell wished that the major hadn't ordered them away before they had finished their work. The bank hadn't been properly looted and stores still held goods they could use later. Whatever phantasm Magee chased was just ahead, or so he'd said, and they had left loose ends dangling.

A marshal and deputy were plenty loose. Now he had to find both of them and kill them, as he should have done back in town.

"Keep the men on the flanks alert. We'll keep goin' up the stream till we find them. I want to personally gut-shoot them and watch them die real slow."

The scout shrugged. It made no nevermind to him what Kimbrell wanted. Lasker got the same share of the loot whether they tortured people to death or ended their miserable lives with a single shot to the back of the head.

"Don't think there's much in the way of hideouts for 'em," the scout said. "Only problem's the damn weather." Lasker pulled up his collar against the cold rain. It would have felt good later in the day, after they had stewed like prunes in the heat. This early in the morning only turned everything the rain touched to shivery cold.

"There's not gonna be any problem," Kimbrell said. He pulled his rifle from its sheath and cocked it. "How far ahead you reckon they are?"

"No more sound of horses' hooves. Can't be more than a quarter mile. Maybe less. I'll keep my eyes peeled in case they crawled up in tree limbs, thinkin' to ambush us."

Kimbrell rode up beside the scout in the water and listened hard. He thought he heard a horse neighing not too far off. It might be a horse of one of his men, but probably wasn't. They had run the bastards to ground.

"I'll take the lead," Kimbrell said, putting his heels to his horse's flanks. The horse sprang forward at a trot that kicked up froth and water from the streambed. Kimbrell was ready for some serious killing.

When he spied a horse tethered to a tree, he knew the

fight was at hand. He raised the rifle to shoot the horse, just to see what ruckus would occur, when the pounding hooves behind him caused him to glance back along the stream. The rain veiled the rider, but he knew who it was. He cursed and turned back to kill the horse. Limbs weighed down by the increasing rainfall hid the horse now. Before he could ride a few yards farther upstream for a decent killing shot, a man called his name.

"Kimbrell! Albert! Got orders. The major wants ever' one back in camp pronto."

"Soon," Kimbrell said. "I got work to do."

"He ain't kiddin'. He said *now*. In that tone of his."

"Go to hell."

"You'll be there a long time 'fore me if you don't break off and come on back. The others are already gallopin' back to camp."

"All of them?"

"Ever' last one, includin' Lasker. They don't want to see the major mad again. You know what happened last time he got really pissed." The courier sawed on the reins and got turned around. He had delivered the message and didn't much care if Kimbrell obeyed Major Magee's order or not. If he reported he had given the message and Kimbrell wasn't there, Hell would be a nice spot for a leisurely vacation compared to the wrath and destruction Magee would bring down.

Kimbrell had seen the major skin a man alive for disobeying orders. Better to desert and never stop riding than to cross Clayton Magee.

With a savage snarl, Kimbrell lifted his rifle and emptied it through the leafy branches of the tree in the general direction of the horse he had spotted. He had no idea if any of the lead he spewed forth hit its target, but the invective had to. Only a deaf man could have missed the cursing as he shoved his rifle back into its saddle sheath and galloped off, leaving behind two men he knew were going to pop up again, just like a damned prairie dog from its burrow. Magee would be sorry he hadn't finished off those two lawmen.

Kimbrell overtook the courier within a mile, and beat the man back to camp by almost a minute. Even then, he was skirting the edges of Magee's ire. The major paced back and forth, hands clasped behind his back. His face was more florid than usual, and his bushy mustache twitched.

"Discipline," Magee cried, "discipline has been too lax. The sentries will forfeit all the pay for the last month!"

Beside Kimbrell, a man grumbled, "They don't give a shit. They're deader 'n doornails."

"Shut up," snapped Kimbrell. He was in no mood to mince words. If Magee tried to dress him down, there just might be a showdown. The only reason he hadn't shot Magee a long time back was the major's uncanny ability to lead men. If Kimbrell took over, more than half the gang would simply fade away. Those remaining might be good enough to pull a stagecoach robbery or hold up a train, but razing entire towns and looting them would be out of the question. Kimbrell liked the killing as much as he did the plunder from banks and businesses. One town—he never did know the name of the place—had a stagecoach depot that offered up more than three thousand dollars in gold. Not very much of that had made its way into the general coffers. As with so much of what he stole, it got stashed along the way so he could return later and retrieve it.

Kimbrell was going to be a very wealthy man by the time somebody shot Clayton Magee. And the dead major would get the blame for everything because he wore the major's uniform and issued the orders to attack. Nobody would remember Kimbrell. That was about as perfect as any robbery could be.

"We lost a great deal of our ammunition, although our food and other supplies remain untouched," Magee said. "That means we must be more careful in our next assault."

"You got a new place all mapped out, Major?" asked Kimbrell. His heart beat a little faster at the notion. If he couldn't leave those two lawmen stretched out dead for the buzzards, burning down another town might put him in a better mood.

"A scout returned just after you lit out, Mr. Kimbrell," Magee said.

Kimbrell tensed. That meant the major had sought him and hadn't found him.

"What'd the scout report? Did he see 'em in town? The two women?"

Magee remained as closemouthed as could be, but Kimbrell knew the best way of deflecting any anger was to mention the women. As always, it worked. The look on Magee's face changed from anger to anticipation. Or was it eagerness to kill? Kimbrell didn't care. Magee was not going to chew out his ass, and that was all that mattered.

"The scout saw one of our quarry in a nearby town. We are short on ammunition, so we must make our raid as quick and efficient as possible."

"We don't shoot nobody?" asked one of the newer recruits.

"Kill whomever you please. Spare me the women."

Kimbrell knew that wasn't really how it worked. Killing the women was just fine, as long as they started with the whores in the saloons and worked their way up through clerks and waitresses who weren't blond. Even then, Kimbrell knew the killing was fine because they would never set eyes on the two Magee chased all the way across Oklahoma. They might be figments of his crazed imagination, or if they were real, they were already well on the way to California.

Or Kimbrell might have put bullets in them before he raped them in some town weeks ago. He didn't care.

"We ride in ten minutes. Mr. Kimbrell, I want a word with you."

Magee fixed him with his steely gaze, but Kimbrell did not flinch. There was no reason to. If anything, he ought to be mad at the major for pulling him away from the fight just when he had caught the varmints responsible for raiding the camp.

"What is it, Major?"

"I am sure this is it. We were so close before, but this

time, this town, this is it. Make no mistakes. I want them alive. Do I make myself clear, sir?"

"Surely do, Major. But we might have trouble since most all our ammo's been blowed up."

"The guards responsible have been dealt with, I assume?"

"Yeah, punished," Kimbrell said, distracted. "I had the two who'd snuck into camp cornered. If you hadn't pulled me back, I coulda had both of 'em."

"This is more important," Magee said. "This is the reason we are in the field." The major pulled up his collar against the steady rain. "We must overtake them now. If they get away in this rain, there will be no tracks, no catching them."

"Everything else is the same?" The major nodded once. "Why's this different? Are you sure the scout saw the women?"

"One of them. He saw a pretty blond woman in the town who was not a local."

"Might be just passing through," Kimbrell said, feeling ornery. There was no reason to argue with the major, but he was still pissed off that he had let two lawmen get away. The best he might have done was shoot one of their horses. That just wasn't the same as shooting them.

"She was not a local and there is no easy way to 'just pass through,' as you put it. The town has no railroad depot or stagecoach service. From the scout's report, she was a stranger to everyone in town."

"What was she wearing? That might make matters a mite easier findin' her."

"A striped gingham dress. That was all he said."

"More 'n we usually have to go on," Kimbrell said, deciding it was time to appease Magee and get on over to the town. "How far do we have to ride?"

"Not more than twenty miles." Magee indicated the direction the scout had come from. "We can make it by mid-afternoon riding steadily."

Kimbrell gave a sloppy salute, then bellowed, "Into your saddles. We got a lot of ridin' to do today!" He left Magee and went to see that the entire gang was ready. Twenty miles in the rain would be a chore, but it was better than sitting on his ass and being chewed out for minor infractions. Kimbrell snorted. He might as well be in the army.

A slow grin came to his lips as he touched his vest pocket and traced over the severed finger there. He pressed down firmly when he felt the West Point ring. After he and Magee parted company, one way or the other, he intended to wear this ring. He might not have gone to West Point and learned all their fancy tricks, but he was as good as any officer that ever graduated. He was certainly better than the man he'd taken the ring from.

"Move out!" He waved his arm around and then pointed in the direction Magee had indicated. Kimbrell might not have any idea where the town lay, but the scout could backtrack.

Then they could all kill.

The rain came down fitfully, obscuring the tiny town with a torrential curtain one instant and then blowing clear the next. Kimbrell wiped rain from his face as he looked the town over. It might have been any of the other tiny towns they had raided in the past month. One main street lined with businesses. A couple smaller streets running parallel, with a few cutting through at right angles. Mostly those were jammed with tar-paper shacks where people lived. Toward the outskirts of town he saw a few more substantial houses. They would hit those first. The men in them probably had enough money for both guns and ammunition. In the past, though, he had found that the poorer men in a town couldn't scrape up the money for even an old black-powder pistol, much less the lead and powder.

Killing them wasn't as much fun, but Kimbrell wasn't much for keeping score like that. The shooting mattered most. And the robbing. A slow smile came to his lips. The raping wasn't so bad either. Truth was, he enjoyed it all, and Clayton Magee was giving it to him for the taking.

"The scout is moving through the town hunting for the woman again," the major said.

"We kin flush her if we attack straightaway," Kimbrell said.

"Soon, Mr. Kimbrell. I feel this is the place. In my bones, I feel it. They will be here."

Kimbrell almost asked why Magee wanted the two women when he could have any of them in any of the towns they pillaged. He held back because asking questions might delay the attack. More than this, he didn't give two hoots and a holler.

"There's the report coming now," Magee said. Kimbrell turned in the rain and saw how intent Magee was. His eyes were fixed on the returning scout. Nothing else mattered to him but the response from the scout.

"Cain't find 'er now, Major," the scout said. "She's prob'ly somewhere in town, though. The livery stable owner said she was ridin' a sorrel, but took the horse 'bout two hours back."

"She left town two hours ago?"

"Might jist be sightseein'."

"In a nowhere town like this? In the rain?" Kimbrell could only scoff. The place was fit for burning, not taking in the attractions.

"Attack, Mr. Kimbrell. We might be too late. Attack and hunt for her."

"Yee-haaaaaa!" The cry ripped from Kimbrell's lips, and he motioned for the thirty-two men left in the gang to attack. They each drew a pair of pistols and guided their horses using their knees only, so they could fire to both sides as they rode, unencumbered by reins, which they held in their teeth.

The first rounds from their six-shooters sounded like distant thunder. Then it was obvious to everyone in town that this thunder was more deadly. Lead preceded the reports and people wilted like drought-stricken flowers. They collapsed into the muddy streets and across rain barrels, but die they did. Everyone in the way of the onslaught perished.

Kimbrell gritted his teeth as he held the reins between

his teeth. His first two six-guns emptied, and then the second pair. He shoved those back into his belt and drew the last pair of the six he carried.

The reins fell from his mouth as he stared.

"Jesus Christ," he muttered. He lifted his six-shooters and fired until they both came up empty, then went for his rifle. Louder, to be heard over the rain and gunfire, he shouted, "Cavalry! We got cavalry on us!"

His rifle fire brought down the guidon bearer. A sergeant bent low and scooped the guidon up before it hit the muddy ground. Using the pole like a lance, the sergeant galloped forward. Kimbrell fired twice, missing the enlisted man both times. He realized he was going to get skewered if he stayed where he was. Kimbrell grabbed up the reins and got his horse turned around. He galloped back through town yelling his warning.

The troopers were at his heels, hitting at the precise worst instant for the outlaws. They had expended the rounds in their six-shooters and now relied on their rifles. When those came up empty, they had nothing to fall back on. Usually, the town would have been wiped out by this time. But for all the dead townspeople, there were soldiers coming at them spoiling for a fight. Kimbrell bent low as the bullets from the army carbines whistled through the rain all around him.

"Clear out, git outta here!" Kimbrell saw that more than one of the gang had already retreated, leaving their partners to fight the soldiers. If they had presented a solid front, they could have turned the attack. There weren't near as many soldiers as there were outlaws in Magee's gang.

"No quarter," came the order from the officer leading the charge. "Cut them all down, men."

Kimbrell's horse began to falter. It had been a long, tiring ride to reach the town, and the initial attack had been done at full gallop. There wasn't any reserve left in the stalwart horse's legs. Flanks lathered and sides heaving, the horse slowed.

Kimbrell let out a yelp of pain as the sergeant caught up with him and tried to impale him with the company guidon. The metal tip on the pole grazed his thigh and caused him to almost tumble from the saddle. The flag flapped against his arm and caused him to drop his rifle.

"You son of a bitch!" Kimbrell snarled. He swung his fist at the sergeant, but missed and almost accomplished what the soldier had not. Clutching the saddle horn, he hung on until he regained his seat.

The harder he pushed his horse, though, the slower it moved, until he felt as if he were slipping through thick molasses.

"Give up and you'll get a fair trial 'fore we hang you," promised the sergeant. The soldier grabbed and caught Kimbrell's sleeve.

The coat rather than the man went fluttering away. Kimbrell swerved to his right and the sergeant raced past. Working furiously, Kimbrell began reloading one of his six-guns. He was sorry now he had killed so many earlier. It would have been more fun killing soldiers. The town would have been icing on the cake.

"To me! Men, to me!" came the loud cry.

Kimbrell wasn't sure if he was glad to see Major Magee taking charge. Of all the men he had ever ridden with, Magee was the cleverest field commander, but the man didn't have a lick of sense. Nothing mattered to him but finding the damned women. Kimbrell almost kept riding, but saw the sergeant coming around after him. If he wanted to get out alive, he had to rejoin Magee and the survivors of the attack. Only by presenting a solid defense could any of them hope to escape. Otherwise, the army column would track them down and kill them one by one.

"This way, boys. Rally to the major!" Kimbrell did what he could to herd the few outlaws around him toward Magee. By the time he got to the major, about twenty men had gathered, and Magee was positioning them to repel the soldiers' attack.

"Take the left flank, Mr. Kimbrell," Clayton Magee said in a voice so calm he might have been discussing the weather. "My section will advance. You lead your men to the left flank and hit them hard. Everything you can bring to bear."

Kimbrell wasn't sure what this would accomplish, but Magee sounded confident.

"Reload, men, reload as many pistols as you can. We don't have much time."

Behind him he saw the captain in command of the troopers struggling to regain some order and position his men. The sergeant with the guidon rode about, relaying orders, then trotted back to take a position opposite the spot where Magee had ordered Kimbrell to attack. Fear closed on Kimbrell's throat like fingers choking the life from him. He had to fight the madman who'd tried to skewer him with a flagpole. Fumbling, Kimbrell reloaded, dropping as many shells as he shoved into chambers.

"Now, men, full assault! Forward. Attack!" cried Major Magee.

Kimbrell saw the sergeant staring right at him. The soldier dipped the guidon in a mocking salute, then bellowed his own order to attack. At this instant, Kimbrell almost faltered. Then he touched the lump in his vest pocket with the severed finger and West Point ring. He had two vest pockets. It would be nice to get himself a second ring. To do that he had to kill the sergeant and then finish off the captain.

"Fire, fire, fire!" Kimbrell barked. He put his spurs to his tired horse and raked bloody grooves in the animal's flesh to begin the attack.

11

"It must be a trap," Marshal Vannover said. "I don't hear so much as a rabbit stirrin' out there in the woods."

"I'll see what I can find," Slocum said, slithering like a snake over the rotted log and down to the stream bank. The rain was coming down harder now, making it difficult to see more than a few feet. The sound of the rain pounding on the leafy canopy above his head drowned out any possible sound, other than outright gunshots. Moving slowly, Slocum came to the spot where he knew the outlaws had to gather for an attack.

The rain had wiped away any trace of prints in the soft ground. Puddles obscured even the ankle-deep grass in places as water pooled before running down into the stream. Slocum moved quicker now, taking in a huge swath of the forest, and found no trace of the outlaws. He went directly back to where he had left the horses.

His paint pawed nervously at the ground, as mad at being in the rain as having been shot at. The limb where Slocum had looped the reins was damned near shot clean off the tree. He jerked the reins free and swung into the saddle. It took him another minute to fetch the marshal's horse and ride slowly back to where the lawman crouched behind the log.

"It's me, Marshal," Slocum called. "I got your horse and I'm mounted."

The lawman rose and wiped rain from his face, then pulled his hat lower to keep more from getting into his eyes.

"Thanks for the warning. Reckon you're not being led around with a ring in your nose, Slocum. What happened to them owlhoots?"

"They cleared out. Don't know why since they had us dead to rights."

"Never question luck. I've drawn to inside straights, I've shot the center out of a quarter at ten paces, I've even gotten laid by a beautiful woman who didn't ask for money. Accept luck when it comes your way."

The marshal dragged his injured foot behind him as if it had become a stump. Grunting and swearing, he pulled himself into the saddle. The horse sagged under his weight, but was otherwise game.

"We need to get some rest," Slocum said. "For the horses, if not ourselves. And you need a doctor to look at your ankle. If it's busted, you need to get it splinted up."

"The doc in Charity's dead. I saw him with a bullet in the side of his head." Vannover chewed at his lip as he thought, then said, "Cimarron Junction is the next closest town, and it's quite a ride from here. Maybe twenty miles."

"I don't think Magee is heading back to Charity," Slocum said. He had no idea if the major was likely to destroy another town, but he felt the need to warn as many folks as he could. "Which way's Cimarron Junction?"

"That way," Vannover said. "If we go up into the hills and cut straight through, it makes for a strenuous ride, but we can cut three or four hours off takin' the road."

"If the road's turned to soup, going across country might be easier." Slocum pulled up his collar against the rain, then surrendered to the inevitable. The rain came down so hard and at such an angle that it was going down his neck no matter what he did. He kept the hat pulled low to keep the water from his eyes. Other than this, he was going to be riding along miserable all day.

Within an hour the rain let up, and within two he was damp but not soaking. Ahead in the direction of Cimarron Junction, though, rain clouds still threatened.

"You hear that, Slocum?"

Slocum looked up. He had been riding along, lost in thoughts of how wet he was and how he wanted to get into dry clothes. The clouds ahead of them warned him not to put on his spare shirt from his saddlebags. He had kept a lookout for the outlaws, but had not seen hide nor hair of them and had been content to push on as fast as his tired horse would take him. The marshal had been right about the hills being steep, but every time they crossed a road, he was glad they had chosen this route. A horse walking in that mud would sink in over its fetlocks. That would force them to find grassy spots along the road itself. This way was quicker, as well as being easier going in the long run.

"It's not thunder," Slocum anwered.

"Guns. Lots of guns. You thinkin' Magee and his boys are shootin' up Cimarron Junction?"

There was no other explanation. Slocum snapped the reins and got his horse climbing a steep, wooded hill. Halfway up, a fine mist made the going more difficult, and by the top of the ridge, it was raining again.

"Holds down the gun smoke, if nothing else," Vannover said wryly. "See that? Looks like we got two armies about to plow headlong into one another."

"Flanking move. Magee's attacking the soldiers' flank," Slocum said in grudging admiration. From what he could tell of the fight, Magee was in no position to press the attack straight through Cimarron Junction, and if he tried to retreat, the cavalry troopers would chew up his ass. By the counterattack, Magee bought himself time, and might force the cavalry officer to draw back. The instant he did that, Magee would get away with most of his men.

"That's Kimbrell leading the charge," Slocum said. He watched as Magee's lieutenant led the charge directly into a squad of exposed troops. The soldiers fought well, but were forced to retreat. When they began withdrawing in ragged twos and threes, their officer had no choice but to retreat alongside to keep his force from being cut in half.

"Magee's getting away," Vannover said. "We can follow him. We got to, Slocum, or—"

"Is your horse able to walk without staggering? Mine neither. And in this rain, his tracks are going to be washed away within minutes. Let him go and be content that he didn't destroy Cimarron Junction like he did Charity and the other towns."

"Damn, but I want his hide nailed to the barn door," Vannover said.

"Let's see what brought the cavalry to this town at the right time," Slocum said. "From up here, the officer struck me as a decent enough field commander, but not one with a whole lot of imagination."

Vannover looked hard at Slocum before speaking. "You always thinkin' this hard? I didn't expect a drifter to be so observant."

"Makes my head hurt if I think too much," Slocum said.

"Reckon it hurts all the time then. Maybe we can convince a barkeep down yonder to offer up some medicine for what ails us—your head and my ankle."

They rode down the steep hill and angled into town, bypassing the muddy, bloody field where the major portion of the fight had occurred. Slocum saw that for every soldier that had been brought down, an outlaw had, too. Such an even swap was bad for Magee. The cavalry officer need only telegraph Fort Gibson and get out a full company to reinforce him. Sheer numbers would wear down Magee's gang until it was no longer a threat.

At least, Slocum hoped it would work that way. He was sick in his gut at seeing entire towns massacred.

"Whoa, don't go pluggin' us, Private," called Vannover. "I'm a marshal and this here's my deputy." He held up his badge so the guard could see. "Can you take us to see your cap'n?"

"Captain Langmuir's seein' to the troops."

"What about your sergeant?" asked Slocum. "He put up quite a fight back there."

The private beamed. "Sergeant Benedict is a real firecracker. Best noncom out of Fort Supply."

Slocum nodded knowingly. This was all it took to settle matters with the young private.

"Git on off them horses and advance slowlike. Keep yer hands where I kin see 'em."

"You got him trained well, Sergeant Benedict," Slocum called.

"It's all right, Private. I know the marshal from a visit I made to Charity a while back," the sergeant said. Slocum saw that Benedict walked with a limp matching Vannover's. The sergeant's leg was bloody where he had taken a bullet.

"Whole damn boot's filled with blood. Don't dare take it off or I'll never get my foot back in," Benedict said, seeing Slocum eyeing him.

"Got the same problem, only I got a swole-up ankle." Les Vannover pointed to his own leg.

"Heard tell they got a doc who didn't get hisself killed. Why don't us two gimps go see him?"

"Lean on me," said Vannover, "and I'll lean on you."

Slocum watched the two hobble away. He looked around, and had no trouble finding where Langmuir had set up his command post. He went through the batwing doors into the saloon and saw the captain hunched over a faro table at the rear, a map spread in front of him. Two guards brought their rifles up when Slocum entered, but went to order arms when Langmuir spoke to them.

"As you were. What can I do for you?"

"Captain Langmuir? Got some information you might find interesting."

"Unless you're scouting for the whole damn force out of Fort Gibson, I can't imagine what that'd be. Who are you?"

Slocum introduced himself, then explained what had happened and how Magee had lost most of his ammo.

"Might be why he decided to hit Cimarron Junction," Slocum finished.

Captain Langmuir shook his head slowly and pulled out a water-soaked lavender-colored envelope.

"The reason I came was this. You know anything about it or who might have sent it?"

Slocum picked up the envelope and sniffed. His nostrils flared when he caught a familiar scent. It matched that in the Cherokee Springs church and over in Charity. He opened the envelope and quickly read the warning that Magee was going to destroy Cimarron Junction.

"A woman's hand," Slocum said. He did not mention recognizing the perfume. "You don't know who she is?"

"I thought it might be the woman who had warned me in person about Magee and his butchers, but I don't think so. I didn't believe her, but this was . . . to the point."

Slocum slipped the letter back into the envelope and returned it to the captain. The officer had a way with words. "To the point" referring to a letter that detailed the most gruesome destruction imaginable in so few words and sparked action on the cavalry's part. Apparently, the other woman, who warned Langmuir in person, had understated the matter.

"Good thing you believed the warning," Slocum said. "You saved an entire town from being destroyed."

"I need to find out what's going on. That wasn't an ordinary outlaw I faced out there. It was as if I had been thrust into the war."

"Major Magee is supposed to be quite a tactician," Slocum said. "Mostly, all he has to do is ride into town and shoot anything that moves, but he seems capable of executing real military maneuvers."

"I need answers, Slocum. Who might supply them?"

"Not me. Marshal Vannover might. He talked to two women back in Charity about Magee. The pair of you might piece together something. He's with your Sergeant Benedict getting their wounds tended to."

"You have any idea where Magee would retreat?" Langmuir tapped the map on the faro table.

"Vannover's the man to see. Or the town marshal here." Slocum saw from the expression on the captain's face that wasn't likely. "He get killed?"

"One of the first. He walked out to parley with them after the first few shots were fired."

Slocum didn't have to ask how that had worked for the marshal. He hoped he would get a decent headstone that didn't include words like "damn fool" or "suicidal."

"I'll talk to Marshal Vannover. Don't leave town without seeing me first, Slocum."

"All I want is a hot bath, some food, and to get my horse tended to."

The captain nodded brusquely and swept out of the saloon, his aides trailing behind, struggling to fold the map and keep up with their commander.

Slocum settle down in a chair and looked around. The saloon was uncharacteristically empty for this time of day. The owner barkeep might have been among Magee's victims. Slocum got up and reached behind the bar to pull down a full bottle of whiskey. He held it up and approved of the color. This might actually contain Billy Taylor's Finest, like the label said, rather than trade whiskey poured into the bottle.

He went up the rickety stairs at the back of the room and poked around. Several cribs where the soiled doves had brought their drunken clients were all empty. None looked too appealing to Slocum, so he went down the back steps and wandered about until he spied the bathhouse at the rear of the hotel. He took a few swigs of whiskey as he worked to light a fire and heat water for a bath. He downed another mouthful of liquor and began to feel mellow. The aches and pains faded and the bath would erase them entirely.

When he was done, he could go into the hotel, get a meal and a room, and sleep until Captain Langmuir decided to roust him. Slocum hoped the captain wasn't a stickler for protocol and observed reveille at dawn.

He finished heating four buckets of water for the large galvanized tub in the small bathhouse. Slocum sloshed out most of the cold, dirty water already in the tub and added his own. He stretched and got muscles working enough to slip out of his clothes. Making sure his six-shooter was close enough to grab if he needed it, he got a brush, some soap from a box on a shelf, and settled down into the hot water.

The searing water caused him to tense, then began working on his muscles until he relaxed and leaned back. His eyes closed of their own accord, and he drifted away, only to come instantly awake when he smelled it.

Rose perfume.

He reached for his six-gun, but froze when he saw the woman standing at the foot of the tub. A small grin turned her bow-shaped lips into something approaching perfection. She wore her blond hair tied back into a ponytail that fell to mid-shoulder. It took Slocum a few seconds to move past her high cheekbones and button nose and piercing blue eyes, but he did. Her shirt was unbuttoned, giving just a hint of white swell from her breasts. She was dressed like a man, but there was nothing manly about those flaring hips and trim waist. From where she stood, he could not see her legs.

They probably matched the rest of the perfect package.

He inhaled deeply, then let the breath out slowly.

"I've smelled you before," he said. He was rewarded by her cornflower blue eyes opening wide. The smile turned to openmouthed surprise. She tried to speak, no words came out. Then she clamped her mouth shut and worked to get her confusion quelled. To Slocum, this made her even lovelier.

"I don't understand," she said.

"Your perfume. I caught a whiff of it in the church back in Cherokee Springs. Then again in Charity, in the restaurant after Magee shot it up. You seem to be a chip bobbing along on a stream."

"And the stream is Clayton Magee," she said. All hint of amusement drained from her now.

"I reckon it's more of a flood."

She put her hands on the end of the tub and leaned forward. Slocum got an even better view down her cleavage.

"I hope I'm not interrupting," she said. She looked from his face down to a spot in the frothy bathwater. The pixie smile returned. "Perhaps I am doing just the opposite."

"You're helping to churn up my bathwater," Slocum said. He sat a little straighter so his erection would sink back below the surface of the bath.

"I hope that's not all I'm helping to churn," she said, bending over even farther. Now he could see more of her breasts. The only blemish on her perfect female form was a large mole on the top of her left breast. Slocum thought that was something he wanted to examine closer.

"You warned Captain Langmuir about Magee raiding Cimarron Junction," Slocum said.

"I did. Is that all you want to talk about?" She moved around and perched on the side of the tub, partly turned toward him.

"I'm John Slocum."

"I know. I asked. One of the soldiers told me."

"If I asked all the soldiers, would they tell me your name?"

"They don't know it. Not even the captain."

"That's a shame. I'm sure you have a lovely name. Rose? Your name is Rose."

She laughed and shook her head. More than her head swayed from side to side.

"Violet? Daisy? Peony?"

"Do I look like a hothouse flower?" She laughed so hard now that she slipped and fell backward into the tub with Slocum. He made no move to break her fall. She landed on his lap with a huge splash that sent water upward, where it hung suspended for a moment, then came rushing back to drench the parts of her that had not been soaked already.

"You look like a well-watered one," Slocum said. He reached out and laid his hand on her breast. The water plastered her shirt to her so that her nipple protruded. His fingers parted and then scissored back together, catching the sensitive nub.

"Oh, oh, my," she said, closing her eyes and splashing about just a little. "I had not counted on this."

"Like hell," Slocum said. Her eyes snapped open. Her angry look faded when she met his gaze. The smile returned.

"Perhaps, I had hoped just a little. You've done so much tracking of Clayton Magee that I wanted to see you with my own eyes."

"What's your beef with Magee?"

"Sarah Beth is my friend. I want to help her. She and her mama are running from him, and I want to help them and—"

Slocum silenced her by bending over and kissing her full on the lips. For a moment, she sputtered, then relaxed, and finally returned the kiss with full passion. More water sloshed about as she turned toward him.

When she broke off the kiss, she whispered hotly in his ear, "Catherine," her tongue following the name into the channel of his ear. Before he could protest, her tongue slid away, around, down to the lobe, where she nibbled. She added, "Duggan."

"So, Catherine Duggan," Slocum said, his hands roaming her body. "You'll catch your death of cold in those wet duds." He moved his hand under her shirt and peeled it away from her skin so his hand rested on warm, bare flesh. He pressed down and felt the nip getting harder. She ground her chest into his hand, moaning louder now.

"I shouldn't" she said.

"You already have." He slid his hand down lower and found her belt. He managed to unfasten it. The button holding her jeans was next to go. He worked down, unfastening buttons until her pants were loose around her trim waist.

She put her hands on his shoulders, lithely turned, and stood so one foot was on either side of him in the tub. He reached up and grabbed the waistband of her wet jeans and began pulling. They resisted until Catherine began a slow, sinuous movement of her hips, then started bucking back and forth to aid him getting them over her ass and down her slender legs. She stepped out of them and stood above him, naked from the waist down. Her shirt hung open, giving tantalizing glimpses of her breasts.

"You have to decide," she chided. "What do you want? These?" She cupped her breasts and jiggled. "Of this?" Her hand ran down across her belly to the tangle of wet fur between her legs.

Slocum reached up, got his hands around her waist, and pulled her to a kneeling position over his waist.

"Why not both?"

"Oh!" She gasped as his hardness slid upward between her nether lips and into her heated interior. Catherine gasped even louder when Slocum bent forward and began licking and sucking at her pink, rubbery nubs.

"I . . . I can't take much of this."

"You in a hurry?" Slocum asked. He was beginning to enjoy it. The water cradled him as surely as the warm female flesh around his erection. She bent forward and almost smothered him with her marshmallowy breasts. His hands worked around her back, up under her shirt, then down lower to cup her firm buttocks.

She let out a tiny trapped-animal sound as she sank even lower and took more of him into her core. There wasn't much room for movement. There didn't have to be. She rose and dropped only a couple inches, but this was enough to arouse them both. The tightness of the passage, her heat, and his hardness generated increasing carnal friction until she threw back her head, ponytail snapping like a whip, and let out a long, loud cry of release.

Slocum wanted this to last, but the way she clamped down around him threatened to crush him flat. He groaned and felt the heat deep within begin to build. The pressure was not to be denied when she tensed and relaxed all around his hidden length. He exploded like a stick of dynamite.

She cried out again, put her arms around his neck, and pulled him close. Slocum was caught in a sexy web he did not want to escape. And then she let go of her hold around his neck and rocked back. He slipped from within her.

"That's the way I'd like to take a bath all the time," he said.

This brought another smile to her lips. She looked positively radiant now. The smile added that much more to her beauty.

"I've never done anything like this before," she said.

"I wondered when you would start."

"What? Start what?" She looked startled again.

"When you'd start lying. This wasn't your first time. You knew what you wanted and, if I'm any judge, you got it."

"Oh, I did, I did," Catherine said. She worked her way backward and then up to sit on the edge of the tub at the foot. Her legs were parted just enough to give Slocum a tantalizing look at her blond bush. He reached out, but she swatted his hand.

"Naughty, naughty," she said. "I meant I don't jump into bed with a man the first time I lay eyes on him."

"Your virtue is still intact then," Slocum said. "You jumped into my tub, not my bed. It's always good to save something for later."

"Are you bragging?" She looked down at his crotch. The water had sloshed out of the tub and left him exposed to her gaze now.

"Anticipating," he said.

"You are an arrogant man, aren't you?" She swung around, got her feet on the floor, and found her jeans. She began wringing them out the best she could so she could put them back on. Slocum enjoyed the show as she struggled to get back into the wet pants.

"Not arrogant," he said. "Confident."

"Then find Magee and stop him. Even better, help me find Sarah Beth and her mother so we can help them."

Slocum said nothing as Catherine finished dressing. She had made love to him to enlist his aid finding Magee's daughter and mother. As he watched her leave the bathhouse, he decided it had worked. Catherine Duggan was one beautiful woman, and she knew how to pleasure a man. Slocum could do a lot worse in the way of bribes.

He finished his bath the best he could in the few ounces of water remaining, then stood, shook himself like a dog to get the water off, dressed, and went to find Catherine. They had a powerful lot to talk over.

And he wanted her to bribe him some more.

12

Slocum had no trouble following Catherine Duggan because she left wet tracks in the dirt all the way to the back door of the hotel. Slocum went inside and down a short hallway into the lobby. He almost laughed when he saw the woman trying to rent a room. The clerk was paying almost no attention to her request because her clothing clung so tenaciously to her trim body.

"Could I help?" Slocum asked.

"He says there aren't any rooms. The people on the outskirts of town have come in because they think that monster Magee will return at any instant."

"You must have a room for the lady," Slocum said. "Me, too." He laid his six-shooter on the counter. For the first time, the clerk's attention strayed from Catherine's half-buttoned, clinging wet shirt. He stared at the worn ebony butt of the Colt Navy, licked his lips, then looked up into Slocum's cold green eyes.

"I, uh, we don't have nuthin', mister. Honest."

"Not even a single, solitary room? For the one who saved your hide?"

"What do you mean?"

"Who do you think alerted Captain Langmuir to the attack on Cimarron Junction?"

"You?"

Slocum said nothing, letting the clerk come to his own conclusions.

"We got a small room. Not got a bed big enough for a man as tall as you." He stared up at Slocum's six-foot frame. "But it'll be better 'n nuthin', I suppose."

"Good." Slocum glanced out of the corner of his eye at Catherine, who fumed. When the clerk shoved the key in Slocum's direction, he pushed it across to Catherine. "She's the one who got the cavalry here in time to save your hide."

"Her?"

"Her," Slocum said.

"Where do you think you're going to sleep?" the blonde asked.

"He said it was a small bed. Might be crowded." Slocum enjoyed the way she bristled at the notion they were going to share the bed. "Not as crowded as a bathtub. That right?" Slocum directed the question to the clerk, but never took his eyes off Catherine.

"Reckon that might be so," the clerk said, frowning. He didn't understand what Slocum was getting at.

"I'd rather sleep in the mud," she said.

"Be sure to avoid drain spouts," Slocum said. He took his gun off the counter, picked up the key, and headed down the narrow hallway to a spot near the back door. He had thought this was a closet when he came in. Opening the door and peering into the dark, damp room convinced him he wasn't far wrong. He stepped in, and immediately what light filtered in from outside was blanked out. Catherine Duggan stood in the door.

"That's the bed?" she said in a weak voice.

Slocum sat on the bed and bounced. The ropes holding the straw-filled mattress creaked under his weight.

"Looks to be," he said. "Here." He tossed her the key. Catherine caught it and stared at it. He got up, put his hands on her waist, and turned her around so she was in the room and he was in the doorway. "There might be bedbugs in the mattress." Without another word, he stepped into the hallway and opened the rear door leading to the bathhouse.

"Wait, where are you going? This is your room."

"It's yours. You weren't getting anywhere with the clerk."

"Where will you sleep?"

"You offering the bed?" He grinned at her shocked expression. Slocum couldn't figure her out. She was willing to strip down to the buff and share her ample bounty when he was in the bath, but not now. Something about her dithering amused him. She was all manners and righteousness now, trying to live down what she had done before so impulsively.

"All yours," he said.

"But where *will* you sleep?"

"It won't be the first time I've bedded down with another companion."

"Oh. There's someone else?"

"My horse, the livery stables, nice clean straw," he said.

"Wait, don't go."

Slocum hesitated. He was not certain what she was offering.

"You were after Magee before he destroyed Charity. You were in Cherokee Springs, too. What's your interest? I told you why I want to stop him."

"You don't want to stop him, you want to get his daughter and wife out of his way," Slocum said.

"I suppose that's so, but I want him dead. That's the only way Sarah Beth and Mrs. Magee will ever be safe. What's your interest? You don't know them, do you?"

"Never heard the names till I got to Charity," Slocum said. "I made a promise. That's why I'm after Magee." He didn't want to go into the promise he had made Nickson back in Cherokee Springs.

"It must be a promise to a dear friend," Catherine said.

"I take such things seriously," Slocum said. "Enjoy your room." He touched the brim of the hat and closed the door behind him. He waited a moment to see if Catherine would open it and come after him. He expected her to offer to share the bed—and all that meant. But the doorknob did not turn. He shrugged it off. Some women would do things in private they would never fess up to in public.

Catherine Duggan's reputation would take a beating if it came out she was crowded into the same room—and bed— with him. Slocum stepped out behind the hotel and looked at the sky. The rain had stopped, but the dreary, lead-gray clouds remained.

He walked around Cimarron Junction and thought on what he saw. Mostly, he thought about Catherine and how she had so mysteriously and emphatically come into his life. She had been in Cherokee Springs and Charity where he had caught more than a whiff of her distinctive perfume. The letter warning of Magee's attack on Cimarron Junction carried her indelible scent, too. She was doing a powerful lot of traveling, just a step ahead of Clayton Magee.

Slocum frowned as he considered this. How did Catherine Duggan do that? She hunted for Sarah Beth Magee and her mother, but she was behind them by about as much as she was ahead of Major Magee. That took quite a bit of detective work on her part.

"She must be a powerful good friend to risk her life like this. What is it she thinks she can do if she catches up with Sarah Beth and her ma that they aren't already doing?" To that question, Slocum had no answer.

Slocum glanced into the saloon and saw a few men there. He doubted they were leaving payment for the whiskey they swilled any more than he had when he'd taken the bottle. Slocum shrugged it off. The booze was their due, as it had been his. Facing Magee and surviving deserved some small reward.

The next morning, he wandered about until he found the doctor's surgery. Two men sat outside, slumped against the wall. Their bandages were fresh, and they didn't appear to be in much pain. Slocum went inside, and had to step over three men stretched out on the floor. Their condition was a considerable amount worse than those outside.

A harassed young man, hardly into his twenties, looked up. He wore a white coat stained with blood. His hands were bright red, and he held some sort of surgical instrument.

"If you're able to walk, find somebody else to patch you up. I got men who have real injuries."

"You the doctor?"

"Not the town woodcutter, though that would be more appropriate." The young doctor looked back at the man on his surgical table. Slocum saw three bullet holes as the doctor worked on the man's other side. He must have caught at least four slugs.

"Looking for the Charity marshal. Name's Vannover."

"Don't ask their names. What was wrong with him?" The doctor glanced at the corner of the room where three men were stacked like cordwood. Not all the doctor's patients survived to sit outside.

"Swollen ankle. Might have been a broken bone in his foot."

"Him. He's in the back room." The doctor pointed with the forceps, then opened them to drop a bullet into a small tin coffee cup. The tinny ring in his ears, Slocum went to the curtain separating the rooms and pulled it back. Marshal Vannover sat on the window ledge, his leg thrust out in front of him.

"Dammit, they cut off my boot. Perfectly good boot, too. Only had it six months."

"Get the town to buy you a new pair."

"Damned cheapskates wouldn't go for a pair."

"Get them to buy you a replacement for the one boot."

"It'd likely be for the wrong foot. Mark my words, Charity's town fathers are a penny-pinching lot, and not too bright either."

Slocum had to laugh. He stepped over more patients laid out. These were either sleeping or in a coma. He leaned against the wall next to the marshal.

"You talk to Captain Langmuir to find out what he's going to do next?" Slocum asked.

Vannover shook his head. "Been locked up here since we got to town. That doc's doing the work of three men. Might be he'd want to come to Charity."

"Especially since you lost your doctor," Slocum said. This erased any joking the two men engaged in.

"Reckon there's no point stayin' here. I need to get back to Charity," the marshal said. "Trouble is, I don't know if I can ride or not. Every time I stand up, I get all dizzy and want to fall over. Can't imagine what it would be on horseback."

"There's nothing keeping me here," Slocum said. "I'll ride with you."

"Why's that? You're not nursemaidin' me. Not out of the goodness of your heart." Vannover fought to focus his eyes. Slocum saw how bloodshot those once-sharp gray eyes were. The marshal needed to rest, but Slocum understood his need to get home. That was always a powerful draw. Home.

"I don't think Magee will be back here," Vannover said. "Not sure why he came roaring into Cimarron Junction, but it was a mistake since he butted up against the cavalry."

"Don't know for sure, but he might have been lured here," Slocum said, thinking that Catherine Duggan was blond and might have been mistaken for one of the Magee women. If she did use herself as bait, getting Magee to attack and hoping Captain Langmuir responded to her letter, she played a far more dangerous game than Slocum ever thought.

"If he comes back, Langmuir's not got a celluloid collar in hell's chance of fighting him," said Vannover. "From what the doc was sayin', Langmuir lost half his men. Don't know what casualties Magee took, but he probably outnumbers the soldiers by two or three to one now."

"Magee looks to be a decent field commander. Too bad he got the taste for spilling blood and liked it," Slocum said. "I'm going to look over the bodies of the men he lost."

"You huntin' for something, aren't you, Slocum?" Vannover winced and turned pale with pain.

"Aren't we all?" With that, Slocum made his way past the bodies. This time the doctor did not even look up. He tossed aside an instrument and began bandaging a wound he had just sewn shut. Slocum had seen too many field hospitals for this to be a revelation to him, but getting outside, though the sun refused to shine and rain threatened again, was a relief.

He found Sergeant Benedict and asked after the outlaws' bodies.

"We got 'em piled over yonder. Not sure what to do with them," the sergeant said.

"Mind if I poke around?"

"You thinkin' on robbin' the corpses?"

"I'm looking for one thing in particular. If I find it, I'll let you and the captain know. Otherwise, they've got nothing I want."

"The captain's decided any money on the bodies goes to the families what lost loved ones here."

Slocum nodded agreement. The sergeant escorted him to where a private stood guard, and let the youngster know Slocum was allowed to hunt to his heart's content. The private looked as if he was going to lose his last meal as his head bobbed up and down in assent.

"Much obliged, Sergeant," Slocum said. Then he got to work. An hour later, he was sorry he had taken a bath and then searched the bodies. He smelled of blood and death once more. Worse, he had not found Nickson's ring. Disgusted, he bade the private adieu and returned to the surgery. Marshal Vannover was sitting outside now, making room for others inside.

"You look like you been in a battle and lost, Slocum. Before, you were all sweet-smelling and clean."

"Sweet-smelling," Slocum said, remembering Catherine Duggan and her distinctive rose perfume. "Be a spell before I'm accused of that again."

"You'd really shepherd me back to Charity? I'd really

appreciate the gesture." Vannover moved his splinted leg around. The doctor had cut off the marshal's pants leg just above the knee. From the knee to the ankle, he had taped two sturdy splints. Vannover could hobble along stiff-legged, but riding would be even more difficult. There was no way he could ever put his injured foot into a stirrup.

"Suppose I could toss you over a saddle like a sack of flour," Slocum said.

"My belly'd give out before my leg," Vannover said.

"What do you say to grabbing some chow, then hitting the trail?" Slocum looked up at the sky. "Weather's never going to improve."

"I wrangled some supplies," the marshal said. "Got us a pair of slickers, too, for all the good they'd do in a real gully washer."

"Better than nothing," Slocum allowed. He helped the marshal to stand, then let him lean heavily on him as they made their way to a small restaurant. After the meal, Slocum brought around their horses. It took the better part of five minutes to get Vannover into the saddle. Once he was there, Slocum wondered how long the man could ride before he keeled over. But Vannover was game.

"You got folks to say good-bye to, Slocum?"

"Nope, nobody in particular. The captain's no special friend."

Slocum turned to see what Vannover had meant. Standing on the front steps of the hotel, Catherine Duggan fought with herself over whether to wave good-bye. Slocum mounted, politely touched the brim of his hat as he nodded in her direction, then rode off without so much as a backward glance.

"You're leaving behind a mighty fine-looking filly," Vannover said as they reached the outskirts of Cimarron Junction. "The way she was eyeing you, it might be worth staying in Cimarron Junction another day or two."

"I just met her," Slocum said. He couldn't remember ever having "just met" a woman who got him hard and pleasured herself so avidly and who wasn't also a soiled dove. But Catherine Duggan was not a woman of ill repute. Everything about her spoke of wealth and class. It might have been an interesting day or two figuring out her motives, but Slocum was more inclined to track down Clayton Magee and honor his promise to Jerome Nickson, if he could. As he rode, he considered what he would tell the man's son if he was unable to recover the West Point ring.

It had been important enough that his son get the ring for Nickson to make a dying request. Slocum considered finding a ring—any ring—and passing it along if he couldn't find which of Magee's bravos had taken both ring and finger. It had meant so much to Nickson that it had to mean something to his son.

"Slocum," moaned Vannover the following morning. "I'm not feelin' so good."

"You look like you're ready to die," Slocum said, riding closer to the marshal. Sweat beaded the man's face, and he looked flushed. Slocum didn't have to reach over to know Vannover was running a fever. His eyes were bright and his hands shook.

"Wish I would. That'd put me out of my misery. Your misery, too. You wouldn't have to nursemaid . . ." Vannover began swaying. Slocum strained to grab a handful of the marshal's jacket before the man toppled to the ground. "Thanks. I'm right as rain again."

Slocum knew he was anything but right as rain.

"Where's the nearest town?" Slocum asked. "We've been riding so long, I'm not sure going back to Cimarron Junction is the quickest."

"Signpost a ways back," Vannover said. "A town's not too far. Not sure which or where, but it's got to be along the road." Vannover gestured vaguely, telling Slocum he had no idea at all where the town lay. For all Slocum knew, the marshal was hallucinating.

Slocum tried to remember the times they had crossed the muddy road. As before, they had lit out across country and found the traveling to be easier. Now he was sorry they had done this. The road meandered up and down the valleys, and often followed a good-sized stream.

"If we cut to the left and make the crest of that ridge, we ought to see this town," Slocum said. "You don't know what it is?"

"Ought to."

Slocum grabbed again to keep the marshal from tumbling out of the saddle. The man slumped forward and clung to the saddle horn with both hands. This was barely enough to keep him astride his horse. If Slocum didn't spot another town, he knew they had to head back to Cimarron Junction and the doctor there. From the way Vannover was burning up with fever, he might not make it, but Slocum knew the doctor would never leave town to tend a patient out in the countryside. There was still too much work to do in the aftermath of Magee's raid.

Keeping a close watch on the lawman, Slocum led the man's horse to the top of the ridge. He heaved a sigh of relief when he spotted the small town nestled in a hollow. He had been right about the stream. It ran near the town. The road was barely a pair of muddy twin ruts, though, the rain erasing all hint of how much traffic came through the area. In the distance, Slocum saw the cornfields and some cattle grazing contentedly in grassy meadows. Clayton Magee's plague of destruction had left this town untouched.

"Come on, old-timer," Slocum said, tugging on the reins to the marshal's horse. "We need to find a doctor to get you all fixed up."

Vannover did not offer even a murmur in reply. Slocum hoped the man hadn't upped and died, but he wasn't going to check to see until they reached town. He had seen enough dead bodies lately without taking it upon himself to bury another up here on the hillside.

13

Clayton Magee paced back and forth with his hands clasped behind his back. He seethed with the indignity of being defeated in such a manner, and by a mere captain of cavalry.

"We're gonna lose a few of the men, Major," Albert Kimbrell reported.

"To injury or desertion?"

Kimbrell seemed to balance his answer. Magee would have none of that. His men had to be honest or there was no point in having them in his chain of command.

"Spit it out, sir!"

"More are deserting than are injured. Mostly, the injured died on the spot. There might have been a couple who didn't escape, but we managed to get most of those who weren't seriously injured away from that town."

"Good. We must cleave together or they will destroy us one by one."

"Easier said than done, Major," Kimbrell said. "Everyone's mighty disheartened."

"I know." Magee's mind raced, turning over possibilities and determining what he could do and what he could not. A smile crept to the corners of his lips. He faced Kimbrell and said, "What post did that captain ride from?"

"Where was he stationed? Don't know. I didn't recognize the insignia on the company pennant."

"We know the insignia of Fort Gibson."

"Reckon he wasn't from Fort Gibson then," Kimbrell said, obviously not understanding what the major meant.

"There are only a few other possibilities, the most likely being Fort Supply."

"That's somewhere to the west of here, ain't it?"

"It is. With this captain in the field, their garrison is reduced by at least twenty men. It is not unusual for a post commander to send out more than one squad to patrol any given area. Fort Supply is not large. There can be only a handful of soldiers remaining to protect it."

"You're not thinkin' on attackin' the fort? That's crazy!" Kimbrell bit back anything more.

"You might think me crazy, but we are out of ammunition." Magee let the criticism of his second in command hang for a moment before going on. "We need supplies. Too many of our horses were injured in the skirmish."

"We got maybe fifteen or twenty men left, Major."

"It's time to buck up their spirits with a resounding victory. If we do not strike quickly and well, more will desert." Magee heaved a sigh of resignation. "If only this were the army. I could catch, try, and hang deserters. There is nothing holding them to my company, however, other than loyalty. Therefore, I must show that I deserve their courage and blood and sacrifice."

"By attackin' Fort Supply?"

"Precisely," Magee said. "Get the men onto the trail immediately. We ride for Fort Supply!" The fervor of a daring maneuver executed well burned once more within Magee's breast. He had not found Louisa and Sarah Beth at Cimarron Junction. The scout had been wrong and that misinformation had almost led to their downfall. The man had paid for his carelessness with his life. Magee had seen the scout shot from the saddle. His death would light the way for greater victories!

Clayton Magee would once more be united with his

wife and daughter. No matter how their kidnappers hid them, he would free them and they would again live as a cherished, happy family.

First, he would raze Fort Supply.

"The men are too tired to fight, Major," Kimbrell complained.

Magee glared at him. It had taken much hard riding to reach Fort Supply. The cavalry post stretched out over the prairie, virtually undefended. Unlike most posts in the region, it sported a ten-foot palisade with guardhouses at each of the four corners of the wall. The fort depended on sentries in those lookout posts to raise the alarm should they be attacked by Indians, but he knew from careful observation that only one of the rear lookout posts and the gate had sentries. There were far fewer soldiers than normal at Fort Supply.

Magee was a student of such matters, and could not remember the last time a fort in Oklahoma had been attacked. Although guards would be marching along their posts, there would be no alarm raised if he employed a coordinated attack, front and rear.

Fort Supply was complacent and ripe for the picking.

"How much ammunition does each man carry?" Magee asked, ignoring the complaint about exhaustion. Armies that marched into battle never had enough rest. That was a given condition of combat. Seldom were they completely prepared, often lacking adequate training and supplies, when they faced death in battle.

Clayton Magee was willing to endure all that to free his family and see them once more at home.

"Not more than fifty rounds. They scavenged what they could from the men who left and those that died."

"Good work," Magee said, nodding in approval. "Fifty rounds each, twenty men. We should have an adequate amount of ammunition for the task."

"If we ride down their throats, they're likely to keep firing at us from up on them walls. They've got an entire armory chock-full of rifles and all the ammunition they can carry."

Magee waved this objection aside. Fort Supply, in spite of its name, had the same problems as all other frontier posts. Chronic undersupply, mistakes made in supply shipments, it was all the same whether in peace or war. If anything, such lackadaisical resupply might be more of a problem in a peacetime garrison. No one died immediately to raise ire back at headquarters.

"See how they patrol only along the eastern wall?" Magee asked.

"They got a man stationed at the west wall, too," Kimbrell said. "I can take him out with a single shot. How are you gonna get through the gate?"

"The wall is sturdy enough for soldiers to crouch behind and fire. If we committed to a frontal assault, a handful of them would certainly repel us. Instead, we have a few men ride up and engage the sentries in conversation."

"Then shoot 'em down?"

"Exactly. Attack will come from three sides, with the bulk of our force moving in from the north and south to scale those walls. A few ropes over the palisade spikes will suffice for climbing. Those on the east will do little more than kill the guards. You will act as sniper for the lone guard at the west wall."

"You called that a pincer movement," Kimbrell said. "That worked real good before, on the first town we hit."

"There has been no need to use the same tactics since," Magee said, sniffing in disdain. "There has not been sufficient opposition anywhere else."

"When do we hit 'em?"

"It is almost sundown," Magee said. "Twilight will cover movement north and south. Eight men to either flank. You will go around to the far side. I will take three men with me to query the guards."

"When do I shoot the guard?" Kimbrell was already eager for the fight. Magee appreciated that, but hoped his lieutenant would not jump the gun. If he did, they would have a serious fight on their hands, with all the soldiers being alerted. He hoped to take most of them by surprise since his own ranks had been decimated.

"There will be gunshots when the guards are taken out," Magee said. "When you hear the shots, do not hesitate. Attack right away."

"What if I can't get the guard?"

Magee flushed with anger and almost his pistol. He stayed his hand. No wonder they had not found Louisa and Sarah Beth yet. He was surrounded by fools and incompetents.

"Attack when you please," Magee said. "I will coordinate my attack to match yours. Is that clear enough for you?"

"Don't ever talk to me in that tone," Kimbrell snapped. "I won't tolerate it." His head rocked back as Magee slapped him hard. Kimbrell staggered and went for his pistol, only to find he was staring down the barrel of the major's six-shooter.

"Obey my orders and you will continue to profit. I know what you do in the towns. I don't care. All I care about is finding those I seek."

"Your damned family," growled Kimbrell, rubbing his jaw. "You didn't have to hit me."

"To your horse, sir, and move into position. You have very little time. We must take the fort before night falls." Magee watched Kimbrell slink off, still grumbling to himself as he rubbed his jaw. Magee had not wanted to strike a subordinate, but sometimes authority had to be enforced. He opened the gate on his six-gun and made certain he had a full cylinder. Then he waved over the three men who would accompany him. He wanted to get this done before night worked against him.

Magee and the three rode slowly toward the break in the low wall where two guards stood. The guards talked idly until one spotted the riders approaching. Magee did not vary his horse's gait. He rode forward as if he intended nothing more than to inquire after the post commander's health.

"Halt!" called the shorter of the two guards. Although

he did not level his rifle, he did turn it in Magee's general direction.

"May I advance and speak to you? I have business with the post commander." Magee saw that the guard high on the wall looked down curiously, making an easy target from the ground.

"Come on ahead," the guard said, foolishly lowering his rifle.

"Good evening," Magee said, leaning forward slightly. This allowed him to put his hand on the butt of the six-shooter slung in a cross-draw holster. "Just the pair of you on guard duty tonight?"

"Mason got the shits," said the second guard. "I do declare, we're all gonna die from eatin' in the mess hall 'less we git a new cook soon."

"No," said Magee, "that's not true."

"What's not true?" asked the first guard, stepping forward.

"The food won't kill you. I will." Magee drew and fired three times. The guard was dead before he hit the ground. Magee turned his weapon on the stunned second guard. A single shot to the head ended his life. Turning his attention upward, he emptied his pistol. One round caught the guard on the wall. He landed with a loud thud inside the fort. Magee motioned for his three men to join him.

"I hear gunshots, Major. Comin' from both sides of the fort."

"Have your six-shooters ready," he ordered. Magee counted slowly, every number corresponding to an event. Inside. Shoot any soldiers found. Ride closer to the compound. Shoot curious soldiers coming out of their barracks. Ride to the armory. Kill the guard there and cut off the soldiers from their weapons.

He heard a loud outcry. The soldiers finally realized they were under attack. If there were enough remaining at the post, they could swamp his handful of stalwarts.

"Attack," Magee ordered. "Make every shot count, but be sure you stop anyone wearing a uniform." He put his heels to his stallion and rocketed out onto the parade ground. He burst out into the center of the open area, and saw three howitzers lined up near the flagpole. The few soldiers running around, frantically trying to find a noncom or officer to tell them what to do, all died under Magee's accurate gunfire.

The roar of six-guns blazing reached him from both sides of the fort. Then the sounds died out. Only a few moans of pain remained. His men had successfully scaled the unguarded walls and made the attack a success thus far. Kimbrell rode up through the gate, shouting.

"Got the son of a bitch, Major. No more guards on the walls!"

With that succinct report, Kimbrell dismounted and walked around, finishing off the wounded soldiers. Magee started to order him to save his ammunition, then decided to let Kimbrell continue. After he had been humiliated before the attack, Kimbrell needed something to bolster his spirits.

They all did.

Magee rode past the commanding officer's quarters. He did not bother looking inside. He wanted the armory secured before making a room-to-room search for survivors.

He slid from the saddle and went to the armory door. It was heavily chained and padlocked.

"Open it. No, don't try shooting off the lock. Get a crowbar. Pry off the lock." Magee shook his head in wonder. These men thought the heavy padlock was just like the ones used on stagecoach strongboxes. One thing the army did not scrimp on was locks. A bullet would only smear itself across the face of the heavy brass lock. Worse, it might foul the mechanism. Better to begin with a pry bar.

Magee waited impatiently as a man returned with a long iron rod. It took almost a minute to force open the door. Magee pushed the man aside and went inside. The dying light from the sunset made it difficult to see what was stored there.

"There. Get that outside. That and that also. Take it to the parade ground."

His men obeyed. Magee posted three men, two to stand guard and the third to dispense ammunition and rifles from the armory, then went to the howitzer nearest the flagpole.

"Do as I say." He guided two men through loading the cannon and turning it toward the officers' quarters. "You will face away and yank the lanyard when I order you," Magee said to a frightened young man. "You will enjoy the experience, I promise."

"It'll blow up something."

"It will."

This made the man grin wolfishly and do everything Magee told him to do.

Magee sighted the cannon in, then gave the order. The man yanked hard at the lanyard and the howitzer fired with a satisfying roar. Then all hell broke loose. The cannonball smashed into the officers' barracks. The resulting fireball exploded upward into the twilight, dazzling anyone looking in that direction.

"You were right, Major. That's 'bout the most fun I've had in a coon's age."

"Reload. Aim in *that* direction," Magee ordered. He trained the cannon on the building where the post commander, his executive officer, the quartermaster, and others had their offices. He smiled ruefully when he saw muzzle flashes coming from doorways and windows. Some of the officers had either worked late or had taken refuge in that building. Magee gave the order to fire. The officers not killed by the first shot were blown apart with his second.

The cannon's roar continued to echo in his ears, but Magee knew the fort was eerily silent now. His men had completed their task. All the soldiers were dead. Using the cannon had eliminated the officers with grim efficiency, and he was now in control of the fort.

"What you want us to do next, Major?" Kimbrell strutted up, his face sooty from gunpowder. "Burn the place to the ground?"

"No, we occupy and use its facilities for the night. Be wary of the food. It's likely to be contaminated."

"How'd you know that?" Kimbrell asked.

Magee laughed. "I'm your commander. It's my job to know these things." In a lower voice, he said, "You may loot the paymaster's office while the men are eating. Then have them rest up."

"What's next?" Kimbrell looked at Magee suspiciously.

"There is a town not a mile away that caters to the fort and its men. We will attack it at first light. But first, we eat, we rest, we resupply."

Magee looked long and hard at his lieutenant.

"And we loot."

Kimbrell let out a yell of triumph and ran off to tell the men. Magee stood alone in the middle of the parade ground, unsure what to do. Louisa and Sarah Beth would not be here. They wouldn't be in the town that would be destroyed in the morning either. He walked away from the cannon slowly to be by himself and to dream of the day when he was reunited with his family.

14

Slocum didn't much care what town this was. It was intact and that meant it had avoided Clayton Magee's devastation. Which meant there was likely to be a doctor who could look after the marshal. At least, Slocum hoped it would be that way. Vannover was delirious now and barely able to hang on to his saddle horn. Slocum considered tying the man in place or even draping him over the saddle to complete the ride into town, but that could take more out of a man than being unconscious.

As they rode down the main street, curious faces pressed against windows and more than a few children rushed out, hollering and jumping about.

"Where's the town doctor?" Slocum asked the nearest of the children. The boy looked at Slocum with wide eyes and then ran off, screaming. "Do you have a doctor?" More of the children ran away. "A vet? This man's in bad shape. He needs tending to!"

By this time a woman had come from the bakery. At first Slocum thought she was a ghost, then saw she was doused from head to toe in baking flour. She dusted off her hands and created a tiny tornado all around her.

"Who you got there, mister?"

"He's a town marshal over in Charity. Where are we?"

"This here's Foreman. Charity's a couple days' ride, maybe more. With a man in his condition, it might be a forever ride."

"He can't ride much farther than the side of the street," Slocum said. "He banged up his ankle. The doctor over in Cimarron Junction did what he could for him, but there's a powerful lot of wounded he had to tend to. The marshal here probably caught an infection."

"Yup, that's so," the woman said.

"A doctor?" Slocum prodded.

"Ain't got one. Not a vet either. Mostly, we look after our own. Or . . ." She turned and looked toward a small cemetery with a knee-high white picket fence around it at the edge of town. Slocum had been all too aware of it when he had ridden in.

"A midwife? Somebody?"

"Midwife's not what this gent needs. He really a marshal?"

Slocum reached over and straightened a burning-hot Lester Vannover so his badge shone brightly in the sunlight.

"I know him! He *is* a marshal. Over in Charity."

Slocum looked from the woman decked out in baking flour to another, who stood in the doorway behind her.

"You sure, Louisa?" asked the baker.

"As certain sure as I've ever been."

"Then get him on down. I don't have much in the way of a cot here in the bakery."

"The room with Mrs. Post. Sarah Beth can look after him."

"You go help her, Louisa."

Slocum's eyes narrowed. Louisa? Sarah Beth? He was not one to believe in coincidence, but here it was staring him in the face. These had to be the women who had spoken to Vannover back in Charity, warning him of Magee's attack. If not for them, the entire town would have been destroyed.

"You happen to be in Charity before the attack?" Slocum asked. Louisa's face blanched whiter than the flour.

"You know about that?"

"It's why I'm riding with the marshal."

"You tell me about this later on, Louisa," said the baker.

"Thank you, Maggie. This marshal tried to save our lives. It's only fitting we try to save him, if we can." Louisa Magee tossed her apron back into the bakery and hurried off. Slocum tugged on the reins of the marshal's horse and got it following the woman as she retraced the path he had just ridden.

"There," Louisa said. "There's where we can take him. Let me ask first to be sure it's all right with Mrs. Post. But she can't deny a lawman help when he's so badly hurt."

Slocum wasn't so sure of that, but he said nothing. Some folks got their dander up at the mere sight of a badge. He knew. He was one of them. He dismounted and went to stand beside Vannover. The man swayed about in the saddle, eyes closed. He muttered something incoherent. The fever had completely possessed his senses, and unless something was done to break that fever, Lester Vannover would soon enough be out in that pretty little cemetery.

When Louisa waved to him from the front porch, Slocum grabbed Vannover by the arm and tugged. The marshal fell into his arms. Slocum staggered back, and finally got a grip on the semiconscious man. Lugging him up the walk, he got to the porch.

"Where can I put him?"

"There," Louisa said, pointing to a divan just inside the door. Slocum turned and heaved. Vannover sank down, opened his eyes, and smiled.

"Heaven," he muttered, "never thought it'd look so sweet." Then he collapsed back onto the divan.

"I do declare, I never thought inviting you into my house would cause such a commotion." The older woman coming from the kitchen carried towels over her arm and a pan of water. She put it down on the floor beside Vannover and began applying damp compresses to his forehead. "This should help. If it doesn't hold his fever, we might have to dunk him in the stream out back. This time o' year, it can be downright chilly."

Slocum glanced up when another woman came into the room. He looked from Louisa Magee to the younger woman and knew instantly they were mother and daughter— and the reason for Major Magee's rampage across Indian Territory.

"Could I have a word with you? Both of you?" Slocum saw the fear rising in Sarah Beth Magee's eyes. Her mother was similarly distressed at his request, but hers was better hidden.

They went onto the porch while Mrs. Post murmured and tended to the marshal. Slocum wasn't sure which worked better with the man because the marshal smiled just a little as the woman offered her sympathies to him. The cool compresses tended to his body, but the soothing words of the woman worked on his soul.

"Marshal Vannover and I were on Major Magee's trail," he said, watching the reaction. If there had been any question who these two were, it disappeared completely.

"Clayton shot him up? The marshal?" Louisa looked more distraught now, while Sarah Beth composed herself. Slocum wondered if their level of anxiety was always the same, only shifting in intensity from one to the other.

"Can't say it was the major who did it because it started with Vannover twisting his ankle. He got some sort of infection over in Cimarron Junction after the major struck that town."

"Oh," Louisa said in a tiny voice.

"How did you escape? Was . . . was Captain Langmuir there?"

He looked sharply at Sarah Beth.

"His soldiers saved the town from complete destruction.

Truth is, though, your pa was the better soldier and managed to escape. The marshal and me, we saw the fight."

"Was the captain hurt?"

"Nope." Slocum watched relief flood over the young woman's face. He had to ask. "How do you know the captain?"

"We tried to warn him of the danger Clayton posed," Louisa said. "He wasn't convinced. At least, I didn't think so."

Slocum realized they had no idea that it had been Catherine Duggan's note that sent the captain and his troopers to Cimarron Junction. He started to tell the women about their friend when he was interrupted by Mrs. Post.

"Get yourselves on in here. Right now."

Slocum followed the Magee women inside. Vannover's eyes were open, but the fever made them bright and intense.

"I gotta get back to Charity, Slocum. Please. I'm dyin'. I know it. I want to die at home."

"With your boots off?"

"Somethin' like that. Please, Slocum. It means ever'thin' to me." The marshal's words trailed off. He snapped back when a new compress was placed on his forehead. "I can make it. I promise not to die till we get back."

"That's not something you'd have a whole lot of control over, Les," Slocum said.

The marshal looked at him without a hint of fever-induced madness.

"I know, but I can make it. Never broke a promise, 'less I had to or wanted to." Vannover smiled weakly.

"Is there a wagon I can put him in? It's only a day or two to Charity, isn't it?"

"Traveling slow enough for him, it might be three or four days—unless you had someone along to care for him. Then you could make it in two." Louisa looked at Slocum and her offer was obvious.

"You want to leave Foreman so soon?" he asked.

"Might be best if we keep moving," Louisa said, looking

to her daughter. Sarah Beth rubbed her hands nervously on her skirt, then nodded once.

"You two just got to town. You can't up and leave this quick," Mrs. Post said indignantly. Slocum saw that the old woman had found herself decent boarders and was not willing to let them go traipsing off.

"We might be back," Sarah Beth said. "I've got so much cleaning to do. And dusting. I promised to do the dusting, and you have so many knickknacks, Mrs. Post."

"I'll hold you to that," the older woman said. She looked fiercely at Marshal Vannover and shook her finger in his direction. "And I'm holding you to your promise not to die. You might get home and find you want to stick around awhile longer."

"I'd like that," the marshal said. This brief discussion had tired him out and he sank back, whiter than bleached muslin.

"Get what you need. Take it from my pantry," Mrs. Post told Sarah Beth. "You can use the old wagon out back. I even got a horse to pull it, but you have to see that I get it back."

Before Slocum could say a word, Louisa piped up. "I'll get it back to you. You've been so kind to my daughter and me. And now a complete stranger."

"He's a lawman. His life's hard enough without having to die on an old lady's divan. Now git, you all git!"

Slocum went around back and found the tired draft horse and the wagon. As unwilling as the horse was, the wagon rolled easily on well-greased axles. One wheel wobbled a little, but it was nothing that would keep them from making good time to Charity. All Slocum needed was a direction to drive and he was all set.

It took the better part of an hour to load what supplies they had been given. Getting Lester Vannover into the wagon and stretched out on a couple of blankets took the longest. It was sometime in early afternoon when Slocum rolled away from Mrs. Post's house, Sarah Beth beside him and Louisa in the back keeping wet compresses on the marshal's face and wrists.

"You're a prince among men, Mr. Slocum," Sarah Beth said.

"Been called a lot of things but never that. Why do you say so?" He drove the wagon along the rough road, avoiding the worst of the rocks and potholes to give Vannover the smoothest ride possible. Even so, the wagon jolted along and hit enough rocks to jar Slocum's teeth together. He didn't want to think how such impacts affected Vannover.

"Why, look at how you have taken care of the marshal. And you only a deputy. You must be great friends."

"Never met him before a week back," Slocum said. "And I don't cotton much to the notion of being a deputy either." He looked at Sarah Beth. She sat primly, hands folded in her lap and looking straight ahead. "Tell me about yourself."

"There's not much to tell."

Slocum felt her folding up like a flower at sundown. Whatever he might have learned about her pa was closed to him now. Still, he had to try to figure out what drove the man other than insane rage.

"Why's he want you and your ma so bad?"

"He's stark raving mad," Sarah Beth said. "I don't want to talk about it."

"How about your friends?"

This got the woman to look at him curiously. She pushed a strand of blond hair back and fixed her bright eyes on him.

"What of my friends? I have very few since . . . because . . . due to the way he acted. Anyone coming over would be treated like the enemy. I had no real friends."

"You've got one," Slocum said.

Sarah Beth graced him with a smile and reached out, her fingers closing warmly on his arm.

"Why, thank you, John."

"I didn't mean—" Before he could mention Catherine Duggan, he heard a cry of pain from the wagon bed. He craned around and saw Louisa Magee trying to hold Vannover down. Louisa looked up imploringly at him.

"We'd better stop," Slocum told Sarah Beth. "If we press on much longer, he's not likely to make it." Louder, Slocum called, "How's his fever?"

"It broke, I think," said Louisa. "He is a strong man, but the fever took a lot of the stuffings out of him. I'm not sure why he cried out like that."

"Might be I jostled his ankle. The doc splinted up the leg, but it's his ankle that's hurt." Slocum looked around and saw a grove of elm trees that looked mighty inviting. There was still an hour or more of light, but it was better to pitch camp now than risk Vannover's life.

He pulled up in the shade of a tree with low limbs and jumped down. He started to help Sarah Beth down, but the woman had already dropped to the ground and was pacing about. She pointed to a spot away from the tree limbs.

"That's a good place for a campfire. The sparks won't set fire to the tree above."

"Go fetch some water," Slocum said. "Your ma and I'll see to getting the marshal out of the wagon."

Sarah Beth went off humming to herself, a bucket swinging in her grasp. When they had begun the trip, the bucket had been full, but the constant bouncing around had emptied it quickly, leaving only Slocum and Vannover's canteens. Somehow in the confusion, Slocum had forgotten to fill those. It had gotten mighty thirsty during the day because he had not wanted to stop to search for water.

He heard the gurgling of a stream not too far off.

"Grab him around the waist," Louisa said, sliding Vannover along on the blanket until Slocum could get a grip on him. "His leg should not be allowed to flop about."

"Climb down and take care of that," Slocum said, struggling with the marshal's deadweight. If it had not been for his ragged breathing, he might be dead already. When Louisa got into position, Slocum slid the man the rest of the way out of the wagon.

As he swung about, he hesitated.

"What is it?" Louisa asked. She cradled the marshal's injured ankle and guided it around.

"Saw a glint of sunlight off something shiny."

"It's probably just Sarah Beth. She's like a crow, always picking up shiny things and working them into her hair. I can't imagine why she started doing that. Her pa always discouraged such frivolity."

"Might be she saw a friend doing it."

"She doesn't have any friends. Her pa chased them all off." Louisa sighed. "When she got of an age that boys were important to her, her pa almost horsewhipped a boy to death for just speaking to her. Nobody would come around after that, much less speak to her."

"Might be she had a friend her pa didn't know about."

"That would be the only way," Louisa said. Slocum saw tears welling in the corners of the woman's eyes. He was poking and prodding at memories with scabs on them.

Slocum got Vannover safely to the ground, blankets once more under him to form a rude mattress. He backed away as Louisa tried to make Vannover more comfortable, and looked toward where he had seen the sudden flash. From behind him he heard Sarah Beth singing a hymn. He glanced over his shoulder and saw her coming, bucket swinging at her side and water sloshing out.

"I've got plenty. We can fill your canteens next," Sarah Beth said.

"That's a good idea," Slocum said. He looked away from her to the wooded area where he had seen the flash. He set off in the direction Sarah Beth had come from.

"Wait, John," the young woman called. "Here. I'll show you where the stream is." She held both canteens. He had forgotten them.

"Thanks," he said. To Louisa, he called, "You be all right with the marshal?"

"He's resting more easily now that he's out of the wagon. It's as close to a natural sleep as he's likely to get, this side of a real mattress."

Slocum and Sarah Beth slipped through the woods, the sound of the stream louder with every footstep.

"Isn't this about the nicest place you can imagine?" Sarah Beth asked. She turned and put her hands flat on his chest and looked up into his green eyes. She licked her lips and suddenly appeared shy.

"Fill the canteens," Slocum said.

"Mama couldn't hear anything going on here, nothing at all. And she's busy with the marshal. It'd be a while before she thought on it."

Slocum knew what she was saying and what she was willing to do. If the situation had been the least bit different, he would have bent over and kissed her to see if she really meant what she was dancing around saying. That simple flash of light had changed everything, though.

"You are about the most beautiful girl I ever laid eyes on," Slocum said.

Sarah Beth looked up at him with shock on her face.

"Don't get the wrong idea," Sarah Beth said. "I didn't mean that we—you—oh!" She stamped her foot. "I want to *talk* to you without Mama overhearing."

"We're not alone." He turned slightly to get a better view out across the meadow where he had seen the metallic glint.

"Mama!"

"Not here. When we pulled up, I saw somebody about a quarter mile off. It might be nothing, but with your pa roaming the countryside shooting up entire towns, we can't take a chance."

"It might be the captain. Captain Langmuir," she said. A dreamy look came to her eyes. Slocum knew then what the young woman had wanted to ask him about. He had seen the captain more recently than she had and must have details to pass along. Slocum was not prone to gossip, especially with lovelorn girls.

"If it were any of the captain's men out on patrol, they wouldn't have hidden," Slocum told her. "I don't want to scare you. Whoever I saw might just be passing through and afraid of dealing with strangers."

"Strangers," she said weakly.

"It might be a scout your pa has sent out, too. I need to find out. It's probably nothing more than a cowboy on his way down south." Even as Slocum said the words, he wanted to ride in that direction and get away from Major Magee and his depredations, but he couldn't. He had responsibilities—and had made a promise to a dying man.

Slocum rocked back on his heels when he realized he had made the same mistake with Vannover that he had with Nickson. He had promised a dying man he would accede to their wishes. Finding whoever had stolen Nickson's ring might be impossible, but he had to try. Getting Les Vannover back to his home was a sight easier to do.

But not if one of Magee's men spotted them and reported back to the major.

"What are we going to do, John? I have to tell Mama!"

Slocum grabbed Sarah Beth's arm and stopped her.

"I can circle and get a better look at him. Don't warn him by doing anything out of the ordinary."

"But he'll tell Papa and—"

"All the more reason not to let him know we're on to him," Slocum said. "Fill up the canteens. Take your time doing it. Then go back and tell your ma what's going on. Don't even look in that direction. Start a fire right where you said. That's a fine place. Cook some food. Tend to the marshal."

"And you'll kill that man out there? The one scouting for Papa?"

"I'll take care of him, but you can't give me away. It means all our lives."

Sarah Beth got a grip on her emotions when he said that. He wondered how long she had been hiding things from her father—and probably her mother. However long, she had undoubtedly gotten good at it. If the penalty was having a friend horsewhipped, Sarah Beth had had reason to get very good.

"Will it take you more than a few minutes?"

"As long as it takes." Slocum slid the leather thong off

the hammer of his six-shooter, started away, then turned back to her.

"What is it, John?"

"Captain Langmuir looked to be in fine shape last I saw him."

Only then did he make his way through the forest like a ghost. The look on her face at his words gave him added incentive to stop anyone spying for Magee. More than one happy future depended on it.

15

"It'll be good getting back to the post," Captain Langmuir said. Sergeant Benedict only nodded as he rode alongside his commander. "My ass is stiff and sore from living in the saddle."

"Been a while since feet touched ground, sir," the sergeant agreed. "The men and horses aren't gonna be worth much for a day or two. What do you make it we've ridden? Forty miles?"

"Something like that. A good unit can travel fifty miles a day. This is a damned good unit."

"What's left of it," muttered Benedict. He got a sharp look from his commanding officer. "Sorry, sir, didn't mean nuthin' by that. It's just that . . ."

"As you were, Sergeant," Langmuir said. He did not want to hear about their losses fighting Clayton Magee. He had thought he could tangle with a ragtag bunch of outlaws and emerge victorious with little loss. Magee's tactical skill and the way his men obeyed like they were a well-disciplined army had taken Langmuir by surprise. He could well imagine Magee had been a major in some army or another. It left a bitter taste on his tongue thinking it was the Union army. To have fought alongside a man with such field experience would have been worthwhile.

To fight against someone now so depraved who had once fought for a noble cause made Langmuir sick at heart.

"Sir, take a deep whiff."

"What is it? My nose is stuffed up." Langmuir tried to take a breath, but the trail dust and all the weeds growing alongside the road back to Fort Supply worked to rob him of one of his senses.

"Smells like gunpowder, sir."

"There might have been a parade. Cannons fired. That sort of thing," Langmuir said, dismissing his sergeant's obvious worry. The fort was a place of refuge and training.

The thin curl of smoke coming from the distance across the prairie in the direction of Fort Supply caused a cold knot to grow in his belly. Sergeant Benedict might not be wrong at all.

"Send out scouts. Three of them. Have them approach the fort from different directions."

"Sir, we ain't got three men capable of much more than sittin' astride their saddles, not after this forced ride from Cimarron Junction. Men and horses are purty near dead."

"Column, halt!" Captain Langmuir held up his hand and brought his patrol to a halt. He looked back at the survivors. They had left the most seriously wounded in the care of the Cimarron Junction doctor. Although young, the man had impressed Langmuir with his no-nonsense approach and ability to do field surgery that had saved more than one soldier's life.

"What do you reckon's goin' on, Captain?" Sergeant Benedict fingered the pistol slung on his right hip.

"Are the men up to a fight?"

"Sir, they was born ready. We're mighty low on ammunition, though. And if we have to do more than stagger along, the horses will die under us. Might be one or two of the men who'd perish, too, from exertion. But there's not a man among 'em whose spirit's not willin' and whose courage won't carry 'im forward at your command."

"It is not my intention to lead a suicide mission. See that the men are ready for a fight." Captain Langmuir took a deep breath. "It might be the fight of their lives."

"Seems like that's bein' said a whole lot lately," Benedict said. He added "sir" as an afterthought before trotting down the column, seeing that the men shared what ammunition they had left so every soldier carried at least a few rounds.

Langmuir watched the smoke rise into the distant sky where it quickly blew away in a brisk north wind. There wouldn't be rain with a northerly wind. All the real storms built down south and raged northward at this time of year, but that didn't mean he and his men wouldn't fight the weather as well as the enemy.

"The enemy," murmured Langmuir. It couldn't be Magee, but who else might be ahead? The amount of smoke told him that this was no mere campfire. A conflagration chewed away at a considerable pile of wood—maybe the size of Fort Supply.

"All ready, sir," reported the sergeant.

Langmuir silently motioned for his troopers to ride on. They reached the top of the low rise overlooking the broad, flat prairie land holding Fort Supply. He had steeled himself for what he might find. He caught his breath. The walls were intact but the fires raged within them. The buildings could be replaced. The men and materiel were irreplaceable.

"Sir, don't see nobody actively fightin' down there. We mighta got lucky."

"How can the destruction of our fort ever be lucky?"

"Just sayin', sir, that we couldn't whip a three-day-old kitten in a fair fight."

Langmuir walked his horse down the road toward the fort. He saw two guards slumped at the gate. Both were obviously dead. Flies swarmed about them and a buzzard or two had pecked choicer hunks of flesh away.

"You want a burial detail for 'em?" asked Benedict.

"Later. There will be a considerable number of graves to dig," Langmuir said. Wary, Langmuir went through the open gate and looked around at the devastation. His horse shied as they neared the parade ground. He drew rein and slowly surveyed the ruins. The armory door gaped open. The barracks and offices were destroyed. From the look of what remained, they had been leveled by cannon fire. All of the outbuildings were ablaze, but many of the larger structures had escaped destruction. But something chewed at him. He struggled to figure out what could be worse. Then it hit him. Two of the three cannons were gone.

"Sir, Boydston and Larson say the Gatling gun's missing from the armory."

Langmuir looked at his sergeant with a bleakness in his eyes that knew no bounds. Two cannons, a Gatling gun, and whatever else the outlaws could steal.

"Get what supplies you can. Is any ammunition left?"

"A considerable amount, sir. Don't rightly know why they didn't take it all."

"They couldn't carry it. The real question's why they didn't blow it up so we couldn't use it against them." Then Langmuir realized the answer lay in Magee's view of the world—he had escaped Langmuir once. That made the captain and his men inferior soldiers and not a threat. Langmuir began to seethe at such impudence; then he calmed a little and thought hard.

"What's been taken from stores?"

"Wasn't much there to steal," Benedict said. "Supply train's late, as usual, and we was runnin' low."

"Take anything that can be useful in the field," Langmuir said, coming to a quick decision. "We're going into town—and a fight."

"No question 'bout it, Captain," Sergeant Benedict reported. "Caissons and a couple cannons rolled this way not too long ago. Last rain was yesterday maybe, so the tracks weren't washed away."

Langmuir looked at his disheartened soldiers and knew they had a hard row to hoe. Magee's men numbered about twenty, and Langmuir commanded only half that. Worse, Magee's gang would be heartened by their successful raid on Fort Supply. They had ammunition and weapons—oh, how they had weapons! Cannons and the damned Gatling gun. Langmuir had never faced such a weapon in battle. He had been instructed in its use, but not in fighting against such a potent killing machine.

"We have to recover the Gatling. When we see it, all attack," Langmuir said. "If an inexperienced artillerist is firing it, chances are good a round will jam."

"If a round don't jam, we're all buzzard bait, sir," the sergeant pointed out.

"We might be even if we recapture the Gatling," Langmuir said. He worried about the cannons. Whoever had fired them back at the fort had destroyed two targets with two shots. That might have been luck, but he doubted it. He could picture Clayton Magee standing behind the field piece, sighting it in and giving the order to fire.

It might be better if they spotted Magee and charged him rather than the Gatling gun.

"Listen, sir," Sergeant Benedict said. "Gunfire."

"Not much. The battle's about over. Or they might be celebrating." The small town only a mile from Fort Supply survived strictly on business with the army. Two saloons were always filled to overflowing with soldiers wanting a taste of whiskey and a whore. Langmuir had come to a meeting of the minds with the saloon owners about getting his men too drunk for duty. Threatening to shut the gin mills down had worked. He sometimes had a soldier unable to appear for morning muster, but the town had come to realize how much more profit everyone stood to gain by taking care of the soldiers, as long as they had a few coins in their pockets.

"Sounds more like celebrating," Benedict agreed. "There wasn't nobody in town who could put up much of a fight."

"They depended on us for that."

Captain Langmuir warily approached the town, set in a

hollow by a stream. Before he got a good look at the town, he saw how the stream ran red with blood. When he and his men rode down into the town, he realized that the gunfire had not been in either anger or celebration. The few survivors were shooting horses and other animals that had been severely wounded during Magee's assault.

"Where'd they go?" Langmuir asked the first man he came to. The man held a still-smoking rifle. Five horses were laid out along the street, each with a bullet in its head from the man's rifle.

"You're a bit late, ain't ya?"

Langmuir saw the standing buildings were riddled with holes.

"Did they use the Gatling gun for anything more than hurrahing you?"

"Wiped out a dozen folks who came to see what the noise was all about. Then they used their pistols. I swear, ain't seen so many pistols on a rider since I spotted a Jay-hawker tryin' to sneak back north during the war."

Langmuir pushed aside the desolation he felt and asked, "Where are they now? They didn't finish with the town."

"Didn't finish? Nope, reckon not. A rider came up whilst they was reducin' everything to splinters. The one wearin' a major's uniform ordered them to break off and retreat. Good thing, too."

"Why's that?"

"He was bringin' up a cannon. If he'd fired that, you wouldn't have found a solitary soul alive."

Langmuir looked around and saw that Magee had come close to exterminating all the townspeople without firing his cannon. He looked over at Benedict when the sergeant cleared his throat.

"Sir, we got the tracks leadin' away. Looks like they're makin' a beeline toward Foreman."

"Why not?" Langmuir found himself too tired to figure out what caused Magee to bounce around like a child's ball from destroying one town to the next. The pretty blonde, Sarah Beth, and her mother had claimed Magee was doing it to get the pair of them back under his roof. Langmuir found it hard to believe any man could kill scores of people and burn entire towns to the ground for such a simple reason. Sarah Beth had claimed her pa was crazier than a bedbug, so there might be something to it. Langmuir discounted both women's claim in favor of something more.

Clayton Magee sought something other than his wife and daughter and was on a rampage until he found it. As pretty as Sarah Beth was, and she had inherited that beauty honestly from her mother, Langmuir could not believe Magee didn't seek vengeance for some terrible crime committed against him.

"There's no reason to go to the fort for help," Langmuir told the man with the rifle. "That's where they got the Gatling gun and the cannons. Killed all the soldiers at the fort." Langmuir looked around. "Best stay here. Unless you want to do a powerful lot of burying at the fort."

"Got plenty to keep me busy here," the man said. "You payin' for the soldiers at the fort to be buried?"

"Yes," Langmuir said. "The usual rate is five dollars per body."

"Beats plantin' the bodies here for nothing," the man said. Then he looked up suspiciously. "You got the authority to order this? You got the funds?"

"Send messengers to all other nearby forts," Langmuir said. "I'll give you letters of authorization to present."

"Cost you a dollar a day fer each messenger to deliver your reports," the man said.

"Here." Langmuir emptied his pockets of all the money he had with him—hardly ten dollars, but it satisfied the man. The captain took another fifteen minutes to scribble out a brief report and passed three copies to the man. "Make sure at least one copy reaches Fort Gibson. Take the others wherever you think best."

"Fort Reno, Fort Cobb, maybe the one out west."

"See that you get the reports on the road immediately," Langmuir said, his mind already following Magee. What remained of the army contingent numbered half of

Magee's gang—and lacked the firepower to match a Gatling and cannons, much less raiders festooned with pistols. A direct fight was not possible.

Isaiah Langmuir had to find a way to stop the renegade major, a way that was not entirely suicidal. Somehow, this was not a lesson that had ever been taught at West Point.

16

Slocum circled wide and from the opposite direction came on the man spying on the Magee women and Vannover. Or he thought he had, until he reached the spot where the man tethered his horse. The horse neighed, uncomfortable at the approach of someone it did not know. Slocum slowed his advance and waited until the horse settled down. The cat might have been let out of the bag; Slocum didn't know, but had to believe the spy, was too intent on the camp to notice as long as his horse finally calmed itself. After all, a wolf or even a fox might cause a similar reaction.

Stewing at the delay but knowing it was necessary, Slocum lay in the undergrowth and waited as twilight turned to utter darkness. The stars poked through thick layers of clouds but cast no real light. He wasn't sure when the moon would rise, or if it would give him much illumination when it did.

Working his way forward gradually, Slocum tried to catch sight of the other man. He frowned when he realized he had not heard the horse in several minutes. Slocum got to his feet and slipped through the grove, using one tree after another as cover.

"Damnation," he said when he got close enough to see

where the man had been. A pair of field glasses dangled from a limb, but the scout using them was nowhere to be seen.

Slocum started to step forward, then froze. The man's horse ought to be somewhere near. He bent and found a small stone. He sent it sailing through the night to land with a thud some distance away. Slocum spun, hand going to his six-shooter when he heard the horse neigh behind him. Somehow, Magee's spy had led his horse away and had gotten behind Slocum.

Colt Navy coming out of his holster in a smooth movement, Slocum retraced the path he had just taken. This time the curse that slipped from his lips was more venomous than before. The man was riding away and had somehow eluded Slocum's keen ears and night vision.

A million things raced through Slocum's head. If he went back to camp and got his horse, he would probably lose the trail in the dark. Since the man was riding slowly, there was a small chance Slocum might overtake him on foot. If he tried and failed, the man would definitely report to Magee. And that report would give the renegade major exactly what he sought.

Without realizing he had come to a decision, Slocum walked fast through the forest going after the man. The rider could probably go faster in the open, but Slocum was more nimble, dodging low limbs and the thick brush to keep him parallel with his quarry.

When he realized he was falling behind in spite of his small advantages, Slocum scooped up a handful of stones and tossed them ahead of the horse as hard as he could. The rattle of rock against leaf achieved what he needed most. The rider slowed and then stopped. He drew one of the several six-guns he carried and peered into the dark forest ahead.

This gave Slocum all the opening he was ever likely to get. He shoved his pistol back into his holster and ran as hard as he could. He made enough noise to alert the man, but by then it was too late. Slocum dug in his toes and launched himself forward. His fingers groped and closed on the outlaw's gun hand, pulling it down. Slocum grabbed with his left hand and caught a fistful of cloth. Jacket, vest, shirt, it didn't matter. He pulled downward as hard as he could and unseated the rider.

They tumbled to the ground together, both flinching when the horse began crow-hopping around them. The hooves added an element of danger—but not that much more for Slocum. He knew what he faced and still had surprise as his ally.

He swung a clumsy fist at the outlaw, and then fell flat when it missed. Slocum's luck was at a peak, though. The man reared up, six-shooter in his hand, and was about to shoot just as his horse kicked out. A shod hoof caught the man on the back and drove him to the ground. Swarming over him fast, Slocum got on top and wrestled the gun from his hand. The man was pinned to the ground, facedown, and unable to breathe. When his struggles turned feeble, Slocum lifted his head and let him gasp for breath.

Dirt and mulch spewed from the man's mouth and nose as he struggled to breathe.

As Slocum turned the man's gun against him, he got a good look at the outlaw. He could well believe this man was capable of about any kind of murder. His face was crisscrossed with a history of old knife fights, and a round scar on each cheek showed where someone had shot him through the mouth. The look of pure hatred he gave Slocum would have melted a brass statue.

"You're gonna die fer this, mister," the outlaw snarled.

"I've got your gun and I've got the upper hand. If anyone's going to do any dying, it's you."

"You ain't got the balls to kill me in cold blood." The man changed his mind when he saw the look on Slocum's face. There wasn't anyone riding with Clayton Magee who looked more capable of such a deed than John Slocum.

"I want to know a few things," Slocum said. "Tell me and you might live."

"If I tell you, chances are real good I won't."

"If Magee finds out?" Slocum watched the outlaw's face

for reaction. One of the man's scars turned pinkish to show his reaction. Then a muscle twitched. Slocum had guessed right. He had caught one of Magee's scouts.

"Screw Magee. It's Kimbrell who's gonna kill me if I spill my guts to you."

"Albert Kimbrell," Slocum said, remembering that the marshal had a wanted poster on the desperado.

"You know him then. Nothing you can do to me would match what he'd do if he finds out I told you anything."

"All you have to do is ride off. Magee and Kimbrell can't go on destroying towns and murdering everyone in them forever." He watched closely, then asked, "What's in it for you? Looting the banks and businesses?"

"What else? I don't care for the killin', not like Kimbrell. He takes real pleasure in it. But we all get hundreds of dollars after every raid."

"Hundreds or thousands? Or maybe Kimbrell keeps more than his fair share? You take the risks, he keeps the money you steal."

"I'm doin' all right," the man said sullenly.

"Magee," Slocum said, getting back to what he thought was more important. "What's he want?"

"The women. The ones I saw in camp yonder. Both blond, one old enough to be the other's mother, matches the description Magee gave."

"What are they to him?"

"He never said. We made a lot of guesses. Seein' 'em, the gossip about them being his wife and daughter's probably right. They run off, or so goes the story, and he wants 'em back. Bad."

"Bad enough to kill hundreds of people?"

"Don't matter to Major Magee. He's seen Antietam and who knows what other battles. People gettin' kilt ain't nothing to him."

Slocum asked, "What else is there about the women?" He saw the hesitation and knew there *was* something more.

"Don't know. He's never even called 'em his family.

Just that he wants them and will pay a big reward for whoever finds 'em."

"Where's Magee now?"

"Don't rightly know. That's the truth!" The man shouted
when he saw Slocum lifting the six-gun to put a slug between his eyes. "I was supposed to scout around and join
up at Charity."

"Charity? He already hit that town."

"Sometimes I think he can see the future. He said all us
scouts was supposed to report back to him at Charity. He's
heard something to get him back there. That's all I know."

Slocum fumed at the information. They were riding
squarely into the teeth of the lion. Magee had left part
of the town standing because he thought his wife and
daughter were at Cimarron Junction. He had razed that
town and given Marshal Vannover a small chance to go
after him and his gang. But if Magee returned to Charity,
there'd be nothing to keep him from finishing what he
had started.

"On your feet. We're going to Charity."

"Kill me, mister. Shoot me and leave my carcass right
here for the bugs to eat. If Kimbrell sees me ridin' back as
your prisoner . . ." The outlaw shivered with real dread.

"You keep thinking on what I asked. You might come up
with something that'd convince me I ought to let you go
free."

"You're a deputy. You'd never do that."

"I'm not a deputy," Slocum said with such force that the
man's eyes went wide. The outlaw started to say something, then clamped his mouth shut.

Slocum shoved him in the direction of the camp. If Vannover ever came out of his stupor, he could give some ad-
vice on what to do with the prisoner. One thing Slocum
knew that could never happen was letting the man go. If the
outlaw had the chance, he would hightail it straight back to
Magee, if not to collect the reward, then to keep from getting himself tortured and killed for spilling his guts.

Slocum doubted it mattered much to Kimbrell if the scout had uttered a word. Torture and killing mattered more than truth to Albert Kimbrell.

As they walked, Slocum with the man's six-shooter pointed at the middle of his back, an uneasiness grew. Ahead blazed the small campfire, but something wasn't right.

"Were you alone?" Slocum asked.

"I ain't gonna tell you squat."

Slocum pushed the man along faster until they reached the campsite. Slocum stared at the fire burning cheerily within its ring of fist-sized rocks. But no one sat around it. No coffeepot boiled its fierce bitter brew. The wagon was gone along with both women and Lester Vannover.

17

"Blow it to splinters," Kimbrell said hotly. "There's no reason to sit on our asses and just watch the damned place!"

Clayton Magee stared at his lieutenant dispassionately. Before Kimbrell could loose another rant, Magee said calmly, "We watch. We wait. They are not in Charity, but they will be. I feel it in my bones."

"You're the master tactician. You always go by intelligence reports. Where're the facts?" Kimbrell refused to be mollified.

"I will get them. My scouts are ranging across this entire stretch of Oklahoma. Sooner or later, one will find them. They are so close." Magee closed his eyes and smiled just a little. "I know it. I *feel* it."

"I want to feel that Gatling gun kicking back on its tripod as I crank off a hundred rounds," Kimbrell said. "There's nothing to be gained by doin' nothing!"

"There is," contradicted Magee. "They will come to Charity, and I will once more be reunited."

"Reunited?" Kimbrell looked hard at the major. The man had his eyes shut and the grin on his face grew as if he had already accomplished his goal of finding the two women.

It shouldn't matter to Kimbrell what the reason was. Magee was a master at planning and was making Kimbrell a rich, rich man. This hesitation to use the fabulous weapons stolen from the army post, though, was a line in the sand. Kimbrell knew it was about time to part company and let Magee take the blame for everything while he recovered the loot he had been hiding and hightailed it for Mexico.

He had been keeping a fairly good accounting of all the gold and paper money he'd stolen, and he figured it had to be about ten thousand dollars by now. Magee ignored such things in his search for the two blond women, but Kimbrell did not. He only dispensed what was necessary to keep the gang on his side and fighting. No one else fought for the sheer love of it, like Kimbrell. They demanded to be paid, so he doled out a little here and there. A few hundred dollars to each man made them think they were kings. If they only knew what the real take was, they would string him up by his balls to make him divvy up what he had stolen from them.

It was definitely time to ride away, but . . .

They had broken off the attack on Charity once before because Magee had received word of the women being in Cimarron Junction. That meant the bank had not been looted, nor had any of the businesses been cleaned out. Kimbrell figured he could scoop up another thousand dollars if Magee would ever give the order to level the town. Kimbrell smiled. The marshal from Charity was dead—he had to be. That left the town wide open for looting.

Kimbrell looked at the Gatling gun with its tall magazine just waiting to be emptied. He could rip through that magazine and send a hundred bullets into Charity before anyone realized they were under attack. Or the cannons they had taken from Fort Supply. Both were ready for use. Hell, he had not even properly looted the fort of everything valuable. Magee had wanted to check the small encampment supplying the fort. Once more, they had broken off a devastating attack because Magee had heard a new rumor about the women.

Albert Kimbrell was fed up with not finishing what they started just because a rumor about the women reached the major's ears.

He considered telling the men to attack Charity without the major's knowledge. By the time Magee realized they were attacking, there would be nothing he could do about it.

"Who has come and gone from the town, Mr. Kimbrell?"

"What's that?" Kimbrell looked at the major, and realized Magee's reverie was long past and the analytical mind worked hard now. The cold eyes bored into him like drills. He wondered if Magee knew what he was thinking. It felt that way.

"Has anyone in our cordon of the town reported?"

"Nobody. The people in Charity are working hard to rebuild. The town's cut off since we blew up and burned most of the towns to the east, and Fort Supply isn't going to be much help, if it ever was."

"There are other forts. And a cantonment is not too distant," Magee said. "We must guard against soldiers from any of the forts finding out what has happened here."

"They've got to figure out it wasn't no tornado blowin' through when they see all the people we shot and how we burned down the buildings," Kimbrell pointed out.

"Let them think it was a renegade band of Indians. The entire territory is filthy with the redskins," Magee said without a trace of malice in his voice. "It is part of my plan to shift blame to the tribes whenever possible until I find . . . them."

"The women? Your family?"

"My family," Magee said. He looked up sharply. "You will personally lead a small party to be certain the army does not learn of what's happened in Charity."

"Find a scout, kill a scout?"

"As you see fit," Magee said.

Kimbrell smiled wolfishly. He knew the major was trying

to manipulate him by offering blood sacrifices. There were always army patrols. Finding one and killing the soldiers would be child's play. Before, Kimbrell would have relished it. Now he looked on it as a chore standing in his way of finishing the pillage barely started in Charity, so he could be on his way.

One last town, one final score to settle with the world.

"You won't raid the town without me, will you, Major?" Kimbrell tried to keep his tone light and joking, but he felt deep down that he had to be in the thick of the battle. The smell of gun smoke and the feel of his six-shooter recoiling in his hand were almost better than sex. The sight of men and women dying by his gun *was* better.

"You are a vital part of my force, Mr. Kimbrell. Together we will succeed."

"I won't need more than two or three men."

"Take whoever you feel is appropriate to the task," Magee said, already dismissing him. Kimbrell hated that, but accepted it.

He stalked off, barking orders as he went. He wished he could take the Gatling gun, set it up near a road, and see what it could do to a man astride a horse. Or a stagecoach. They had fired it a few times, but never in the heat of battle except at that dinky town outside Fort Supply, and that hardly counted. Kimbrell had not even emptied the magazine before the fight was over and Magee had ordered them here to Charity.

"Just us, boss?" Barger towered over Kimbrell and tried to intimidate him, but it never—quite—worked. Kimbrell was tougher, and they both knew it. But if he had to have someone watching his back, it would be Barger.

"You and One Ear. Where is he?"

"Got his good ear to the ground," Barger said, laughing at his joke. "Might be I should cut it off so he can carry it around in his pocket so he won't lose it, too?"

Mention of severed body parts made Kimbrell reach up to his vest pocket and trace over the desiccated finger with the ring on it. He considered putting the ring on, but he would save that for the showdown with the major. It might not be such a bad thing taking over the gang by killing Magee. Wearing the ring would lend some authority to his position, if he did become leader.

Who'd ever know he hadn't graduated from West Point? Nobody in the gang had enough imagination to think anything else but what he told them.

Kimbrell moved his hand away from the finger with the ring in his pocket. This was his little secret for the time being.

"Saddle up. We're goin' on patrol," Kimbrell told Barger. "And find One Ear. I want him, too. He'll sit in camp and get drunk otherwise."

"Hell, I wouldn't mind doing that. Can we sneak into that town and steal a few bottles of whiskey? My throat gets mighty parched out here."

"We keep people from going in or out of the town," Kimbrell said. "Mostly, we hunt for soldiers."

"They must be plenty pissed at us for destroyin' their fort like we did. Maybe we should go back and occupy it."

"What do you mean?"

"Use it as our base. I get mighty tired of ridin' around all the time. It'd be good to have a hideout."

Kimbrell snorted in contempt. "You idiot, don't you think after a while that even the army'd figure out that the men on those walls weren't soldiers and do something about it? We couldn't hide in the fort because everybody knows it's there."

Barger pursed his lips as he thought. "Reckon you might be right, but it'd surely be nice to sleep on a mattress more 'n once in a blue moon."

"Don't git too comfy, Barger. We got a lot of fightin' ahead of us."

"Where's One Ear? I want to get on the trail. Hey, One Ear! Get your ass on over here!" Barger grumbled and strode off to find his partner. Kimbrell readied his horse.

When the two returned, One Ear visibly drunk, they mounted and rode off.

"We patrol the outskirts?" Barger asked.

"We could, but I want to have a look-see at the country-side. Don't want no soldiers sneakin' up on us, do we?"

Kimbrell and his two henchmen rode for almost an hour before speaking again. That suited him just fine. Barger and One Ear were anything but good storytellers, and that was about all that mattered with a good trail companion. That and sharp eyes. Barger spotted the trail about the same instant that Kimbrell did.

They looked at each other and reached for their six-shooters. One Ear was trifle slower to respond, but he did, too, when he saw hoofprints in the soft ground.

"Good thing it's not rainin'," Kimbrell said. "We might have missed the tracks entirely."

"Looks like rain, though," Barger said, glancing at the clouds building to the south. "We'd better find them and kill them 'fore it gets too inclement."

"Only a single rider," Kimbrell said as he followed the trail. "This ought to be like shootin' fish in a barrel."

"Could be most anyone," One Ear pointed out. " 'Cept it ain't. It's a cavalry sergeant."

"Now how the hell do you read that in the tracks?" demanded Barger.

"He's not lookin' at the ground, you idiot," Kimbrell said. He pointed ahead to where a cavalry sergeant stood, staring down in the direction of Charity. As he turned, he lowered his field glasses. Kimbrell got off a quick shot that only surprised the trooper and alerted him to the danger. Kimbrell didn't care. He might have got a good shot at the soldier's back if he had been quiet and snuck up close enough to be sure of his aim. This was more fun.

"After 'im!" Barger spurred his horse to full gallop. One Ear and Kimbrell were not far behind. They had the advantage of already being in the saddle and riding down hard. The cavalry sergeant had to mount and get his horse up to a gallop.

They overtook him quickly.

"He's headin' fer town. Don't let 'im!"

Kimbrell did not need Barger's warning. He veered to the left as One Ear went right. They got even more speed from their horses and moved to cut off the soldier's retreat to the town. One Ear's horse flagged quickly, but Kimbrell cut in front and drew his pistol. He saw the sergeant's grim expression and laughed as he fired. All six bullets missed, but caused the soldier to slow. His horse broke stride, and that meant it was all over for him.

The three outlaws circled the soldier, who was desperately looking for a way out. The sergeant whipped out his pistol and emptied it, then went for his carbine. By now Kimbrell had a second six-gun out and firing as he charged straight for the sergeant. One round hit the soldier's hand and knocked the rifle from his grip. Then Kimbrell raced past, his six-shooter empty. He drew a third one and went in for the kill.

"He's all mine, boys," he shouted.

"I'll see you in hell!" roared the sergeant as he lowered his head and drew a long knife from his belt. Holding it like a lance, he galloped forward to meet Kimbrell.

Bullet beat knife.

The soldier toppled from his saddle and crashed to the ground. The impact knocked the knife from his grip and he lay gasping, staring up at the gathering storm clouds. Then Albert Kimbrell filled his field of vision.

"Who are you? Least I can do is let your commander know who died this day."

"Benedict," the sergeant said with his last gasp before Kimbrell blew him away.

"What'd he say, Al?" Barger shoved his pistol back into his belt.

"Didn't hear," Kimbrell lied. "What does it matter? Let's see if there's any more of them bluebellies out here scoutin' and tryin' to set a trap for the major."

The trio of outlaws spent the rest of the day hunting for other cavalry scouts, but found no one. Kimbrell rode back to report to Magee, sorry there had been just the one, but knowing there could be no objection to going into Charity and burning it to the ground now. And if there was, if Magee said anything about his gut telling him his family would be there soon, Kimbrell would put a bullet through that lying gut. It was getting to be time for a change in leadership.

18

Already exhausted, Isaiah Langmuir felt like dying then and there. He squinted into the setting sun as he studied the way Clayton Magee had deployed his men around the town of Charity. Langmuir had hoped to get to the town and find some allies, but if he tried to ride into that town now, Magee's gang would destroy him and his handful of soldiers.

He sucked in a deep breath and tried to steady his nerves. Keeping his hands from shaking was already beyond his ability, but he needed to get a grip on his desolation. There had never been a class at West Point teaching how to feel or react in such a situation. They had studied battles and victories and looked at defeats as what you meted out to the enemy. Nothing was said about being driven into the ground and still having to fight against overwhelming odds.

The sight of the Gatling gun pulled off the road and partially hidden by trees worried Langmuir the most. If a company came riding from Fort Gibson, they would be cut to ribbons before they realized anything was wrong. He had not found where Magee had placed the two howitzers, but he knew Sergeant Benedict would find them.

The sergeant had ridden a wider route, circling to cover the far side of the road leading into Charity. When he reported, Langmuir would get a better picture of what they were up against.

From what he had seen, though, any attack on Magee and his gang would be suicidal and gain nothing. Why the renegade major simply sat and waited rather than attacking the town—finishing it off after his initial attack—was something Langmuir hoped his sergeant would discover. Magee's men lounged about, joked, and rested. Even if the cavalry got into position to attack, the pitiful ten remaining soldiers would be going up against rested, ready, and better-armed brigands.

If even one of his men felt better than he did, Langmuir wanted to know the secret. He touched a coat pocket where he carried a small silver flask. It had been filled with brandy—for medicinal purposes, he told himself. A few drops to his dying men had not been wasted. After he had dispensed those paltry few ounces, he began drinking the rest himself. Keep up his courage. Kill the aches and pains in his battered body. To make himself more alert and a better leader. He had used all those excuses, and now the brandy was gone.

Langmuir was running out of excuses, just as he had drained the last of his liquor.

He tried to make notes on a scrap of paper so he would not forget, or if necessary so the observations he had made could be passed along should he be injured or killed. Langmuir sighed deeply. That implied that his body would be found. If Magee or any of his killers got to him, he doubted he would ever be received into a consecrated grave.

Seeing the last of the outlaws begin their cooking for the evening meal, Langmuir slipped away and found his horse. Rather than mount, he led the horse away from Magee's camp so he would not be heard as he rode off. He had to rendezvous with Benedict; then they both had to find their way back to where he had left his ragtag band of soldiers. Langmuir hoped they would have time to recuperate and get themselves into fighting trim, but combat would be hard without adequate ammunition. He cursed Magee for stealing from the fort the supplies that they needed most. But this was war and he could not fault the major for his actions.

He could only damn him for killing so many innocents.

Langmuir swung into the saddle and rode slowly, but had gone only a few hundred yards when he heard a scuffle in the darkness. He stopped and put his hand on his pistol, not sure what to do. If this was only a disagreement between two outlaws, he was better served letting them settle their dispute. One might kill the other and save him the trouble.

The shrill cry told him it wasn't an outlaw being chased. Knowing his duty lay in reporting back to his troops and hating himself for not obeying standing orders, Langmuir wheeled his horse around and trotted in the direction of the fracas.

"Yer quite a fighter, ain't ya?"

"Get your filthy hands off me!"

The man laughed at the woman's objections to manhandling her. Langmuir heard cloth rip and knew his mission had just changed. He was entrusted with protecting the people of the Indian Territory. Fighting Magee and his butchers was a part of that, but this was more immediate.

"Stop, oh! Don't touch me there!"

"You ain't a virgin. Don't go tellin' ole Jaycee that you don't want what I got to offer. Lookit." The man laughed harshly as the woman screamed.

Langmuir followed the noise, and quickly came upon the scene he had envisioned as he rode. One man held a thrashing woman down on the ground. Her skirts were pulled up to expose her privates. The second man watched and cheered on his partner, waiting his turn at rape.

Langmuir did not even offer them the chance to surrender. He aimed his pistol and fired. The man holding the woman's legs apart let out a tiny sound and then collapsed forward onto her. Before the second man realized anything was wrong, Langmuir shot him in the head.

"You horrible man, you—" The woman suddenly discovered that the outlaw atop her was deadweight. Really deadweight. She shoved him off and sat up, looking around wildly.

"We've got to get out of here," Langmuir said. "The shots will bring the other outlaws running."

"You—you're the cavalry officer! The one I sent the note to back in Charity warning of the Cimarron Junction massacre."

"You did? The note wasn't signed." Langmuir looked at the woman suspiciously, but she had no reason to gull him. He watched as she got to her feet and stumbled a step or two before getting her balance. She tried to smooth her skirt, but it had been torn in too many places. The blond woman looked up at him.

"I did. The perfume on the letter was mine. Rose."

"You sent it. Why didn't you sign it? I thought it was one of the other women who had come to me. I found their story to be less than credible, but—"

"We have to get out of here," she said. "My name's Catherine Duggan. Please, Captain, let me ride with you. If I can't, then . . . then I'll ride that way." Catherine pointed westward. "That way they won't catch both of us. Not easily."

"How'd they catch you?"

"I was on my way to Charity. I think Sarah Beth Magee is heading there. At least, it makes sense that she would. Her and her ma."

"The ones I didn't believe," Langmuir said, feeling as if he had stepped off a cliff. Nothing he had done was right. He could have stolen a march on Magee if he had believed the two women when they told him their story. It had taken the note, apparently sent by Catherine Duggan, to get him into the field. Too late. Everything he did was too little and too late and—

"Is that the direction you intended to ride?" she asked. "I can go in another. Just tell me."

"Here," the captain said, reaching down for her. "We'll find these two owlhoots' horses. You can use one of them, unless yours is nearby."

"It ran off. Tracking it would take too long. Where are their horses?" Even as Catherine asked, a loud whinny came from a copse not a dozen yards away.

Langmuir took Catherine's hand and pulled her up behind him. He appreciated the feel of her arms circling his waist, but there was no time to enjoy her nearness. The rose scent of her perfume matched perfectly that from the warning letter. Putting his heels to his horse brought them to the stand of trees and the outlaws' mounts. He made a quick decision and grabbed the reins of a mare.

"Take this one. And it'll be safer if you ride with me. I'm heading back to my squad."

"Squad? That's all?" Catherine quickly vaulted onto the other horse and spent a few seconds coaxing it into allowing her to stay astride.

"Magee has wiped out both my fort and most of my men. I was reconnoitering his position."

"He's in Charity?"

"Outside the town, waiting. Is it the two women he's waiting for?"

"I must have been right that they'd head there, thinking he had already razed the town and would never return." She laughed harshly. "I'm getting to think just like them—and him."

"What's your part in all this? You're not one of them he's looking for?"

"Hardly," said Catherine. "I need to talk to Sarah Beth but—"

She clamped her mouth shut when loud cries rose from the spot where the two outlaws had tried to rape her.

"They've found the bodies," Langmuir said. "I was afraid the gunshots would bring them running. And they did."

Langmuir looked around and found an opening in the woods. He rode straight for it, Catherine keeping pace.

"Where are we going? Do you know where your men are camped?"

"This leads away from Magee's men. I'll have to get my bearings after we get far enough away from them to take a breather."

The words hardly left Langmuir's lips when gunfire erupted all around. His horse stumbled, but did not go down. He looked over his shoulder and saw that Catherine Duggan had not been so lucky. A bullet had caught her horse just above the shoulder. The horse had run another few strides and then collapsed under her. She struggled to get out from under the weight of the horse pinning her leg to the ground.

Cursing, Langmuir pulled hard on the reins and got his horse turned to go back to the trapped woman.

"No, no, get away. Save yourself. There're too many of them!" Catherine waved at him, then twisted about to look back into the woods where half a dozen riders, all waving their six-shooters, galloped forth.

Langmuir knew he had no chance against so many outlaws. He had only a couple rounds left in his pistol. And no more ammo at all in his saddlebags.

"Get away. Come back for me when you can," Catherine pleaded. "Don't get killed or there'll be no one to rescue me!"

Langmuir knew she spoke the truth, but it tore at his very soul to turn tail and run, leaving her to those murderers and rapists.

But that was what he did. It was all he could do. Tears ran down his cheeks as he galloped away into the night, Catherine's cries finally fading when he topped a rise and went down the far side of the hill.

19

"Don't make me waste a round killing you," Slocum said to his prisoner. The man grumbled, but kept moving through the dark. Slocum wondered if he ought to have taken the time to find the man's horse so they could make better time, then decided he had done the right thing.

Sarah Beth and Louisa Magee had driven away with the marshal, of that he was sure. Not finding any sign of a struggle told him they had not been kidnapped or taken away at gunpoint. Slocum doubted he had been absent from camp long enough for any of Magee's men to sneak in and capture them. If Magee had others in the area, they would have come to the rescue of the spy Slocum had taken prisoner.

"I can't see where I'm puttin' my feet," the man complained.

"Slow down and I'll shoot you," Slocum said without rancor. He walked a few paces behind the man to give himself a better view of the ground and the twin ruts left by the wagon wheels. The direction confused him. They had been on their way to Charity so Vannover could die at peace with the world in his own bed, but the tracks angled away from the town.

"Which way?" asked his prisoner.

159

Slocum saw they had come to a road. In the dark, either direction could have been taken by the wagon. He knelt and studied where Louisa had driven the wagon onto the road. From the angle and depth of the ruts off the road, Slocum figured the wagon had gone southward.

"Which way?" asked his prisoner.

Slocum saw they had come to a road. In the dark, either direction could have been taken by the wagon. He knelt and studied where Louisa had driven the wagon onto the road. From the angle and depth of the ruts off the road, Slocum figured the wagon had gone southward.

"What's in that direction?" Slocum asked, pointing south. All he got was a shrug. If the scout had given him any kind of answer, Slocum would have worked to decide how truthful it was. The shrug took some of the worry out of following the women.

He swung into the saddle and pulled his lariat free from the saddle. He spun a loop around his head a couple times and dropped it neatly around the outlaw's shoulders. A quick tug cinched it tight.

"What are you doin'? I ain't no cow!"

"You'll be buzzard bait if you try to get away," Slocum said. "Start walking. That way." He tugged on the rope to get the outlaw stumbling in the right direction. His paint had been trained as a cow pony and knew how to keep the rope just taut enough. If his prisoner slowed, the horse did, too. If the prisoner tried to veer one way or the other, the horse corrected, pulling harder and harder on the rope to keep the man on the road where Slocum wanted him. The only maneuver Slocum had to watch for, for which the horse could do little, was the man turning and running for him. This would loosen the rope enough to let the man get free and attack.

But armed only with his bare hands, he was no match for Slocum's six-gun.

"How long we got to follow this damned road?"

"Until we get to the end," Slocum said. He snapped the rope and got the man walking faster. Within ten minutes, he was glad he had urged a quicker pace because they came to a long stretch of road across a grassy valley. A quarter mile ahead Slocum spotted the wagon. It was too dark to see the driver, but he thought he made out one person in the driver's box and another in the wagon bed. That was as it should be.

If there had been any other silhouetted passengers in the wagon, Slocum would have had a fight on his hands.

"Those are the women you were spying on."

"The ones Magee wants," the scout said. "I woulda been rich. He'd have paid through the nose for them."

"Your nose is big enough. Keep going. Faster."

"I can't."

"Then I'll have to drag you." Slocum came up alongside and trotted a yard or two ahead, keeping the tension on the rope. The outlaw saw that Slocum meant what he said, and began to run along doggedly. His spurs jangled with every step and his breath gasped in and out like a tuberculosis victim's. Slocum wanted only to reach the Magee women and see if Vannover was still alive. What condition the outlaw was in when they overtook the wagon didn't matter a whole lot to Slocum.

Louisa must have seen him behind, because she tried to whip her horse to great speed. The horse was as exhausted as the people riding in the wagon. Slocum came up within hailing distance in less than five minutes.

"Hold up, Louisa, it's me, Slocum."

"Who's that with you?"

"The spy. I caught him. Stop the wagon!"

"There's no danger?"

"Stop the damned wagon."

She reluctantly pulled back on the reins. The horse let out a grateful whinny and stopped dead in its tracks. Slocum came alongside the wagon and looked hard at her.

"Did you see something?" he asked.

"I didn't want to get caught. You can handle yourself so well. We . . . we can't."

"You've done a mighty fine job up until now," Slocum

said. He glanced into the rear of the wagon where Sarah Beth knelt beside the marshal. The man looked pale, but otherwise seemed to be doing as well as could be expected. Vannover rolled from side to side, moaning, but he sounded more like a man having a nightmare than someone awake and in pain.

"He's sleeping," Sarah Beth said.

"Pull the wagon over there, off the road," Slocum said. There was a depression a couple dozen yards away that would let them get out of sight. Sooner or later, an observant rider along the road would spot them, but maybe not in the dark. By daybreak, he intended to be rolling again, headed for Charity.

"How come you didn't take the road to Charity?" he asked after Louisa had tied the reins around the wagon brake and climbed down.

"I got a feeling," she said. She looked over at her daughter, then chewed on her lower lip in anguish. "It's not easy to put into words."

"You think Magee is waiting for you there?" Slocum asked.

"He could be. The man's able to read minds. He must know we're going there."

"So you think you can read *his* mind? He sent out scouts to look for you. This one found you. That means Magee doesn't know where you are and is still looking."

"He's like a spider in the middle of a web. A strand trembles, and he reacts." Louisa shuddered and put her arms around herself as if she were freezing to death.

"We've got to go somewhere," Slocum said, then looked hard at his prisoner. The man had his head tilted to one side to hear better. Slocum didn't say another word and went to the man, looping more of the rope around his arms and then cinching it down hard. He tied a few quick knots and shoved the man to the ground.

"What are you doin'? You can't do this. What if the team spooks?" The outlaw struggled to get free as Slocum lashed him to the rear wagon wheel.

"Reckon you'd spend a while going round and round until an arm or head came off," Slocum said. He looked into the wagon bed and saw that Sarah Beth still tended to the marshal. "You watch this varmint," he told her. "I'm going to gather something for dinner. Don't think it would be too smart to shoot anything, not with your pa's scouts all around."

"Will he stay quiet or should you gag him?" Sarah Beth asked, looking over the edge of the wagon at the captive.

"He'll stay quiet, won't you?" Slocum nudged the man with the toe of his boot. "If you let out so much as a peep, I might just slit your throat."

Sarah Beth gasped and then sat back, staring at Slocum as if she didn't believe him. Then she saw that he meant it, and hastily turned back to putting a damp compress on the marshal's forehead.

Slocum backed away and went to see what he could find in the nearby grove that might do them for dinner. A few roots would boil down with greens. It wouldn't be as good as a rabbit or deer, but it also did not require him to shoot and maybe draw unwanted attention.

He was poking about at the base of a tree when he heard soft movement in the grass behind him. His hand went to the butt of his six-gun, and then he relaxed.

"Not too smart sneaking up on me like that, Louisa."

"Sorry, John. I didn't want to startle you. It was worse trying to come up without making a sound, wasn't it?" She came around and settled down, back to the tree, so she could look at him. "You think I'm crazy running from Clayton like this, but I'm not."

"I see what he's doing to catch you. I know which of you is crazy. You want to be left alone and he's killing people by the hundreds, then burning down the towns where they lived."

"It's not all his fault," she said. "He's thrown in with some desperate men."

"Like Albert Kimbrell?" Slocum saw the woman shiver again.

"He's one of the bloodthirsty murderers Clayton hired," she admitted. "Kimbrell enjoys killing. All Clayton wants is for Sarah Beth and me to return home. I'd rather die before that. I'd kill my own daughter before I'd let that happen!"

"It was hard living with Magee?"

"Impossible. He treated Sarah Beth and me like slaves. He told us who we could see, where we could go—which was seldom anywhere—and even what to think. When he started beating me, I knew I had to leave. And Sarah Beth had to come with me or he would begin treating her as he did me." Louisa tried to keep from crying. She suddenly turned and grabbed Slocum, hugging him close.

He held her until the quaking stopped. She laid her head against his shoulder. When she said something he did not understand, he asked her to repeat it. Louisa pulled away, her face only inches from his.

"You're so strong, John. I need your strength now."

He kissed her. It wasn't right. She was a married woman, even if she was married to a man capable of any crime. Her lips quivered as they pressed into his; then passion built and they clung to one another hard.

Her hands gripped hard at his back, fingers curling about to scratch at him. Slocum didn't mind. If anything, it made him more inclined to keep kissing her—and to do more.

The thought made him break off the kiss.

"This isn't right. We—"

"It's right, John. I want it. I *need* what you offer me. Don't lie and say you don't want me, too."

He kissed her again, and this decided the matter. Her fingers moved over his back and came around between them. She greedily kept kissing as she unbuckled his gun belt. It fell away, but her fingers kept working to get his jeans unbuttoned. One by one, the buttons popped free. And then her fingers circled the thick, hard, shaft that protruded up from his groin. He gasped as she squeezed down on him.

"It's been so long, John," she said softly. "I want you to do it. Please."

"There's no need to beg me," he said. His own fingers had

been working down the front of her blouse, unfastening the buttons one by one until he was able to push it back off her shoulders. Her frilly slip showed how aroused she was by the twin points pressing hard and hot into the fabric. Slocum caught one cloth-sheathed nipple and squeezed down on it. He was rewarded with a corresponding squeeze around his manhood. He used both hands on her breasts, massaging and pressing, crushing and pulling, until the woman cried out.

"Now, John, please. I want you so!"

"No need to rush things," he said, but she was urgently tugging at him, pulling him toward her. He wanted to take his time. She wanted the opposite.

He slipped his hands down her chest, across her belly, and lifted her skirt. He felt the heat of her flesh beneath. His hands worked around until he cupped the half-moons of her behind and began kneading them like lumps of dough. No bread dough ever produced such a response.

"Oh, yes, John, yes," she said, swarming up and straddling his waist. Slocum was pressed back against the tree as Louisa faced him. She hungrily kissed him as she positioned herself over his groin. Slocum groaned as she lowered her hips and his steely length sank into her heated core.

For a moment, he thought he was going to lose control like a young buck with his first woman. Louisa knew all the tricks that aroused him most. She tensed and relaxed her strong inner muscles. He felt her heat soaking into him and the thick juices leaking from her down around his shaft and tickling his balls.

Then she began rising and falling, slowly at first and then faster and faster, until he closed his eyes and simply reveled in the sensations rippling through him.

She kissed him again, then worked down his neck and tried to kiss his chest. In this position, she was unable to keep her hips flying up and down. As the heat from the carnal friction died, she straightened.

This allowed Slocum to reach out and cup her breasts, giving them more of the tweaking and twisting he had given before.

"That's what I need, John. Don't stop, don't stop."

"You keep moving, too," he said. He was pinned under her weight and could not lift up to meet her downward motion. Although he felt the urge to thrust, he remained still to allow her to set the pace. She was the one who had been denied good loving. He wanted her to satisfy herself—and he was certainly enjoying every instant of their lovemaking.

"More, more, oh, yes, more," Louisa cried out. She began grinding her hips downward and twisting from side to side with him hidden deep within.

When she crushed down so hard that Slocum thought she would mash him flat, he was unable to restrain himself any longer. Deep in his balls he felt the boiling start and then expand upward faster and faster until he erupted within her. She clung fiercely to him, her hips shoved down to take as much of him into her center as possible.

Then she sagged forward and laid her face against his chest.

"Your heartbeat's so strong," she said. He felt her breath against his skin. She moved up and clung to him, sobbing softly. He held her, not knowing what to do.

"It'll be all right," he said. "I'll make sure it is."

"I know, John, I know," she said.

After a while, they disengaged and straightened their clothing. Slocum buckled his six-gun back on, and then they hunted for wild onions and greens to boil down for dinner. A handful of black walnuts would give a bit more to eat, paltry though they were. By the time they got back to the wagon, Sarah Beth had a small fire burning. Slocum was glad to see that she had carefully selected only dry twigs to keep smoke from rising.

Louisa fixed the vegetables, and they ate in silence. Slocum found himself looking from mother to daughter and back. He wondered what the hell he was getting himself into.

20

"Now ain't this a purty sight?" Albert Kimbrell walked around Catherine Duggan, eyeing her like a wolf might a rabbit. "Where was you goin' in such a hurry, little lady?"

"Go to hell," she spat. Catherine struggled to get her leg pulled out from under the dead horse. She was securely pinned to the ground and could not get away from Kimbrell, no matter how she tried.

"Oh, I've been there and I kinda like it. It's my sort of place. But you, now, you don't look like you've seen enough of Hell to appreciate what you have." He reached out and put his grimy, calloused hand on her cheek. She tried to flinch away, but he pressed down hard until the imprint of his fingers remained on her skin.

"Was anybody else riding with her?" Kimbrell looked up at the two men astride their horses watching what he did. They exchanged guilty looks, giving Kimbrell his answer. "Get on after 'im then. There's no tellin' who might have been with her."

"Might be one of them soldiers," opined one outlaw.

"If it is, kill him. You know what the major wants done. Do it!"

Both men yanked on their reins and headed out into the night after their quarry, leaving Kimbrell with Catherine.

"It's not gonna be nice for you 'less you tell me what I want to know. It'll be plenty nice for me, though, no matter what you say."

"You're going to kill me. Why should I say a word?"

"I'm not gonna kill you. You'll just wish you were dead." Kimbrell's matter-of-fact declaration caused the woman to recoil. She renewed her efforts to get free from under the horse. Her leg was beginning to go numb.

"Two of you out there. You and maybe one of them horse soldiers?" Kimbrell grinned when he saw her expression. "Yep, sure was. You were spyin' on the major. Find out where his men are positioned, ride on back to the soldiers, and let them know. Are there enough of them left to matter?"

Catherine turned away. She realized he asked questions to get her to react. She might as well be telling him everything he wanted to know with her words because he was getting the right information from her face.

"Don't matter. My boys'll stop that soldier ridin' with you. Kill him. Won't be a gentle way of dyin' either."

"Why? Because you taught them?"

Kimbrell laughed, beginning to enjoy this. The woman showed fire.

"They watched me, and they learned real good." Kimbrell sat on the dead horse's rump so he was just out of Catherine's reach. She struggled and finally settled down. He wondered if she'd tired herself out, or if she thought to lure him closer so she could rake him with her nails. The brief touch of her cheek had made Kimbrell powerful horny, but there was no need to rush matters. If anything, this made it all the more exciting for him.

"You look like one of the women the major's hunting. You wouldn't be family, would you?"

Catherine looked sharply at him, then shook her head. "My name's Catherine Duggan."

"That's good, 'cuz what I'm gonna do to you I couldn't do to one of his family and live to tell about it." Kimbrell unbuckled his gun belt and put it aside. Then he took out his knife. He enjoyed watching her flinch away, but he only used it to cut off a piece of harness.

"What are you doing?"

"Gettin' ready to free you from under that dead horse," he said. "First, I got to tie you up so you don't run off."

"I can't run," she said before she realized how she was helping him.

"Leg's all numb and tingly, huh?" Kimbrell took the long piece of leather, cautiously approached Catherine, and then caught one slender wrist. As she tried to hit him with her other hand, he snared it, too. A couple of quick turns and he had her hog-tied. "Now I can git down to freein' you."

Kimbrell dug a little in the dirt, then saw an easier way to get the woman out from under the horse. Using his knife again, he cut the saddle cinch.

"Git ready," he warned, then he yanked hard on the saddle. Her foot was still in the stirrup under the dead horse. Catherine screeched in pain as he pulled her out from under, then disengaged her foot from the stirrup. "You got real purty legs. You're gonna love wrappin' 'em around my waist while I have my way with you."

He felt her shiver as he ran his hands up under her skirt, going higher and higher. She tried to fight, but he had secured her hands too well with the leather cut from the bridle. When she tried to scoot away, he followed her until he could clamp his hand down firmly on her upper thigh. This froze her in place.

"You might as well quit strugglin'," Kimbrell said. He wanted her to do just the opposite. He loved it when they thrashed around and cried out and begged for mercy. His hand moved to the vest pocket holding the ring and severed finger. He wondered if he ought to show her. That would scare her plenty.

Catherine kicked out and caught him in the belly. Momentarily off balance, Kimbrell fell back and sat down hard.

"You're gonna pay for that, honey pie."

"You . . . you foul *thing*!"

Kimbrell laughed heartily. She had more spunk than he had thought when he first saw her trapped under the dead horse. He was going to have fun all night long with her. Getting to his feet, he walked to where she kicked feebly, trying to get away.

"Can't stand? Leg still numb? Let me rub it till you feel somethin'." He pounced on her and pinned her to the ground. With her hands bound, she was unable to fend him off as he pinched and stroked along her leg. There was no response. He wondered if she had broken it, but there wasn't that kind of pain. He got his hand back under her skirt and ran it up the leg, and felt the limb begin to twitch and jerk with returning blood. "See? Old Doc Kimbrell knows what ails you and how to remedy it."

His hand touched the juncture of her legs. He thrust his finger upward into her. She closed her eyes and lay still.

"Go on, move around. You're allowed."

When Catherine did nothing, Kimbrell stood and began unbuttoning his jeans. He was getting tired of her. Best to get it over with so he could kill her and then see what to do about the major.

"Hey, Al, we lost him. We followed him fer a mile and then he just upped and disappeared like some kind of Injun."

Kimbrell stopped unbuttoning his pants and stepped away from the woman. He was angry at being interrupted, but he was even madder that the men had not found the spy.

"If he gets back where he can tell the army, the major'll have your balls for it. How'd you lose him?"

"It's night, Al. Fer Chrissakes. Trackin' in the dark of night's a fool's errand."

"I sent the right men, and you weren't fools enough from the sound of it."

"Look, Al, we was on his trail. He rode through a stream. We thought we found his tracks on the other side, like he rode straight across. Only the tracks weren't his."

"Deer tracks," murmured the second outlaw. "We followed a damn deer."

"By the time we got back, there was no way to keep after him. He might have gone in either direction."

"He's an army scout. He went downstream," Kimbrell said. "Like you'd hunt from downwind, he'd go downstream to keep from givin' himself away."

Catherine tried wiggling away like a worm, but Kimbrell saw her. He took two quick steps and stomped down hard on her skirt. If she tried to go any farther, she would tear off her skirt and leave herself naked from the waist down. She sank back to the ground, glaring at him. Kimbrell paid her no heed.

"You sure he was an army scout?" Kimbrell asked.

The men shrugged. They didn't have any idea who they had been after. Kimbrell looked down at Catherine and smiled.

"He was an army scout, wasn't he?"

"No!"

"Might have even been an officer out to find what he was up against. Wouldn't trust any of his men. He'd let them rest up while he played hero. Might even have been thinkin' on gettin' himself a medal for bravery." Kimbrell watched her reaction and knew he was right.

"Boys," he said, "the gent you lost was an officer. Probably it's that captain we almost shot up at Charity. He might have adopted the town as his own since we took everything worth takin' out of Fort Supply. I reckon that was his post." Kimbrell glanced at his prisoner again, but she didn't react now. She had no idea about the officer's command.

"What are you gonna tell Major Magee?"

"Nothing," Kimbrell said. His heart beat a little faster as he looked from his captive out into the dark night. "I figure we can lay a trap for him that's sure to bring him runnin'."

"What you fixin' to do, Al?"

"What I was gettin' down to doin' when you cayuses interrupted me." Kimbrell turned back and finished unbuttoning his jeans. "Let me get *in* to it."

Catherine began screaming and did not stop as Kimbrell raped her. But over her cries for mercy, he listened hard for another sound. It wasn't long in coming. Kimbrell had not figured it would be.

"Get off her, you animal," came the cold order. "Stop this instant or I'll kill you."

Kimbrell looked up from the now-sobbing woman into Isaiah Langmuir's grim face. The captain held his pistol at arm's length, sighting in on Kimbrell's head. His finger was white against the trigger.

"Now aren't you the knight in shinin' armor?" Kimbrell laughed as he backed away. He was in no particular hurry as he tucked himself back into his jeans and started buttoning up. Then he reached for his six-shooter, which he had laid a few feet away before he had begun raping Catherine Duggan.

"Touch it and you're a dead man."

"Really, Captain? You know why I think you're bluffin'? You would have shot me the instant you had me in your sights if that gun of yours had even a single round left. You're out of ammo, aren't you?" Kimbrell reached for his six-gun slowly. His fingers curled around the butt as he drew it. The six-shooter came halfway out of the holster when Langmuir launched himself in a low dive.

His shoulder collided with Kimbrell's belly and knocked the outlaw backward. They went tumbling over and over together, arms flailing and fists hammering at one another. For a moment, Kimbrell came out on top and landed a heavy punch to Langmuir's torso. Then the cavalry officer kicked Kimbrell and ended up straddling his chest, knees pinning Kimbrell's shoulders to the ground.

"You're worse than an animal, and I'm going to beat you within an inch of your life." Langmuir landed one blow on Kimbrell's cheek, and had cocked his fist back for another when he felt something cold and hard pressed into the back of his head.

"I ain't the only one who's got a bead on you, Captain," said one of Kimbrell's henchmen.

"Don't blow his brains out!" Kimbrell heaved and up-ended the captain, sending him tumbling to the ground.

"You'd have got blood all over me." Kimbrell brushed himself off, then lightly touched the cut that Langmuir had opened on his cheek. "Took you two long enough to stop him."

"Figured you'd want a piece of him, Al. Like you got a piece of her." The outlaw laughed.

When Langmuir got his feet under him and prepared to lunge forward, he heard the metallic click of a six-shooter cocking. He glanced over his shoulder.

"Yup, I said there were two of 'em. You want to die or you want to live—a little longer?" Kimbrell went to Langmuir, judged distances, then unloaded a haymaker to the man's belly. Langmuir gasped and doubled over. "What I thought. You can dish it out but you can't take it."

"We take both of them back to the major?"

"Why would we want to do that?" Kimbrell asked. He rubbed his knuckles. "We're just gettin' started with them, and we got all night."

"Uh, we got all night with her, too?" Both of Kimbrell's henchmen stared at Catherine, who cowered and began to sob softly as her fate became more apparent.

"Sure. And he can watch. You'd like that, wouldn't you, Captain? You'd like watchin' my boys here have her?"

"You—" Langmuir lunged forward. Kimbrell was waiting. He stepped to the side, thrust out his boot, and tripped the officer. Langmuir landed facedown in the dirt. Before he could get back to his feet, Kimbrell clipped him above the ear with the barrel of his six-gun.

"Yeah, we got all night. Help me tie this one up, and then you can take turns with her."

Kimbrell laughed at the reaction he got from Catherine Duggan. He laughed even more when he saw the horror on Langmuir's face when he regained consciousness. It was going to be a long, fun night.

21

"There, all done," Sarah Beth Magee said, putting the last of their cleaned tin plates onto a stack. "What do we do now, John?"

"Yeah, John, what are you gonna do? Screw her, too?"

"Shut up," Slocum said to the prisoner tied to the wagon wheel. The gibe hit close to home. Slocum had not thought it was that apparent what he and Louisa had done while out in the woods gathering tidbits for dinner, but it must have been for the outlaw to pick up on it.

"What's he mean, John?" Sarah Beth asked. She looked curiously at him.

"He wants us to argue. That's about all he has left to do. I could gag him if he's bothering you," Slocum said.

"Yeah, go on, big man. Gag me. Shut me up. I don't blame you and her ma for f—"

Slocum drew his pistol and pointed it directly at the man's face. The bore was considerably smaller than a .44, but had to look big enough to stick a hand down.

"How bad you want to live? You'll swing whenever they get you to trial, so killing you here and now isn't robbing the law of a damned thing."

"You'd kill me in cold blood, wouldn't you?" There was a hint of admiration in the outlaw's words.

"Might not be in cold blood," Slocum said. "Might be I'd like it, just to watch you die."

"John!" Sarah Beth was outraged.

"Hush, dear," cautioned her mother. Louisa put her hand on Sarah Beth's and squeezed it tightly. "We're in a terrible position, with your pa's men all around and the marshal laid up the way he is."

"Was it a terrible position?" called the prisoner. He groaned when Slocum buffaloed him. The barrel of the Colt Navy caught the outlaw just above the right eyebrow and opened a deep gash that spewed blood and blinded him in that eye.

"There's no call to do something like that," Sarah Beth said primly. "Let me stitch it up before he bleeds to death."

"He won't bleed to death," Slocum said. "Not unless I decide to put a bullet in his gut. That's a real slow way to die, isn't it? Painful?"

"You can't scare me," the outlaw said, but he was obviously lying. A wild, animal look came into his eyes. He looked around as if he could take flight. All he succeeded in doing was tugging on his bonds and tightening the knots around his wrists.

"John, don't. You're scaring me."

Slocum slid his six-shooter back into its holster, but kept a steely gaze on the prisoner, ignoring whatever Sarah Beth was doing to try to distract him.

"How's the marshal doing?" Slocum finally asked.

"Better. He's weak, but I don't think he's in any danger now," Sarah Beth said, obviously relieved to have something other than their prisoner's imminent demise to occupy Slocum. "We should head for Charity, I think."

"No!" Louisa Magee shot to her feet and looked around wildly. "That's going to do us in if we do. Your pa's there. I feel it in my bones."

"She's right," Slocum said. "Take a gander at our prisoner and tell me she's not right."

After studying the man's expression for a moment, Sarah Beth nodded.

"He would make a terrible poker player, wouldn't he?" the young woman said. "You were right, Mama. We should go somewhere else. But where?"

"Wanna go home," came Marshal Vannover's weak protest.

"I'll get you there when it's safe," Slocum said. "Let's sleep on where to head and see if the morning doesn't suggest something better than we're likely to decide right now when we're so tired." He shot a look at the prisoner that stifled another of the man's outbursts.

Slocum made a circuit of their camp, went into the wooded area surrounding them, and then returned. By this time, the women were asleep. He looked at Sarah Beth and then at her mother and shook his head. He was getting bogged down where the going should have been easy. A quick look at the marshal showed he was sleeping peacefully. Vannover's breathing came easy now and the paleness had faded on his weathered face. Given another day or two of rest, he might be right as rain.

A final check of the prisoner's bonds and Slocum turned in for the night.

Something awoke him a few hours later. He sat up, sixgun in hand, and looked around. A feeling of wrongness tore at him. He got to his feet and peered over the edge of the wagon. The marshal had not moved, but his breathing remained slow and easy. Slocum looked over his shoulder at Louisa. She was curled up tightly under her blanket, but otherwise was safe and sound. Sarah Beth thrashed about as she fought a nightmare.

Slocum knelt to look under the wagon, and it took several seconds for him to realize the dark outline he saw wasn't their prisoner. He grabbed a handful of blanket and pulled. The ropes that had once held his captive were cut clean through. Slocum cursed under his breath. The man had hidden a small knife. Behind his belt buckle or in his boot. All it took was a few minutes of determined work and the ropes had parted.

Slocum's fingers came away bloody when he touched the ropes. The escape had not been easy.

"How much of a head start do you have?" Slocum rubbed the blood over his fingertips, trying to figure from how dry it was when the man had escaped. Standing, he looked around on the soft ground and found boot prints.

"John? What's wrong?"

"Our prisoner got away. I'm going after him," he told Louisa. "You and Sarah Beth get the marshal out of here come sunup. If I don't catch the prisoner fast, he'll tell your husband where you are. You want to be far away if that happens."

"Where do we go?"

"Your instincts have been good so far. Keep following them."

"How will we get back together?"

"I'll find you," he told her. For a moment, he considered kissing her, but Sarah Beth had awakened from her nightmare and sat up staring at them. "You tell her what's going on," Slocum told Louisa. He grabbed his saddle and went to his paint. The horse protested some when he got the saddle cinched down, but the stalwart horse did not show the slightest hesitation when he began following the outlaw's footprints.

Slocum knew he could only track from horseback for so long. When the man got to the woods, the going would get really hard. The outlaw probably had a good idea where he wanted to go, and all Slocum could do was follow along at a slower pace. Anything like crossing a stream or climbing a tree and jumping from limb to limb would make tracking even more difficult—and time was what mattered most now.

Slocum hoped the man was too intent on getting back to Magee to make much effort hiding his tracks.

When Slocum reached the edge of a heavily wooded area, he dismounted and stood for several minutes, listening hard. He was sure the man had come this far. Now he had to rely on other senses to locate him if he was in the forest. At this time of night, not many animals were out and stirring. Slocum heard an owl flapping after a mouse or other small prey. A soft wind blotted out most other sounds, but when a lull came he heard a distant crunching, as if something heavy moved along the forest floor.

That was the direction Slocum went, moving fast, not trying to find tracks. Gambling was a way to make money—win or lose meant very little. Now Slocum gambled with lives. If he followed a deer or other large animal and allowed the outlaw to reach Magee and his gang, there would be hell to pay.

As he walked, Slocum listened and sniffed the air and tried to feel through his skin if the man had come this way. He kept going, as much on instinct as from any clue. Within fifteen minutes, he heard voices. He sucked in his breath and held it. He had failed. The man had already teamed up with some of the killers from Magee's gang.

Slocum slipped his six-gun from his holster and left his horse behind as he advanced slowly. His gun rose, and he almost squeezed off a round when he saw a man raping a woman. He lowered his six-shooter when he realized at least one other outlaw was in the small clearing, watching.

Or was he? Slocum edged around to get a better look, and saw the second owlhoot had a gun pointed at a man doubled up and tied.

"How long do you think we kin keep this up?" the man who had finished with the woman said. He pulled up his pants and went to where his partner kept the six-gun trained on their other prisoner.

"What do you mean?"

"Hell, Kimbrell had her. I jist did. You will. I don't know if I kin do it again any time soon."

"Might be Kimbrell will be back before then."

Slocum listened with some interest. Albert Kimbrell

had been here, but had left these two with the prisoners. What would get him away from raping and killing? The answer settled like a cold lump in Slocum's throat. The man he chased must have reached these men and had ridden off with Kimbrell to report directly to Clayton Magee.

"I dunno. He was mighty excited when he left."

Slocum needed to know more, but the pair weren't inclined to give it to him. They began talking about different tortures they could mete out to their captives. At this, the man lifted his head. Slocum caught the glint of starlight off captain's bars. It didn't take much guessing to believe that Isaiah Langmuir had fallen into their hands.

The starlight turned the woman's hair a silver white. Slocum reckoned Langmuir and Catherine Duggan had been riding together when they were captured. If it hadn't happened exactly that way, it didn't matter. They were both hostages now. How long either would last depended on how much hate these two had in them.

If Kimbrell had been here, Slocum knew the rape and torture could last all night. These two might not be as brutal, though they rode with a man who ordered them to kill everyone in towns they had never laid eyes on before.

This decided Slocum. They might get tired and simply kill Langmuir and Catherine. He held his pistol at his side and began walking toward the pair. The men didn't see him until he was twenty feet away.

One turned and said, "That you, Al? You're back mighty quick."

Slocum raised his six-shooter and fired. The bullet caught the man in the head. As he fell, the other outlaw realized the mistake. He went for his six-gun, only to discover he had taken off his gun belt when he had started raping Catherine Duggan. He spun and dived for it.

Slocum didn't cotton much to shooting a man in the back. This time he made an exception. The man died as he pried his six-shooter from its holster. He twitched, and Slocum shot him again.

"Thank God," cried Langmuir. He was tied in such a way that his wrists were secured to his ankles. Looking up was painful for him. "See to her, Slocum."

Slocum ignored the man. There wasn't a hell of a lot he could do for Catherine at the moment, and he worried that Kimbrell might be back at any instant. Using his knife, he slashed twice and cut the rawhide straps binding the captain.

"Watch my back. They expected Kimbrell to return sometime soon." Only then did Slocum go to the sobbing woman. He knelt, but said nothing and did nothing. Whatever he said or did was likely to be wrong for a woman in her condition.

She wiped at her nose and rubbed away some of the tears as she looked at him. Slocum tried to read a message in her eyes to guide him in what to do next. She answered for him, grabbing him hard around the neck and burying her face in his shoulder. He awkwardly held her, saying nothing as she cried herself into exhaustion.

"We have to get out of here," he said when a laxness came to Catherine's death grip around his neck. "Do you know where Kimbrell went?"

"A scout rode up. I didn't hear what he said to that monster, but it got him away. H-he left us with th-those two." She began crying again, but there was none of the hysteria there had been before. Slocum kept his arm around her and helped her to her feet.

"Did you hear what was said to Kimbrell?" he asked Langmuir.

The soldier shoved the six-shooters taken from both the dead men into his broad leather belt.

"I was out of ammo."

"You tried bluffing them with an empty gun?" Catherine's eyes went big. "That was stupid!"

"I couldn't let them rape you."

"Never mind that," Slocum said, interrupting. "The man who talked to Kimbrell *rode* up?"

"Yeah, he did. The horse was all lathered as if it had run miles and miles," Langmuir said. "Why's that important?"

Slocum quickly explained how his prisoner had escaped.

"He'd be on foot. The rider looked like an outlier who had found something and was reporting to Kimbrell," Langmuir said. "I think I heard him say something about Magee moving into town."

"Charity?"

"He has cordoned off the town and is waiting for his wife and daughter to return. I have no idea why they would."

"They wouldn't normally. Louisa Magee is able to out-guess her husband. But she and Sarah Beth have the town marshal with them. He's in a bad way."

"Sarah Beth?" Langmuir perked up. "Is she all right?"

"Fine as frog's fur, considering all that's happened," said Slocum. "We have to get out of here before Kimbrell returns."

"He might not if he's reporting to Magee, but you're right. We have to get as far from here as we can."

"Get those two owlhoots' horses. Mine's still in the woods back yonder." Slocum jerked his thumb in the direction he had come. "Can you find your men?"

"There might not be much safety in that," Langmuir said. "Both Sergeant Benedict and I went out on a scout. I'm not certain, but I think they killed him."

"So your men don't have anybody to tell them what to do?"

"They're well disciplined," Langmuir said stiffly. Then he realized what Slocum was getting at. "They might try returning to Fort Supply. Magee raided the fort, killed everyone there, so they might consider it a refuge."

Slocum thought this over. "Get to them. Take Miss Duggan with you."

"Can you ride, ma'am?" Langmuir asked.

"If I have to, I'll ride through hell to get away from this terrible place," she said, looking around. Slocum saw how she looked faint. She caught herself, bit her lip, and then regained some of her gumption. "I want one of those guns you took. If they come back, I swear by God I will kill them!"

"Better let the captain hang on to those hoglegs, Catherine," Slocum said. "You might waste ammo pumping too many rounds into a single man."

"If it's Kimbrell, I won't care!"

"If he's got a couple dozen men with him, yeah, you will care. A lot. Don't let them repeat what happened already."

"What should I do?" Her weak voice was almost lost in the soft whisper of the wind. Slocum started to answer, then clamped his mouth shut and turned to the captain to see if he had heard the hoofbeats, too.

He had.

"Go on, you two try to get back to the wagon," Langmuir said. "I'll decoy them away."

"Wait," Slocum said, but it was too late. Langmuir vaulted into the saddle of the horse nearest him and let out a yell that rattled through the still night. He galloped off.

Slocum watched him ride away, knowing there was no point in trying to follow. He put his hands around Catherine's waist and heaved, getting her up into the saddle. He climbed up behind her and got the balky horse trotting toward the forest to take advantage of the head start Captain Langmuir had given them. On two horses, they might have a chance of getting away from Kimbrell and his henchmen.

Maybe.

22

"We're not going to make it!" Catherine's voice rose to a shrill pitch that carried through the quiet forest.

"Hush," Slocum said. When she started to screech again, he clamped his hand over her mouth to stifle the sound. "You're going to draw Magee's men like flies to shit if you don't hold your tongue."

She nodded and he released her.

"I'm sorry," she whispered. "I can't seem to keep from thinking about what they . . . what they did to me."

"You'll even the score one day. You'll watch them all hang. Langmuir's a mighty determined officer."

"His entire command has been destroyed," she said.

"But he's still in the field. That was a mighty brave thing he did decoying away Kimbrell."

"Mighty stupid. We could have fought them off if we'd stayed together," Catherine said. Slocum wasn't going to argue. She might be right. If it had been Kimbrell alone, or even riding with a couple men, they could have ambushed him and eliminated one thorn in their side. Langmuir's chances of getting away were slim.

Even worse, Slocum thought his and Catherine's chances weren't much better. He guided the horse through the low-hanging branches until he spotted his horse. The paint stood quietly, cropping at grass growing in abundance below the trees where sunlight slanted in during the early morning hours. Slocum had to blink a couple times because the horse's coloration caused it to fade into the forest.

Slocum hit the ground, causing Catherine to jump.

"What's wrong, John?"

"Getting my horse." He paused as he stood beside the paint, then dropped to the ground and pressed his ear down. Indians could tell if they were being followed by the hollow thud carried through the ground. He heard what must be several horses. He got his boot in the stirrup and pulled himself up before looking around. In the darkness, he couldn't see their pursuers. All the sound had told him was that he and Catherine had men on their trail, but not where they might be.

"This way," he said, cutting at an angle through the dense growth. They burst out on the other side and found a game trail. Slocum let Catherine ride ahead while he hung back to tug and pull bushes back over the dense growth they had ridden through. It was a poor way to cover his trail, but was the best he could do. In the dark, Magee's men might overlook it.

"John, we're heading toward Charity."

Slocum cursed his bad luck, but from the sounds behind in the forest, they could not turn back now. He looked both left and right. His imagination worked to beat the band, but he thought riders flanked them on both sides and behind. There was only one direction he and Catherine could go.

Ahead.

"Keep a sharp eye out for Magee's men. If he cordoned off the town, we have to get through his guards."

"Is it smart to go into the town?"

"We don't have a whole lot of choice," Slocum said, hearing voices to their left. They definitely had riders behind them. If he gambled on a quick burst of speed to the right through the forest, there was no telling what they might find. His only hope for staying alive lay in how thinly Magee must have spread his men around the town. With at least a half dozen flanking him and some behind, Slocum knew there couldn't be more than three times that in a ring a mile in circumference.

"We're getting close to the town," Catherine said. "I can smell the burned wood from the buildings."

"Not all the town was destroyed," Slocum said. "There are some buildings still standing." He thought about heading there and seeing if they could take refuge, but the sounds of pursuit were getting louder. There wouldn't be time to hide the horses.

"The woods are thinning, John. We'll be seen."

"Stay low and keep to whatever shadows you can find." He touched the butt of his six-shooter, but knew he could never shoot it out with half a dozen men and come out alive. Then he saw salvation. He galloped forward, nudged Catherine, and pointed. She bent lower and urged her horse to more speed.

They raced for a partly destroyed barn to get out of sight before Magee's men appeared. Slocum saw Catherine jump her horse over a pile of debris. An instant later, he followed. He tugged hard on the reins and got his horse to a dead halt before it collided with Catherine's.

"Down," he said urgently. "Put the horses in adjoining stalls."

"There are only a couple still intact."

"All the better. The barn looks as if it's been completely gutted. They might not even slow down to search the place."

Slocum led his horse into a stall where the straw was only partly singed. Catherine tied hers in the next stall and swung around, colliding with him. He caught her in his arms and swept her up off her feet, and tossed her into a pile of hay that had fallen down from the loft above. She landed lightly and lay still.

Hand on his pistol, Slocum waited tensely as the hoofbeats came ever closer. He peered out between boards in the wall and saw two men pass by fast. A third trotted after them. When he heard the horses coming back, he gripped his six-shooter even tighter, ready for a fight.

The trio of riders departed without ever slowing.

He let out a breath he had not even been aware of holding, and went back to the depths of the barn where Catherine still lay in the hay.

"Should I burrow down and hide?" she asked.

"No need. They didn't go into town. They probably don't want to alert whoever's left that Magee has returned. That means the townspeople might have a chance of fighting them off. Enough of the gang might be dead that—"

"John?"

"What?"

"Shut up and hold me. I need something more than you rambling on and on like that."

"Something more?"

"Something to erase all the bad that's happened." She sat up, grabbed his leg, and pulled hard enough to get him off balance. He tumbled down into the hay beside her. Catherine's hands began moving more insistently, and he found himself responding.

"Are you sure this is what you want?" he asked.

"Just lie there. Let me be the one doing things," she said. Her finger worked to remove his gun belt, and then she began in earnest to free him of his pants. By the time she worked his jeans back, he was standing proudly at attention.

She looked up at him. Slocum tried to read what was in her face but could not. There was no eagerness or fear or revulsion. There was nothing, and that was more troubling than if she had pushed him away and curled up and cried all night long.

"So nice," she said, stroking along the rigid length. Bending over, she gave the tip a quick kiss that sent tremors all the way down into Slocum's loins. "So big." She started stroking up and down with enough friction to make him groan. "And so lonely."

She engulfed the purpled tip with her lips, then slid down

a bit more until she took the entire end into her mouth. Her lips caressed and her tongue teased. Slocum groaned even louder when her tongue began stroking along the sensitive underside. Then she clamped down and scored the sides with her teeth. He forced himself to keep from rising off the hay and thrusting into her mouth. She wanted to be in control, but it was hard for Slocum not to react.

Her tongue whirled about the end and slipped back and forth until he was fighting to keep control. Then she began to suck. Her blond head worked up and down as she took him as far into her mouth as possible and then backed away so that her lips danced on the very tip.

"You're really making it hard on me," Slocum said.

"I know. I can feel it." She gobbled a bit and then said, "And I can taste it. You're doing just fine, John."

"Not so good. Can't hold back too long."

"Let yourself go whenever you want. That's what I want. I want to know what it is that's exciting you."

"You are," Slocum said. He gasped and leaned back as she went down on him again. He wanted to lace his fingers through her blond locks, but instead contented himself with grabbing a double handful of hay. Her head flew up and down faster as she took ever more of him into her mouth. And then there was no way of holding himself back. Slocum shoved upward uncontrollably and spilled his seed. She rode out the rush and kept her mouth around him until he went entirely limp.

"That was tasty," she said. The tip of her pink tongue sneaked out and made a slow circuit of her lips.

"I don't know if you got what you needed, but I surely did," Slocum said.

"There's some more," she said. "Hold me, John. Hold me."

She snuggled into the circle of his arms. Slocum didn't mind that, nor did he mind when she put her hand down on his crotch as if to check to be sure it didn't rise up unexpectedly. It would come back to life eventually, but not at the moment. She had treated it too well for that, leaving Slocum drained.

Catherine Duggan went to sleep while Slocum stayed awake, listening and waiting and worrying that Magee would take it into his head to finish destroying the town of Charity.

Hours later, Catherine stirred and murmured something he did not catch. He took her hand away from his privates and buttoned up. She rolled onto her back and stared up at the loft for a while before speaking.

"It'll never go away, what they did to me, but I feel better now. Not completely whole, but better. Thanks, John."

"You did everything," he said, strapping on his six-gun.

"You let me. You let me do what I wanted at my own pace. That gives me some feeling of control over my own life."

"Thanks," he said.

She laughed. "Men." Catherine sobered and looked hard at him. Then her gaze softened. "You men are not all alike."

"Glad to hear it." Slocum got to his feet and brushed off hay before going to peer outside. It was getting late in the day. From where he stood, he didn't see any of Magee's men, but they must still be lying low outside Charity.

"I don't know if we should go on into town and do what we can to get them ready if Magee attacks again, or if we ought to see if Langmuir got away. If they caught him, Kimbrell will torture him for days."

"He's terrible. I swear, that man makes most Apaches look like Little Goody Two-Shoes." Catherine hesitated, then said, "The captain is resourceful enough to escape."

"He's got his standing orders to protect the people in the territory and is trying to carry them out," Slocum said.

"John," Catherine asked. "He has orders, but what are we doing? I mean, what is the plan? We can't run around like chickens with our heads cut off all the time. If we do that too much, Major Magee will oblige."

Slocum rubbed his neck. He had felt a hangman's noose there on occasion, and had been stabbed there and strangled. The thought of letting someone like Magee hack off his head only strengthened his resolve to stop the mad major.

"I was escorting the Magee women and Marshal Vannover back here when things went wrong," he said.

"Sarah Beth? Louisa? You were with them? Are they all right?"

"They're just fine," Slocum said. "The marshal's got some injuries, but it looked like he was getting over them. By the time I find them again, he'll probably be the one driving the wagon."

"What do you mean?"

"Louisa's been doing a right fine job of being a freighter."

"Louisa Magee?"

"Reckon you know her as a hothouse flower, always being watched over by the major. She's blossomed. Don't think Sarah Beth is the same as she was when you knew her either."

"I've got to get to them!"

Slocum considered the different courses of action. They had risked their lives getting past the cordon Magee had around Charity. To simply ride back through the cordon accomplished nothing.

"You wait here," Slocum said. "I'll see to spreading the alert about another attack. The folks left in Charity are likely to be the toughest. Nothing's scared them off so far, and they're more likely to fight if Magee tries to finish what he started here."

"He must think Sarah Beth is coming here. How would he know that?"

"Guessing," Slocum said. "He and Louisa share the same thoughts, or so it seems. We were coming here because the marshal wanted to die at home, but Louisa veered away because she knew Magee would be here waiting for her. How Magee knew she would come to Charity, or how

Louisa knew he was already here, isn't something I want to think on too much."

"They won't come here if Magee's waiting for them?"

"That'd be a right stupid thing to do, wouldn't it?"

"Where did you leave them?"

"We'll head there straightaway after I warn the town."

"Draw me a map. Here in the dirt." Catherine kicked away straw from the floor and handed Slocum a twig.

"I need to get things right in my head." He thought a few seconds, then began sketching. "Magee's gang is likely to be stretched out in an arc from here to over there. I left the marshal and the women about here. There was a stream." His voice caught when he thought of the stream and how he and Louisa had indulged one another's fancy near it.

"You go on, John. Don't be long now, you hear?"

"Only as long as it takes." He thought of kissing her, but drew back when she made no move toward him. Catherine had been through a hellish torture, and Slocum did not want to do anything to stir up unwanted memories this soon. Given time, they might fade and be less painful—but she would never forget.

Slocum backed his paint from the stall and led it to the rear door. He spent a couple minutes looking for any sign of Magee and his men. When he saw none, he swung into the saddle and rode fast for the middle of Charity. What buildings remained intact were there. He also discovered that it was where the residents of Charity were determined to make their stand. More than one rifle poked through a doorway to follow him.

"You have a mayor? I need to talk to somebody in charge."

"I'm as close to bein' in charge as there is," said a portly man carrying a sawed-off shotgun. He came out onto the boardwalk from the saloon. Slocum saw how he kept the scattergun pointed in his general direction.

"Marshal Vannover's been wounded, but I think he's

on the mend. I'm trying to get him back into town, but Magee's got the whole town ringed in."

"Magee? That the varmint the cavalry warned us about bein' responsible fer burnin' us out?"

"None other than," Slocum said. "He's waiting for the women traveling along with your marshal to come into town—then he'll attack again."

"Let him. This time he'll ride into a wall of gunfire."

"That's the spirit," Slocum said. "Just don't get too trigger-happy and shoot up the marshal."

"Never cottoned much to old Les Vannover, but compared to the others, he's a prince among men. Won't shoot him, not if his gun will join ours defending the town."

"Count on it," Slocum said. "I've got to get back to where I left the marshal. Can I get some ammo and enough food for a couple days? I can fill my canteen from a watering trough."

"Go on. Get your water, and I'll fetch you some ammunition. Not sure what we've got in the way of food we can let you have. Town's supply is mighty scarce right now."

"Some jerky or dried beans will do me just fine. I've lived on worse."

"We can spare that much," the man said. He ducked back into the saloon while Slocum got his water and let his horse drink. By the time he and the horse had their fill, the man returned.

"Here you are. Use those cartridges wisely."

"On Magee and his men," Slocum said, tucking the box into his saddlebags. "Much obliged."

"Get that varmint Vannover back here, and we'll call it even."

Slocum touched the brim of his hat, mounted, and rode quickly back to the partially burned-out barn where he had left Catherine. As he neared, his sixth sense began to act up. He always listened to it. Since the war, it had saved his hide more than once.

He left his horse twenty yards away from the barn and

advanced quietly on foot, Colt Navy drawn and ready. With a sudden move, he swung around the rear door and leveled his six-shooter at . . . nothing. The barn was empty. Catherine was nowhere to be seen and her horse was gone.

23

Slocum followed Catherine's horse for several hundred yards, then lost the trail in a gravelly stretch. He rode around, wary of being seen by any of Magee's scouts. Knowing the major's entire gang of murderers was somewhere just out of sight made Slocum increasingly uneasy about hunting for Catherine's trail. She had not been forced to leave. The solitary set of hoofprints proved that. Whatever had caused her to run had put her in great danger.

The longer Slocum hunted for her, the more likely he was to draw attention to himself—and to her. Wherever she had gotten off to.

The sun was setting, giving him a chance of sneaking back through Magee's sentries and once more riding with Marshal Vannover—and the Magee women. Slocum kept thinking about how the pair of them looked. Sarah Beth was beautiful, but her mother had something the younger girl lacked. There was a steely determination to Louisa that appealed to Slocum. She knew what she wanted, what needed to be done for the good of her child, and she did it. Slocum doubted Sarah Beth would ever have run away from her pa's dictatorial ways, no matter how brutal he became to her, without her mother's approval.

That Louisa had led the way only made her the more attractive.

Slocum shook his head in wonder. How could he be thinking of Louisa when he had just been with Catherine? Something about Catherine Duggan bothered him, but he could not figure out what it was. She was lovely and had shown great courage in the face of torture. More than this, she had sought out his company and seemed sincerely drawn to him.

There was something amiss. Slocum found himself thinking again of Louisa and worrying that even her courage would not be enough to save her daughter and Marshal Vannover from her husband.

He considered retracing the route he had taken into Charity, but figured that would be watched closely. The trio of riders that had followed him was enough of a warning that he knew he should heed it. Let them watch that game trail. That meant fewer of them to keep lookout everywhere else.

Slocum cut across a broad, grassy plain, and then found the hills rising to meet him quickly. He cut this way and that, more to cover his back trail than to find a way through the dense undergrowth. Once, he heard men talking, and sat silently astride his horse, waiting tensely. When the men making all the ruckus faded away in another direction, Slocum started his trip again. This time, he came out of the woods near a road. He closed his eyes and pictured the land lifted onto a map until he got his bearings. The clouds were hugging the sky now and blotting out the stars he might have used to guide him.

Before the hour was up, he knew where he was and where he had left the wagon with the marshal and the women. He rode faster now, and finally came to the spot. He was not surprised that Louisa had chosen to move on. Staying in one place, especially with her husband's henchmen all around, might prove dangerous.

But was hiding out as dangerous as getting on the move? Slocum didn't know. He circled the area a few times, trying to make sense out of the wagon tracks. The deep ruts showed they had headed toward the northwest. The only thing in that direction that he knew of was Fort Supply, and it had been overrun by Magee's horde.

Heaving a sigh, Slocum started on the trail, but had ridden only a mile when he got the feeling of being watched. The hairs rose on the back of his neck, and occasional small sounds that did not—quite—belong to the woods at night put him on edge. It might be nothing, but he dared not make a mistake now.

Riding through the woods, he began hunting for a branch at about the right height. When he saw it, he heaved hard, grabbed the limb, and pulled himself up. The paint dutifully trotted on, as if it had not lost its rider so suddenly. Slocum flopped out along the branch, and waited only a few minutes until the dark-cloaked rider following him came closer.

Slocum held his breath and tried not to look away. He had been in situations where he had been alerted because someone was looking hard at him. It was nonsense, but a man learned to live by the little things, superstition or not. He didn't want to warn the man on his trail by staring, yet he had to if he wanted to make his attack quiet and precise.

The rider stopped and looked around. For a heart-stopping moment, Slocum was certain the man felt eyes on him and was responding. Then he rode forward, directly under the limb where Slocum waited like a mountain lion ready to pounce.

Slocum counted slowly, and when he reached five he dropped. Both of his hands gripped the man's shoulders, controlling his movement in the saddle. With a hard, wrenching jerk, Slocum unseated the man and fell on top of him. Using his six-shooter would be dangerous with Magee's men everywhere. Slocum whipped out the knife from the top of his boot and prepared to strike.

He stopped just inches away from Isaiah Langmuir's throat.

"Howdy, Captain. Didn't expect you to be sneaking around behind me like that."

"Slocum, get the hell off me."

Slocum did as the officer requested.

"I thought you were one of Magee's men." Slocum did not bother apologizing because he saw nothing to apologize for. If he had slit the captain's throat, he might have felt sorry for a while, but this was dangerous territory, thanks to Clayton Magee.

"I thought you were, too, but I wasn't sure."

"What happened when you decoyed Kimbrell and his men away?"

"I shot it out with them. I think I winged one, but they wouldn't stop coming after me. I finally lost them in the hills south of here. It was night, and Kimbrell wasn't inclined to make a career out of running me to earth."

"You see the women? The marshal and the wagon?"

"I found the clearing, apparently after you. I followed the tracks until I spotted you."

"What's in that direction?" Slocum pointed toward the northwest.

"Only the fort. Maybe the women don't know it was destroyed and think they'll find shelter there."

"Might be the only place they can think to go that Magee might not be watching."

"There's no reason for him to leave a guard at the fort. He's already taken all he can—and killed all the soldiers he's likely to, unless . . ."

"Unless what?" Slocum demanded.

"My squad might have returned to the fort when neither I nor Sergeant Benedict returned. There wasn't a soldier above the rank of corporal there." Langmuir looked sharply at Slocum. "I did *not* abandon my men. We needed a scouting report, and Benedict and I were the only ones capable of doing it."

"Not saying you were wrong," Slocum allowed. He didn't bother saying he thought that the captain hadn't been right. Being in command carried responsibilities beyond scouting. Langmuir had made a bad decision that might have cost him all his men. Slocum didn't know if Magee or

Kimbrell had come across the soldiers, but if so, the soldiers would never have put up the kind of defense needed to survive without someone to command them.

"The wagon is heading for a road that will lead directly to Fort Supply," Langmuir said. "If we cut across that ridge, we can gain several miles on them."

"Let's go," Slocum said. In one respect, he was glad to ride with the captain. The man had patrolled this area extensively and knew the shortcuts.

"You think Magee will keep his men over at Charity?"

"I think Kimbrell or one of the others will get tired of waiting, and they will finish the job they started. I warned the folks in town of that possibility, but it will be quite a fight."

"They know Magee isn't a tall tale to frighten children. They'll be waiting for him and his murderous gang."

"Hurts, doesn't it?" Slocum asked. Langmuir looked at him hard. "You went up against a crazy man and barely managed to retreat."

"That fight cut both ways. Magee barely managed to retreat."

Slocum started to say that the major had come out ahead, looting Fort Supply and still being in the field. He might have fewer men, but from all Slocum could tell, he still had the advantage in men, arms, and supplies, too. Something about Langmuir made him want to goad the officer, but no good could come of it.

"There! Look, Slocum, down there!"

At first Slocum didn't see what excited the officer. Then a wagon emerged from around a bend in the road. They had found the Magee women and Marshal Vannover. Slocum was a little late riding down to meet them, too. Captain Langmuir galloped flat out, until Slocum thought the man would kill his horse under him. By the time Slocum reached the wagon, Langmuir was dismounted and talking with Louisa and Sarah Beth.

"Reckon you got to talk to *me*, Slocum," the marshal said from the back of the wagon. Vannover was propped up and looking better.

"Seems like a family reunion," Slocum said, seeing how Langmuir pressed close to the women and peppered them with questions.

"I think he's sweet on her."

"Do tell," Slocum said. Slocum rode closer and looked at the marshal. "You're about ready to get on back to your job. They need you in Charity."

"They may need me, but they don't want me," Vannover said. "Never made many friends, not after I threw the mayor's worthless kid in the clink for public drunkenness a couple times."

"Mayor's dead, and the ones left are hankering for someone to tell them how to stay alive."

"Fancy that," Vannover said. "I'd head on back since that's where I thought we was headin' anyway, but there's not a spare horse. I'm pretty much stuck with bein' a passenger."

"Getting into Charity might be a problem without a company of soldiers at your back, too."

"What are the chances of that?"

"Looks like we'll find out real soon," Slocum said.

"We're going on to the fort right away," Langmuir said in his best command voice. Slocum looked from Louisa to Sarah Beth, and saw that the captain was out to impress the daughter. That suited Slocum just fine, though he wished the officer had some plan to impress Major Magee with how he ought to surrender before fighting a huge battle. It wasn't going to happen, though, and Slocum wondered what Magee's reaction would be if he found out the captain was sweet on his daughter.

For all that, what would Magee do if he found out about his wife and Slocum and their tryst down by the river?

"You want me to watch our back trail?" Slocum asked.

Langmuir looked sharply at Slocum, then nodded.

Without another word, Slocum turned and trotted along the road, on the lookout for any sign that Magee's men were after them. He appreciated the solitude and chance to simply stop riding for a spell. He sat beside a rock at the side of the road and listened hard, watched for anything out of the ordinary, and just thought on what had happened. After a half hour without any trace of the outlaws, Slocum mounted and trotted to catch up with the wagon.

Langmuir had set a slower pace than Louisa wanted from the way the two were arguing when Slocum rode up. The officer wanted to spend a little more time with Sarah Beth was Slocum's guess. Louisa wanted to get the hell away from Clayton Magee.

"Nothing after us," said Slocum. "What's ahead?"

"I scouted the fort," Langmuir said, shaking his head. "I couldn't tell who's taken charge there. The gates were closed, and I saw a guard moving about up in the watch tower."

Slocum had worried over this possibility like a dog with a bone.

"It's not Magee or his men in there," Slocum said. "He is too sure Louisa and Sarah Beth are going to Charity. He's committed all his men there."

"What of Kimbrell?"

"Either Kimbrell's going along with Magee or he's hightailed it. Either way, he's not in Fort Supply."

"You make a sound case, Slocum, but we have to know before we risk the ladies' lives."

"To hell with it," Slocum said, snapping his reins and getting his paint trotting ahead down the road. He ignored both Langmuir's and Louisa's cries for him to stop. When the captain didn't come galloping out to accompany him, Slocum knew Langmuir had decided to remain and protect the women.

"Sarah Beth," Slocum said, chuckling. He hoped that the captain's infatuation with her did not build to match that of her father's.

"Halt, who goes there?"

Slocum slowed and stopped a few yards from the locked gate. The palisade walls rose dark and foreboding. On the walkway above, he saw a head poking up. A rifle balanced precariously, and centered on him only when the nervous sentry trembled in the proper direction.

"Name's Slocum. I scouted for Captain Langmuir."

"I know you. Where's the captain?"

"A mile back down the road. He's got three civilians with him. Who's in charge of the fort?"

After a long pause came an answer that made Slocum wish he had just kept riding.

"Reckon I am. Private Leary. That's me."

"Open up the gate. Captain Langmuir's on his way back to assume command."

"The captain's still alive? Thought he was kilt."

"Open the gate," Slocum said. He turned his paint and galloped back to the wagon, giving a succinct report.

"You're going to have to order the private to let us in," Slocum told Langmuir. "I don't think he'd let his own mother in he's so scared."

"Who can blame him?" Sarah Beth looked at Langmuir. "Without a decent officer in charge, why, the whole fort must be like a ship without a rudder."

"Roll 'em," Langmuir said. He rode ahead of Slocum. When Slocum tried to catch up, the captain rode a little faster. Slocum finally gave up on this pissing match and fell back to ride alongside the wagon so he could talk with Marshal Vannover.

"You'll have a bunk to sleep in soon enough," Slocum told him.

"Think I can convince the captain to send his men to Charity? I wouldn't want to see my hometown burned down." Vannover coughed. "The rest of it, I mean. Some folks wouldn't care if they never saw me again, but I've got an obligation to the whole lot of 'em."

"Langmuir's got to do something about Magee," Slocum said. "He sent couriers to the other forts. At least one must have delivered the bad news."

"With his sweetie safe, Langmuir's likely to risk another sortie after Magee and his gang," Vannover said. "If I can reach Charity, might get a few citizens to take the fight to him. It's to everyone's benefit to get rid of Magee, and hitting him from both sides might be what it takes to finish him off once and for all."

By the time Louisa drove the wagon to the gate, Langmuir had given orders and had it pulled wide open. As they rode into the fort's parade ground, Slocum saw how the main gate hung precariously. It had been severely damaged and would never withstand a real assault. But it might never have to—if Magee thought Louisa and Sarah Beth were heading for Charity.

"How many men you have left?" Slocum asked the officer. Langmuir's expression gave the sorry answer.

"Not enough. Almost ten."

"Almost ten? How close to ten?"

"Seven made it back," Langmuir said angrily. "I'll see that our guests are shown to their quarters."

"Looks like the officers' barracks are all blowed to hell and gone," observed Vannover. Langmuir ignored him. Slocum helped the marshal down. Although he was shaky, the lawman could walk on his own. He motioned for Slocum to give him some support. "Get me on over to the mess hall. I'm hungry enough to eat a horse."

"Not mine," Slocum said. "I still need it."

"Maybe Langmuir's then. That'd give him an excuse to stay with Sarah Beth."

Slocum chuckled at the marshal's observation. The captain personally escorted Louisa and Sarah Beth to the one remaining house at the end of a row of houses destroyed by cannon fire.

"That's more truth than poetry," Slocum agreed. He joined Vannover in the mess hall for a meal of beans and hardtack. After having his belly rub against his backbone for so long, any food set well with him. As they finished, Langmuir came in and sat across from them.

"I am going to hold Fort Supply until reinforcements arrive. There's no way I can justify splitting seven men between maintaining the fort and attacking Magee."

"Three or four men wouldn't make much of a dent

against a force like Magee's," Vannover agreed. Slocum looked at the marshal sharply as he continued talking. "So, Captain, why don't you let me have an escort back to Charity and I'll rouse the citizens? We can do your job for you."

"That is uncalled for, sir." Langmuir shot to his feet and stormed from the mess hall.

"You aren't much for winning folks over to your side, are you?" Slocum said.

"Don't see you going out of your way to do that either, Slocum," the marshal said. "Why don't you mosey on over to where the women are bivouacking and talk to them? If Louisa asked her daughter to ask Langmuir to send troops to Charity, I bet my bottom dollar he'd have his men all lined up lickety-split."

"Nobody ever won the battle by just sitting on their thumbs," Slocum said. "Let me have another plate of beans, and I'll see what Louisa has to say about this." He knew Vannover had figured out what went on between Slocum and Louisa as well as how Langmuir was sweet on Sarah Beth. He might have been laid up with a fever, but he was no fool.

Slocum finished his meal, tossed the tin plate in a bucket at the end of the table, and stepped out into the humid night. Clouds worked their way over the stars, but the waxing moon shone with enough light for him to walk confidently to the fort's guest quarters. A lamp burned in the single window.

Slocum rapped on the door and waited. Louisa opened the door. For a moment she smiled. Then the expression died as she looked past him.

"Did anyone see you? Come in, John. Please hurry. Soldiers gossip like old women."

Slocum ducked inside, and found his arms filled with a warm, willing woman who kissed him.

"I've missed you so," she said, pressing her cheek against his chest.

"We've still got business to tend to," he said.

"Clayton," she said with a deep sigh. "He is always there like some evil dark shadow."

"Could you talk to Sarah Beth so she'll convince Langmuir to abandon the fort and attack Magee? Marshal Vannover is sure he can get a dozen men from Charity to join the fight."

"She does make doe eyes at him, doesn't she?" Louisa stepped back and smiled just a little again. "Like I do with you." She nodded suddenly and said, "I'll talk to her right now. She went straight to bed because I think she wanted to be up before reveille so she could see her hero out in front of his command."

Louisa went to the door leading to the bedroom, paused, and said, "I wish we were in there. Together. All night long." She heaved another sigh of resignation and opened the door. Louisa stood for a moment, then rushed into the room crying out for her daughter.

Slocum went to the door and drew his six-shooter. Louisa frantically searched, but Slocum saw immediately that Sarah Beth had gone out the window. He slid his pistol back into his holster.

"She's not in any danger," Slocum said. "Not with the captain."

"I'll paddle her, I swear I will! She knows better! She knows what this will do to discipline in the fort and how it will undermine the captain's authority with his men."

Slocum went to the window and looked outside. The earlier rain had left the ground soft and the bright silvery moonlight highlighted footprints. One set coming to the window. Two sets leaving.

He drew his six-gun and climbed through the window to follow the footprints, which went directly to a hole that had been shot in the palisade by a cannonball. Sarah Beth Magee had left the fort. And not with Isaiah Langmuir unless he wore a boot the same size as Sarah Beth.

24

"She's gone?" Isaiah Langmuir stared at Slocum in disbelief. "This isn't something her mother put you up to claiming, is it, Slocum?"

"Just to keep you from sniffing around? No, she left the fort. See for yourself. The tracks are plain as the nose on your face."

"I'll rouse the garrison."

"Not much of one to rouse," Slocum said, "but it might be a good idea to put up an extra lookout or two in case Magee has decided to move from Charity."

"You make it sound as if the man has second sight."

"He has scouts out everywhere. Might be one of them spotted the wagon coming into the fort."

"Reinforcement are on the way. Two companies from Fort Gibson will arrive within a day or two."

"That's good," Slocum said, "but it might be too little, too late. Magee has shown his men can ride like the wind and fight like devils once they get to the battlefield."

"You make them sound like Nathan Bedford Forrest's troopers."

"Magee fought for the Federals," Slocum said caustically.

"You ought to appreciate his tactics and skill better than anyone around here."

"He may have fought for the Union, but to insinuate that he and I share anything in—"

"Stuff a sock in it, Captain," said Lester Vannover. "Arguing over the war's not gettin' anybody nowhere. It's not making Charity a safer place to live or Sarah Beth safer or—"

"I get your point, sir," Langmuir said, fighting to hold down his anger. "What are you saying?"

"Slocum's got the right idea. If Magee's scouts have reported to him, he's on his way here. The only thing in that man's demented mind is getting back his wife and child."

"Sarah Beth is not a child. She's a woman."

"Captain, grab hold of your dick and tuck it away until after this fight's done," Vannover said. "We've got big problems brewin'."

"Orderly! Throw this man in the stockade!"

Slocum drew and pointed his six-shooter at the soldier's head when he came running into the room, ready to obey his commander.

"As you were, Private," Slocum said. "We're having a friendly argument, and you don't want to get involved."

"Throw them *both* in the stockade!"

"Sir," the private said, voice quavering. "The sentry on the gate. He thinks he saw a rider along the road."

"Sarah Beth!"

"He said it was a man. He rode up, looked at the fort, and then hightailed it."

"Magee's scout saw the wagon tracks," Slocum said. "They were hunting for the wagon and know it came into the fort."

"Too bad it didn't rain more and wash away the tracks," Vannover said. "You got a spare rifle and any ammo, Captain? I'd like to go down fighting when Magee attacks."

"As you were, Private," Langmuir said.

Slocum watched the emotions play across the officer's face. Slocum didn't have time for any of it.

"Private, sound assembly. Get the entire company to the walls with all the ammunition and weapons they can find," Slocum said brusquely.

"There's not much left, sir," the private said, turning to Slocum.

"Get all you can. Magee will attack at dawn. We must be ready for him before that."

"Yes, sir." The private saluted Slocum and ran out as fast as he had come in.

"You're not in command of this post, Slocum. I am."

"Then act like it, Captain," Slocum said. "There's no time to pine over Sarah Beth. You've got a command to protect unless you want your reinforcements to find a burned-out husk of a fort and dead bodies stacked high."

"Did Magee take Sarah Beth?" Langmuir looked stricken at the thought.

"Hard to say, but I don't think so. He would have kidnapped Mrs. Magee, too." Slocum didn't bother telling the captain that the second set of footprints were too small to belong to any man riding with Magee. Unless Magee had recruited a young child, another woman had lured Sarah Beth from the fort. Slocum had to think Catherine Duggan was responsible.

"She's safe?"

"As safe as any of us, you jackass," snapped Vannover. "Get your men assembled, give the orders, and let's fight!"

Langmuir glared at the marshal, then at Slocum, and hurried from the room. Vannover shook his head at such pigheadedness.

"Where do they get their officers?"

Before Slocum could answer, the ground shook with the explosion of a cannonball ripping through the mess hall. He caught himself, but Vannover was knocked from his feet. Slocum helped the lawman stand.

"Looks like we just ran out of time," Slocum said. "You

get to the armory. Somebody's got to pass out whatever carbines are left."

"You going up to the wall?"

A second cannonball whined overhead to land harmlessly beyond the parade ground.

"They're homin' in on the outhouses," Vannover said. "That ought to be a war crime." He slapped Slocum on the back and hobbled away as fast as he could. Slocum stepped out of the room Langmuir had used as an office and tried to guess what time it was by the stars. The storm clouds had moved in, blocking the moon. If they had to escape from the fort before it became a death trap, a heavy rain would provide good cover. Langmuir didn't have many men left—and Magee's force had been reduced in size also.

A third cannonball missed the fort entirely, sailing over both the front palisade and the rear to explode some distance away. Slocum knew that meant Magee was no longer doing the aiming for his artillery. If he had taken a position in the front of his gang, a sniper might end this fight in a hurry with a single shot.

Slocum had been one of the best snipers in the Army of the CSA. He rummaged through his gear stored in the stables and drew his Winchester. It wasn't what he would have chosen for long-distance work, but it had to do. He dumped a box of cartridges into his coat pocket and climbed a ladder to the top of the wall.

"You're the fellow who scouted for the captain," Private Leary said as he crouched down behind a thick section of the wall. "Hope you're as good a shot as you are a scout."

"Let me see," Slocum said. He found a spot where he could rest his rifle and command a wide arc of fire across the road. If Magee showed up, this would be the spot.

In the darkness all Slocum could see were darting shadows. Rather than waste his ammo, he shifted his field of fire around until he found one of the artillery batteries. A discharge momentarily blinded him. Then came the whistling sound and an impact that shook the entire wall.

For a heart-stopping instant, Slocum thought the cannonball had brought down the entire wall. But whoever had built the defenses for Fort Supply had done a good job. A few timbers fell free and a hole large enough to walk through had been blasted low in the wall, but the structure remained standing.

Slocum sighted in on the cannon, judged distances, and made guesses about windage. They had made a mistake moving the cannon too close to their target. He began firing slowly, steadily, shifting each subsequent shot a little to the right to send out a spray of bullets. He did not hear any sound, but he had the feeling his aim was on target.

"They oughta send another cannonball into us, 'less you got 'em," the private said.

Slocum did not reply. He hunted for a new target, still wanting to sight in on Clayton Magee. When he didn't see anyone mounted, he shifted his rifle a little lower. Magee's gang had gone to ground and were waiting to rush the front gate.

In the dark and dismounted, they would be almost unstoppable.

"Down!" Slocum shouted. "Everyone off the front wall!"

He turned and jumped, landing hard fifteen feet below. He tried to roll, but the impact was too great. He was slammed flat and had the air knocked out of his lungs. This saved him. Magee had brought up the Gatling gun and opened fire, reducing the top of the wall to splinters. Three of the soldiers had not heeded his warning and were dead, two falling into the fort and the other flopped over the top of the palisade.

"Stay away from the gate!" Slocum rolled onto his back and brought up his Winchester as the Gatling barked its deadly cry again. The gate was reduced to splinters in a second.

Not even waiting for what remained of the heavy gate to fall, Slocum began firing. He brought down two of Magee's men and wounded two others. His rifle came up empty. He drew his six-shooter and emptied it, too. By this time, Captain Langmuir and two other soldiers had appeared from their posts along other segments of the wall and poured their fire into the gaping hole in the fort's defense.

"Charge!" roared Les Vannover. "Attack! Go get 'em. Get 'em all!"

No one was mounted or able to obey the command, but Slocum saw that the shouted order was intended only to throw the enemy into confusion. Reloading quickly, he flopped onto his belly and, from this prone position, began picking his targets carefully. He brought down two more before the outlaws got an order to retreat.

When the shooting stopped, Slocum thought he had gone deaf. There was a complete silence that swaddled him like a woolen blanket.

"They've pulled back," Langmuir said, peering around the corner of the gate out along the road.

"They'll wait for daylight and attack again," Slocum said, getting up and dusting himself off. "You have to turn that cannon against them."

"And take out the Gatling gun while you're at it. It did all the damage," Vannover pointed out.

"Is there anybody left who knows how to fire a howitzer?" Slocum asked.

"I do," said Langmuir. "And Private Leary is trained."

"Come along, Private," Slocum said. "Me and you are going to do some skunk hunting."

"Go on, Leary," the captain said, seeing the private confused about whose orders to follow. "There'll be enough left of us to defend the fort."

Slocum knew that wasn't true. If there were three others left, it would be a miracle. He saw Louisa coming from her quarters, carrying a rifle. She looked so determined he said nothing.

"Give me a post, Captain, and I'll do what I can," she said.

"Mrs. Magee, you can't—"

"I will die fighting that son of a bitch husband of mine rather than surrender. Considering his history with towns and soldiers who stand in his way, I'd recommend that you do the same thing."

Slocum nudged Leary and pointed toward the gate. With the clouds hanging low and heavy, he didn't know how long they had before sunrise. Even a small amount of daylight would stop him from doing what he planned.

Leary followed as Slocum slipped outside the fort, found a shallow drainage ditch alongside the road, and walked in a crouch along it.

"What we up to, Mr. Slocum?"

"Was the captain right? You know how to man a cannon?"

"Not the best artillerist in the company, but I ain't the worst either. I can load and swab with the best of 'em."

"Stay low. We are heading for the battery." Slocum used what cover he could find to get within ten yards of the howitzer that had caused so much damage to the fort. His sniping had killed two of the gun crew. The other two stood arguing about what to do. From what little Slocum could overhear, he had killed the only two who knew how to fire the cannon.

"What'll we do, Mr. Slocum?"

Slocum paid Leary no heed. He aimed carefully and fired. One outlaw sank to the ground, dead instantly with a bullet to the skull. The other kept arguing, as if his partner had not simply collapsed. When he realized there was trouble, he was dead, too. Running forward, Slocum reached the cannon and found what remained. There were two cannonballs, wadding, and enough powder for a dozen shots.

"Help me turn it." Slocum lifted the cannon tongue while Leary dug in his toes and pushed for all he was worth. The field piece cut deep into the soft ground, but finally relented so Slocum could get it aimed away from the fort and toward the road.

He silently pointed to what he wanted Leary to do. The private worked with infuriating deliberateness, but Slocum could not fault him for that. Leary had his way of doing things and it worked.

"Get on the lanyard. Fire when I tell you," Slocum said. He jumped to the carriage and climbed to the top of the right wheel, balancing precariously. He waited several minutes, then hopped down and struggled to shift the muzzle a few degrees to the right.

"Three, two, one, fire!" Slocum yelled. Leary turned away as he yanked the lanyard. The cannon leaped up off its wheels and then fell back to the ground heavily. "Get it reloaded!"

"The barrel's gonna melt if we keep firin' it fast," Leary warned.

"There's only one cannonball left. Don't worry about wasting powder. We got plenty." Slocum took another sighting and immediately ordered Leary to fire. Again the cannon spat out its death.

"Load it chock-full of powder and wadding," Slocum said.

"But there's no shot!"

"Do it!"

After Leary had rammed the barrel full of the remaining powder, Slocum lifted the tongue and called to Leary to help. When the private saw what Slocum was doing, he got under the wood support and heaved hard enough to up-end the cannon and drive its muzzle down into mud.

"Get on back to the fort," Slocum ordered. "This cannon's going to be shrapnel in a few seconds."

"But Mr. Slocum, you can't stand here and fire it. It'll blow up!"

"They won't use it again," Slocum said. He heard horses coming. "Now git!"

Private Leary "got." Slocum ran as much of the lanyard cord out as he could, then tugged as he fell into a low ditch. The explosion behind him rattled his teeth and turned him deaf. Hot metal chunks from the brass barrel sailed past him—and also ripped toward the outlaws galloping toward the gun.

Slocum lay for a minute getting his senses back. When he sat up, a loud buzzing in his ears told him he was still mostly deaf, but he was alive and three more of Magee's men were not. The exploding barrel had turned men and their horses into bloody shreds.

Getting his bearings, Slocum moved away from where the main body of Magee's men would be gathered—what remained of them. He moved in a wide circle around the fort until he came to the spot where Sarah Beth had left. It took Slocum only a few minutes to find two sets of footprints leading away from the fort and another ten minutes to locate where horses had been tethered.

Slocum had the trail. All he needed was a horse to follow it.

25

"There's no reason to hold back. What do we do? Sit around on our asses while they laugh at us?" Albert Kimbrell did not try to restrain his anger. "Attack now. Kill them while we can."

"There is need for caution," Magee said. "My family is in there. I feel it in my bones. Two scouts saw them in a wagon heading toward the fort. Where else can they be? I'm so close now. My wife and daughter! I don't want them hurt."

"One cannon blew up on us and the other's no good after its carriage broke," Kimbrell said. "Use the Gatling gun on them some more. They'll give up."

"My wife and daughter might be injured. Or killed!" Magee's eyes flashed with a wildness that Kimbrell had seldom seen. But Kimbrell didn't care. He was furious at losing the chance to kill the soldiers inside the fort.

"There's not that many of those bluebellies left. Use the Gatling. They'll surrender. They're all cowards."

"You should never have fired the cannon or ordered the Gatling up. You disobeyed my orders, Mr. Kimbrell."

"To hell with orders! I want to kill them all! We busted into that damned fort before without so much as a fare-thee-well. You sayin' we can't do it again when there's only half a dozen left? We stole their guns and ammo. They're sittin' ducks!"

"My family comes first. Their safety trumps your bloodlust."

"We sat around doin' nuthin' at Charity. We coulda destroyed the whole damn town, but you thought they were in the town so we held back. If it wasn't for my men findin' the wagon with your wife and kid, we'd still be sittin' outside Charity, jerkin' off and wonderin' what to do next!"

Kimbrell rocked back when Magee slapped him hard with the canvas officer's gloves he carried. Kimbrell went for his six-shooter, but found himself looking down the barrel of the major's gun before he could draw.

"Disobeying my orders is a punishable offense. Should I order a field court-martial for you, Mr. Kimbrell, or will you obey my orders exactly as I give them?"

Kimbrell swallowed hard and rubbed his face. Sullenly, he said, "I'll obey."

"Good," Magee said. "I must plan how best to rescue my family from those that have kidnapped them. There is no doubt they are being held hostage."

"Full-out attack," Kimbrell said. Magee glared at him and he fell silent.

"Dismissed."

Like a whipped dog, Kimbrell slunk off. The farther from the major he got, the angrier he grew, until his towering rage knew no bounds. He had to kill something.

"You look like something the cat drug in, Al," piped up one of his men. Kimbrell glowered at Herk Wilson. Nothing bothered the man. His expression never changed whether he was raping a woman or killing her husband or sitting across a poker table bluffing with a pair of deuces. Kimbrell could depend on Wilson and half a dozen in the gang to follow him, no matter what. The rest were either loyal to Clayton Magee, or would slip away and find their own trails when things went to hell.

"I want to attack that damned fort. I want to bring it down."

"I'll get the boys ready," Wilson said. The stocky man hesitated and asked, "There more in it for us?"

"Double shares. We'll be the only ones attacking."

"That'll make it about one on one. We can handle that," Wilson said, laughing. "And I want you to rename it Fort Wilson, after me."

"I'll name it Fort Shit after you if you don't get the men," Kimbrell snapped. Even this tone did nothing to change Wilson's expression. He went off, humming a song that Kimbrell couldn't quite recognize. With one last glance in the direction of Magee and the map the man had spread out on the ground in front of him, Kimbrell went to his horse and mounted. He settled his six pistols and made certain his rifle's magazine was full. With half a dozen other men riding beside him, there was no reason they couldn't take care of the fort with their first assault.

Kimbrell rode up and looked at Wilson and the others. Without a word, Kimbrell pointed toward the fort. They let out bloodcurdling battle cries and galloped to the attack.

"No quarter, men. Kill 'em all!"

"What about the major's family?" called Herk Wilson. "You said we don't kill no blond women."

"Kill 'em *all*!" Kimbrell was past caring what Major Magee said or did. The old man was getting cold feet when it came to leveling towns now that he thought he had finally found his wife and daughter. With the money Kimbrell had stashed away, he didn't need Magee anymore and could live like a king. After this one last killing spree.

Six-shooters came easily to his hands as he rode with the reins in his teeth. The gate to the fort canted inward at a crazy angle. One of the cannonballs must have knocked it from its hinges. Kimbrell began firing wildly at anyone daring to poke their head up above the top of the wall. On either side rode his cadre of men, all firing, too.

To his surprise, a volley from the fort ripped past. Kimbrell put his head down and kept firing until his six-guns were empty. He grabbed another pair thrust into his belt and got closer, only to find the fire from the fort was growing more intense. Bullets ripped past him. One nicked his horse's leg, causing it to stumble. It took all of Kimbrell's skill to keep from being spilled to the ground.

"Keep going. We can get inside!" Kimbrell saw that the men with him were slowing their headlong attack as the fusillade did not slacken. The closer they got, the better targets they made. The sun was coming up behind them, outlining them in the dawn light.

"Al, two of us are down. They shot our horses." Even as Wilson reported, he took a dive off his horse. He hit the ground hard and skidded to a halt, moaning. Kimbrell emptied his second pair of six-shooters and went for his third, but the attack had been turned. The men on the fort walls continued to fire steadily, accurately.

"Get back," Kimbrell said. "We shoulda had all the men behind us." He saw that he had underestimated the resistance he would meet. He thought the sight of half a dozen men galloping down on them would break the spirit of the fort's defenders. It had done the opposite. It had made them even more determined.

"Where'd they get the goddamn ammunition? I thought we took it all."

"Al, don't leave me!"

Kimbrell looked around and saw that Wilson and two others were down. He considered simply retreating, getting the hell out of there. He didn't need more scalps to make him happy if it was going to be this dangerous, but the way the soldiers fought infuriated him. He bent low, reached down grabbed Wilson's outstretched arm, and pulled him up behind him.

"I owe you," Wilson said. Kimbrell did not bother replying. He was galloping away from Fort Supply, knowing he had to face Magee's wrath.

"You there," Kimbrell said, pointing to the others, also riding double. "Grab more horses. And the Gatling. Take the Gatling. Hitch up its wagon and let's get the hell out of here."

"What are we gonna do with it?" Wilson hit the ground

running, stumbled, and caught himself. Then he was up into the almost empty supply wagon where they had mounted the Gatling gun and carried spare ammo and magazines for it.

"We gotta get out of here right now," Kimbrell said. If Magee sent men after them, the Gatling would come in real handy. And if he didn't, if he let them simply ride away, Kimbrell was sure he could figure out a use for the deadly weapon. There had to be more than one bank waiting to get shot up and robbed between Indian Territory and the Mexican border.

Kimbrell and his men rattled away with the Gatling gun, leaving the rest of Magee's men wondering what was going on.

"Halt!" shrieked Clayton Magee when he saw his lieutenant begin the assault. "I'm placing you under arrest! I'm going to court-martial you, damn your eyes!" Magee ran forward, waving his six-shooter in the air. He slowed and then stopped, watching in the gathering light as Kimbrell and his men began their sortie against the eastern side of Fort Supply.

The attack was all wrong. They were spraying bullets wildly and might injure Louisa and Sarah Beth. The two women had to be inside the fort. They had to be. Nothing else made any sense.

Magee took no pleasure seeing how the handful of defenders rose from behind the walls and began firing methodically, not rushing, but keeping a steady curtain of lead flying outward against Kimbrell and his men. Part of the major appreciated the coolness of the defense, even as part of him hated to see the soldiers successfully repel the assault. It made his task all the more difficult now. He had seriously considered going to the fort commander under a truce flag and offering safe passage for the officer and his men in exchange for Louisa and Sarah Beth. And the men who held them prisoner.

Magee wanted to personally shoot those sons of bitches

responsible for making him do all the terrible things he had done because they had stolen away Louisa and Sarah Beth. No one kidnapped his family and dragged them across Oklahoma without paying for that heinous crime.

Kimbrell's attack faltered as the defenders found the range and took out their horses. Magee saw that the walls would have been breached had all his men participated. But the risk to Louisa and Sarah Beth was too great for that. The soldiers in the fort would be like trapped rats. Magee did not want them lashing out and harming his family. He loved them too much to ever see them harmed.

"You should never have gone from the house against my wishes," Magee said to his wife and daughter, as if they could hear over the gunfire and at this distance. "When we return, I'll put locks on all the doors and windows. You'll be safe. No one will ever kidnap you again, not while there's breath in my body."

He straightened as he watched Kimbrell and his men ride double to escape the withering fire from the fort. How the soldiers could have any ammunition left after their armory had been looted puzzled Magee, but not unduly. He knew how his men sometimes fell down in their duties. They might have looted the fort armory and left ammunition and weapons behind. Enough, as it turned out, for the handful of soldiers to defend themselves.

"A parley," Magee said to himself. "It's still possible. I can tell the commander that Kimbrell was only the leading element, the first strike, a feeler to gauge the resolve of those inside. How can he have any reserve, either in manpower or supplies? Yes, yes, a parley. Then I'll make sure Louisa and Sarah Beth are safe."

He swung back to his map and came to an abrupt halt. A blond woman stood where he had been planning his own assault on the fort. She held a six-gun trained on his midriff. For a giddy moment, Magee thought it was Sarah Beth. Then he saw it was another young woman, somewhat taller but of the same age and coloring.

"Don't move a muscle," the woman said. She held the

three-pound pistol with both hands. The six-shooter did not waver a fraction of an inch.

"Who are you?"

"I'm the woman who's got your daughter prisoner. I swear by all that's holy, I will kill her if you don't give me what I want."

"Sarah Beth? Where is she? *You* kidnapped her and my wife?"

"She's where you'll never get her. If anything happens to me, she's dead."

"You're the one I've been chasing across Indian Territory? You took my family?"

Catherine Duggan laughed harshly.

"That's a pipe dream you conjured up in your own head, Major, but I've got Sarah Beth now and that's all that matters."

"I'll give you whatever you want in return for my daughter."

"Damned right you will. Here's what you'll give me." She began telling him what she wanted.

26

"I will kill her."

The words came to Slocum's ears faint and distant. He shifted direction and made a guess where he had to go to find the speaker. He had tromped through the woods for an hour on foot to avoid Magee's men milling about, following the hoofprints of the horses from the spot where he was sure Sarah Beth and her captor had mounted. The hoofprints veered in an unexpected direction from the direction he now headed, but Slocum felt an urgency about the threat that made him abandon the trail.

He moved silently until he came upon the tableau. Catherine Duggan held a six-shooter on Magee. The major and the woman were separated by a map spread on the ground and nothing more. Slocum wanted to call out to her that she stood too close. Guns were not close-in weapons. Even belly guns were best used before the foe got too close. Such a philosophy would be lost on the woman, however. She spoke in angry, staccato bursts.

"Tell me what I want to know, or I will kill your daughter."

"Who are you?" Clayton Magee moved a little closer. The man might be a lunatic, but he still had a strong survival instinct. Or was it simply that Catherine dangled his daughter's life like a carrot on a stick in front of a mule? Slocum moved around to get a better view as he drew his six-shooter. He wasn't sure who he would shoot.

Killing Magee would end the rampage across Oklahoma, but Catherine had a wild-eyed look about her as crazy as Magee's. Either was capable of killing and hardly noticing. More than this, Slocum wanted to know just what the hell was going on. He edged closer until he came to a rotting tree limb that afforded him some cover. The two were so intent on one another that they did not notice him.

"You don't know me? You don't know *me!*"

"You're the woman with a six-gun trained on me," Magee said, his voice totally lacking in any inflection. "You claim to have my daughter. Where is she?"

"I'll tell you when I find out about my pa."

"Your pa?" Magee looked as confused as Slocum felt.

"Harrison Duggan," Catherine said. "Lieutenant Harrison Duggan. You don't remember him?"

Magee shook his head slowly.

"I swear, I will kill Sarah Beth. She will die if you don't give it all to me."

"Give what? Release my daughter, and we can talk." Magee's mood was changing again, this time becoming that of the analytical tactician who won battles. Catherine was too engrossed with her demands to notice the shift. But Slocum did. He pointed his six-shooter at the major now.

"You ruined him. At Stone River. You accused him of cowardice in the face of the enemy and court-martialed him. He was innocent!"

"I . . . I seem to remember something of that."

"Stone River. He was cut off from his men by Rebel fire."

"And his entire company was killed. If he had been with them, they would not only have lived but turned the tide of battle in our favor."

"He couldn't help it. He's innocent. You know that he is. You hid evidence of how he was too injured to command. I want it."

"I hid nothing," Magee said.

"Liar! You hated him because he was a better commander than you were. He should have been given a medal, but you gave false testimony. You *lied*. I want to hear you say it. He was an honorable man and not responsible for what happened to his company!"

"Eighty-two men died because of Lieutenant Duggan," the major said. He edged to his left. From Slocum's vantage point, he could not tell what was going on, but Catherine turned to follow him with her pistol. This blocked Slocum's view of her face and he had no way to determine how likely she was to pull the trigger.

A thousand things rushed through Slocum's head, but it was as if he was mired deep in mud and could not get free. If he shot Magee, Catherine might never tell where Sarah Beth was because she had been thwarted in proving her father was innocent of desertion charges. If he shot Catherine, he might never find Sarah Beth because the girl's hiding place would die with her, a secret. Slocum knew he might follow the hoofprints and locate Sarah Beth, but Magee's men made any protracted hunt risky.

"I've got her tied up so she'll hang herself if I don't get back soon. Tell me now, Major Magee. Tell me all the evidence you suppressed at my father's trail!"

"There was none. He was guilty."

"You wouldn't say that if he were here today!" Catherine's voice rose shrilly. She was losing control. "I'll let Sarah Beth die."

"The crime is on your head then. You're as much a coward as your father. It runs in the family."

"I'm no coward."

"He turned tail and ran. He abandoned his men because he was afraid. You've kidnapped Sarah Beth rather than face me without that bargaining lever because you're a coward, too."

Slocum saw that Catherine was reaching the point where Magee's death would be just fine with her. She could always search through the major's effects for whatever evidence she sought. If it wasn't there, she was in such a state that she could lie to herself and actually believe she had found everything to prove her pa's innocence.

No matter what, Sarah Beth had to be found quickly. Slocum doubted Catherine would ever let the girl go free, even if Clayton Magee surrendered the evidence she demanded. The chances of him having it with him were worse than drawing to an inside straight. As Slocum decided what to do, he rose from behind the felled tree limb and aimed—and heard someone behind him.

Slocum threw himself to the side, brought his Colt around, and almost fired into Isaiah Langmuir's chest.

"What the hell are you doing here?" Slocum demanded in a harsh whisper.

"Sarah Beth. I followed the tracks like you did, Slocum. There, with Magee. That's the woman who warned me of Magee and his horde. What—?"

"Shut up." Slocum pulled the captain down and hastily explained what had happened.

"She knows where Sarah Beth is? I'll make her talk!"

Slocum yanked hard on Langmuir's arm and dragged him down again.

"You're a damned fool. You abandoned your men. You left your command during battle. You can spend the next twenty years in the Detroit Federal prison for that."

"I love her!"

"I suspect Sarah Beth loves you, too, but you're going to get her killed if you barge in."

"I have to do something."

"Shut your pie hole." Slocum rolled back and peered over at Catherine and Magee. The major had edged around another two feet. Slocum saw a rifle leaning against a stump. For whatever reason, Magee was going for it. If he made a mad grab, Catherine could not miss hitting him. His lunacy must cause him to think he was invincible.

"I will not give you anything to exonerate the lieutenant. He deserved the firing squad."

"He died in disgrace. It's *you* who's a disgrace. You ride around killing hundreds of people and all because those two whores left you. They *left* you!"

"You are the one who kidnapped Louisa and Sarah Beth," Magee said. His eyes grew wide and his face became a mask of rage.

Slocum saw how the delusions were fitting together like a key into a lock and he did not like it.

"We've got to stop—" Langmuir never finished his sentence.

Magee jerked toward the rifle against the stump. Catherine swung in that direction with her pistol, but Magee was already moving the other way. From under his uniform jacket he drew a small pistol and fired four times. Slocum thought that might be as many rounds as the hideout pistol carried.

"I'll get him," Langmuir said, standing. Slocum tried to pull the man back down, but this time the captain jerked free.

"His men! The shots are bringing his men!" Slocum stayed low behind the limb, yet not only Magee but four of his henchmen spotted Langmuir.

"I'll decoy them away. Find Sarah Beth and get her back to the fort. Hurry, Slocum, I'm begging you! Save her!" With that, Langmuir aimed his six-shooter at Magee and began firing. He was seconds too late. The major had rolled back toward the stump and grabbed his rifle. He added several bullets to the air around Langmuir's head even as he was screeching for his men to rally to him and kill the assassins.

Langmuir ducked and ran toward the fort, then cut away and dived into a ditch with Magee's men hot on his trail. Slocum could not fight so many men, but considered a killing shot for the Magee. Cut off the snake's head and the whole body dies. Whether by accident or design, four of the major's men crowded too close to him for Slocum to get a clean shot. Leaving behind the human shield, Slocum slipped back the way he had come knowing he could only do what Langmuir had asked—and what he had stayed away from the fort to do.

Sarah Beth had to be somewhere near. Catherine Duggan had approached Magee on foot. Finding cover, Slocum hurried back to the point where he had chosen to follow Catherine's voice rather than her trail. More than once he had to duck and take cover however he could. The shooting had stirred up Magee's men like pouring boiling water down an anthill. They had been anxious and ready to attack before, confused at Kimbrell's actions, and a little frightened after the cannon blew up. Now they were trigger-happy and shooting at breeze-caressed shrubs.

He found the hoofprints and veered sharply, following them. They were plain enough in the burgeoning light that a blind man could see them. Rather than going to Catherine, he should have pursued Sarah Beth, but he had not known. Slocum hoped he was not too late. There had been a ring of truth in Catherine's threat that she had left Sarah Beth tied up in such a way that she would hang herself unless freed. What worried Slocum even more than Sarah Beth accidentally ending her own life was that Catherine had murdered her before confronting Clayton Magee. In her state, Catherine would have thought it fitting justice if she could have gotten the evidence exonerating her father and then told Magee where to find his dead daughter.

Slocum almost missed her. He was jogging along, watching the trail, when he heard a choked sound and a scraping noise. He spun and saw a flash of blond hair through the trees. He pushed aside shrubs and burst into a spot directly under an oak tree. Catherine had tossed a rope over the limb and then secured it to a gnarled root popping up from the base. The other end was slipped around Sarah Beth's throat. She had been standing on top of a smooth rock. But now she had slipped off the rock and was strangling slowly.

And this was what had temporarily saved her.

The scraping sound Slocum had heard was Sarah Beth's

foot going out from under her. A drop from a gallows would have killed her outright. Now he had seconds to keep her alive. He rushed to her and threw his arms around her thighs and lifted.

"Get the rope off your neck," he told her. He got only choking noises as a response. With her hands tied securely behind her back, Sarah Beth could not free herself. Since he was holding her up to take the weight off the noose, Slocum could not loosen the rope either.

He tried to get her feet back to the top of the smooth rock where she had been standing, but it was too slippery. Slocum couldn't say a word about how it had gotten that way. In her fear, Sarah Beth had pissed herself and made the rock too slick to maintain her balance.

"I'm going to lower you again."

Frantic sounds told how frightened she was of being choked again.

"Only for an instant. I have to get my knife out." He lowered her and tried to hold her upright with one arm, but the slippery rock betrayed her again. Her feet went flying. Slocum moved like a striking snake, though, got his knife from the top of his boot, and slashed furiously in the air above her head.

Sarah Beth crashed to the ground, gasping for breath and sobbing.

"You're safe now," Slocum said.

"I peed in my pants," the woman sobbed out. "I haven't done that since I was a little girl."

"Nobody will ever find out. I promise."

"You promise?"

"We have to get back to the fort."

"Not like this. Please, John, not like this!"

He cut the ropes on her wrists and let her rub the circulation back. But noises in the woods warned of Magee's men getting closer by the minute.

"We have to go, unless you want your pa to catch you."

"No!"

He took her hand and yanked her to her feet.

"Where're the horses you rode from the fort?"

"Th-there," Sarah Beth said, pointing.

"Stay here." Slocum kicked through the undergrowth, making as much noise as he could. He grabbed the rifle thrust into a saddle scabbard, then swatted the horses on the rumps and yelled as loud as he could.

"They're after us! Ride fast!"

Then he ducked back toward Sarah Beth.

"Y-you chased off our horses," she said. "How will we get back?"

"The same way I got here. On foot. They'll chase the horses for a mile or two. By the time they find we're not on them, it'll be too late. Both of us will be all safe and sound inside the fort."

Slocum hoped it would work that way because he had to rely more on luck now than skill to keep them both alive.

27

"John, help him! He'll never get away!" Sarah Beth started toward the open area leading to the Fort Supply gate. Slocum grabbed her and pulled her down to the ground where she would not be seen by the men chasing Isaiah Langmuir.

"He's decoying them away so you can get into the fort safely," Slocum said.

"I don't care. What's the use of me being safe if Isaiah is dead?"

Slocum grabbed her again to keep her from bolting and running. Langmuir was on foot and dodging frantically to keep away from Magee's gang, many of them on horseback. They worked the cavalry captain like a steer to be branded. Always, they let him start toward the gate and then cut him off. This tactic tired Langmuir since it always forced him to run farther than if he simply turned from the fort and tried to find a spot to make his stand.

From the way the captain waved his pistol around, Slocum guessed he might be out of ammunition. Slocum considered firing a few rounds at the outlaws to throw some confusion into their rank, but the distance was too great.

"Don't make his sacrifice for nothing." Slocum grabbed

her arm until he felt his fingers cutting into her reluctant flesh. He knew he bruised her and did not care. If the pain caused her to move, he had accomplished all he had set out to do.

"I won't leave him like this. Without him, my life is nothing!"

Slocum gauged distances and how mad he was getting. Using this as a goad, he turned, scooped Sarah Beth up, and tossed her over his shoulder. She kicked and screamed and he ran. Langmuir had done a good job leading the outlaws away from the fort, and that gave Slocum a chance to run along as fast as he could carrying the struggling woman until he got to the sundered gate.

Panting harshly, he dropped her to the ground. She sat heavily in the dirt, leaned back on her hands, and glared at him for perpetrating such an indignity on her.

"Get her inside," he told the soldier who had poked his head past the gate to see what was going on.

"No, no!"

"There! They're comin'! I see the pennant! It's two whole companies from Fort Gibson!" The lookout high on the wall jumped up and down in his excitement, pointing eastward.

Slocum looked into the rising sun and saw the dust before he saw the soldiers. They were saved.

"If the outlaws see the cavalry on the way, they'll let Langmuir go and hightail it," he told Sarah Beth.

She started to say something, then clamped her mouth shut. Tears ran down her cheeks.

"What's wrong? Captain Langmuir's likely to get back here at any minute."

"Papa," she said in a low, weak voice. "The cavalry will never take him alive. Can you do anything to save him, John?"

"What do you care? He would have beaten you, imprisoned you like he did your ma, maybe done even worse to you."

"He's my father. What can I say? He needs help."

Slocum held his tongue. What Clayton Magee needed

was a slug through the brain. Even that might not cure his craziness.

"Hell, I'm as loony as he is." Slocum ducked past Sarah Beth into the fort and found his paint. He swung into the saddle and trotted back to the gate. Louisa Magee stood on the porch of their temporary quarters, hand to her throat. She waved and smiled weakly as he rode out. Slocum cursed himself as a fool for giving in to Sarah Beth's request. Her father was responsible for untold deaths and the destruction of several towns. No jury on the face of the earth would ever let him go free. If it were possible to hang him repeatedly, even that sentence might not be harsh enough for Major Magee.

Slocum rode past Sarah Beth, never looking at her. He heard ragged shots from the direction of the outlaw camp, and knew the leading element of the Fort Gibson detachment had opened fire. Galloping from the fort, he cut off the road and went directly for the spot where he had last seen Magee. The area was deserted now—except for the map Magee had spread on the ground and Catherine Duggan's body.

Circling the spot, Slocum hunted for tracks, but the area was so chopped up with men and horses passing through that he could not figure which tracks were Magee's. Then he rode closer and looked down at the map. He puzzled over it for a full minute before he got his bearings. A large X had been marked off to the side of the fort. Connecting it to where Slocum studied the map itself was a dotted line.

He looked up and saw a dry streambed leading away. Magee had marked it for some reason, as he had a spot behind Fort Supply. Not having any other notion where he might find the major, Slocum rode down into the dry streambed and trotted along on the pea-sized gravel, gently curving around to a spot behind the fort.

"This is where the X was marked," he said softly. The banks on the stream had shielded him from the sight of all but the most alert sentry on the walls of the fort. With the chaos raging all around, no one would notice a single rider reaching this spot.

The spot where Slocum saw fresh hoofprints indicated that Magee—or someone—had come here within the past hour. Considering the frenetic battle, Slocum guessed whoever had come here had done so in the past few minutes. He dismounted and walked forward, now in plain view of anyone on the fort wall. From the decrease in gunfire, Slocum knew the fight was about over. Those outlaws not killed were on the run. Before the soldiers from Fort Gibson chased after them, they would consult with Captain Langmuir.

Slocum stopped dead in his tracks. The rider preceding him had dismounted and sent his horse running off, only the horse had not gone more than a few yards. Slocum saw it grazing at a clump of particularly juicy grass made tastier by the heavy rains. The horse might have thrown its rider—Slocum found boot prints going to the palisade. It didn't take more than a few seconds of searching to find where someone had dug out dirt at the base of a post so that he could squeeze into the fort.

"Magee," Slocum said. He knew where the major would be.

Slocum was either bulkier than Clayton Magee or not as driven. He lost a considerable amount of skin by wiggling between the rough-hewn posts in the palisade. Slocum got to his feet and ran straight for the quarters where Louisa had waved good-bye to him.

To his right he saw Isaiah Langmuir and a cavalry colonel talking. Not far away Sarah Beth stood, gazing lovingly at her captain.

"Louisa," Slocum said under his breath as he doubled his speed. He neared the small cabin and caught sight of Louisa Magee through the single window. She backed away, hands outstretched in front of her as if to push someone away.

Slocum took the three steps in a single bound and tried

to get the door open. It was barred on the inside. He stepped back and kicked as hard as he could. The door splintered and let him reach inside to pull free the chair blocking its opening.

He stumbled in, six-shooter drawn.

"Clayton, don't do it."

"You betrayed me. There was no kidnapper. No one kidnapped you. That woman took only Sarah Beth. She's my little girl, and she's dead because of you. You're responsible for my little girl dying. You never could do anything right."

"Clayton, she's alive. Look out on the parade ground. Sarah Beth's out there."

"You fooled around behind my back." Magee ignored Slocum and stared at his wife.

"You never let me out of the house! You kept me a prisoner!" Louisa looked at Slocum, silently pleading for him to help her.

"For your own good," Magee said, advancing. He held a knife. "I'm going to punish you, Louisa. It's for your own good. You need to learn to obey your husband."

"Magee," Slocum shouted. "Drop the knife." It was as if Clayton Magee had turned stone deaf. He kept moving toward Louisa. His world had collapsed into just one thing: vengeance on a wife he thought had betrayed him.

"Magee, stop!" Slocum rushed forward and swung his six-gun as hard as he could at the man's head. The barrel grazed Magee's temple, but the man never took notice. Slocum slammed the gun down on Magee's wrist in an attempt to make him drop the knife.

This got the major's attention. Magee snarled and grappled with Slocum, the knife still clutched in his fist.

"You! You're the one she's screwing!"

Slocum found himself pressed back with manic fury. He winced as the knife slicked along his leg, but he kept his balance. Somehow, his six-shooter came up and fired. Magee never flinched and kept fighting. A second shot. Still no effect. Slocum thought he had missed. He dropped his six-gun and grabbed Magee's wrist with both of his hands to force the blade away.

Clayton Magee suddenly went limp and collapsed to the floor. Slocum stared at him in disbelief. How could he have been so dangerous one instant and dead the next?

"You had to do it, John. You saved my life."

"And mine, too, I reckon." He rolled Magee over. Both shots had gone through the man's heart, but it had taken him a long time before his fury gave way to his death. Never had Slocum seen a man so driven by anger and madness.

He heard steps behind him. Slocum turned, ready to use his six-shooter, but saw Sarah Beth Magee in the doorway.

"You killed Papa!" the woman screamed. Before Slocum could say a word, she whirled about and ran from the room, sobbing. Slocum turned and looked at Louisa. He wasn't sure what he read on her face.

It was time for him to be moving on. He slid his six-shooter back into his holster and headed for the door.

28

"That's quite a show," Louisa Magee said. She moved a little closer to Slocum as they watched the troops marching past on the parade ground before stopping in precise ranks to face a small platform on the far side of the grounds. Two buglers dueled each other and a drummer worked even harder to drown them out. The troopers looked crisp and alert in spite of the sultry day as they went through their presentation of arms.

"It's certainly Captain Langmuir's day. He's supposed to get a medal and command of the fort," Slocum said. He also saw how Sarah Beth sat on the platform, her eyes fixed lovingly on the officer.

"It'll be Sarah Beth's, too," Louisa said. "She thinks the captain will propose to her after the ceremony."

"Congratulations," Slocum said.

"She hates you, you know."

Slocum shrugged that off. He had killed Clayton Magee because he had no other option.

"Better me killing the major than her beau doing it. I'm not sure she'd want to marry Langmuir if he had been the one coming face-to-face with . . . that problem."

"There's no need to pussyfoot around it, John. You killed that horrible son of a bitch."

Slocum looked at her. The woman had her blond hair pulled back and neatly tucked under a broad-brimmed hat. From somewhere she had found a decent dress for the ceremony.

"Why aren't you on the platform?" Slocum asked.

"Because you're here," she said, reaching over and taking his hand. She squeezed down hard on it. "I've been through too many ceremonies like this. Clayton forced me to attend too many." She turned and started toward the door leading into the small cabin. Slocum stayed put. Louisa looked at him, but did not release his hand.

"Are you sure?" he asked.

"I want to have a celebration I can appreciate," she said. "I want a celebration for us both. A celebration of life, not death." Louisa tugged harder on his hand. This time Slocum followed her inside. He kicked the door shut and blocked out only a little of the loud drums and bugles. The speeches hadn't even begun yet. From the way the colonel from Fort Gibson went on when he wasn't in front of a big audience, with a captive audience he would take more than an hour before presenting the medal to Isaiah Langmuir. How long the captain would speak was something of a mystery to Slocum.

What wasn't a mystery was how Louisa had gone to the bedroom door and turned, framed by the light behind her. In silhouette, she began to slowly undress for Slocum. She shimmied and the dress slithered down her body, giving Slocum a view of her flaring hips, trim waist, and shapely legs. When she turned sideways, he saw her breasts in profile. Continuing with her striptease, she stepped out of the undergarments and turned back to him, arms outstretched.

"This is the prettiest sight I have ever seen."

"No lies, John. Just make love to me."

"No lies," he said. "You're beautiful." And she was. If Sarah Beth matured into a woman half this appealing,

Langmuir was a lucky man. Slocum went to Louisa and put his hands around the small of her back.

She trembled at his touch. He pulled her closer and felt her breasts crush against his chest. Even through his coat, vest, and shirt, he felt the hard points of her nipples growing even harder with lust. Moving his hands lower, he cupped her firm buttocks. Then he kissed her.

It started as friendly, then got serious. Passion began building in him until he could not control himself. His lips crushed hers and then moved around to nibble and lick at her earlobe. She moaned softly, then gasped as he worked even lower to the hollow of her neck—and lower.

His tongue lavished broad, slow licks across her breasts. He paid special attention to the woman's nips, sucking and kissing and licking until Louisa began to swoon.

"I'm on fire inside, John. I want more."

"More like this?" He dropped to his knees and pressed his face into the woman's fragrant bush. His tongue snaked out and found the rim of her heated center. Around and around he raced until those nether lips trembled. Then he thrust his tongue hard into her.

Louisa staggered back and collapsed onto the bed. She propped herself up on her hands and lifted her feet to the bed, wantonly opening herself to him.

"I want more than your tongue in me. You know what I mean, too."

Slocum shucked out of his coat and vest. He pulled his shirt off over his head and stood bare-chested. Louisa watched his every move. He dropped his gun belt to the floor and then worked to unbutton his jeans. He found that he wasn't working fast enough for her. Louisa sat up and surged forward, grabbing hold and pulling him forward.

It was his turn to gasp with pleasure as she applied her mouth and sucked and kissed. Still, she stopped after a few ecstatic seconds.

Louisa leaned back on the bed again, this time reaching down between her legs.

"Here, John. I want you here."

He did not need to be told twice. His hardness brushed along her nether lips and found the dampness welling out from her heated core. He positioned himself and then moved forward inexorably. She cried out. He stopped, thinking he must be hurting her.

"So good, so good," she gasped out. "Don't stop now, damn you, make me forget. Take me away from all this."

He continued slipping into her tightness until she surrounded him totally. He began a slow rotation while entirely within her. This produced a loud gasp. He felt her tighten even more around him. He wanted to stay like this forever, looking down into her desire-racked face, seeing her tits bob about, feeling her tense and relax around him. It should last forever. But the pressure deep within his loins began to build, warning him of what was to come.

Slocum started thrusting with short, quick strokes that burned them both with erotic friction. He reached around her and grabbed her rump again, this time pulling her up off the bed so he could enter her at new and excitingly different angles. When she began thrashing about, he shoved his hips forward, trying to bury himself completely within her. She cried out as he spilled his seed.

He sank down on top of her, kissed her, and rolled to one side. Louisa turned to circle his leg with both of hers. She rubbed her crotch against him like a cat stropping up against a chair leg. Clinging tightly to him, she simply lay with her cheek pressed into his bare chest.

"How long do you think the speechifying will go on?" Slocum asked.

"Uh? Oh, a while. Why?"

"We've got time."

"For what?" she asked.

He showed her.

"We will track down those outlaws who escaped capture," Captain Langmuir said, "and bring them to justice. There will no longer be such lawlessness in Indian Territory."

Slocum thought the captain's speech was more for the

benefit of Les Vannover, sitting at the far end of the platform, than for the soldiers. Most of the troopers would
return to Fort Gibson now that the danger from Clayton
Magee was past. It would take a month or longer for Fort
Supply to get back to full complement and possibly longer,
depending on those horse soldiers' training, to get out in
the field. By then, any of Magee's men that had escaped
would be long gone.

Slocum looked over his shoulder in the direction of the
cabin where Louisa still lay in bed asleep. He had crept
out like a thief in the night, not wanting to wake her. Or
was that the reason? Trying to figure out such things was
too hard for him.

The captain had his medal. Sarah Beth had her man. Marshal Vannover was recovering and would return to Charity a
more respected man, if not a hero in his own right. Slocum
went to the stable and saddled his paint. He had a promise to
keep, and time was nigh for him to get on with it.

29

Gunfire drew Slocum because it was not a single discharge
but a steady staccato burst from a Gatling gun. For three
days he had tracked the wagon carrying the stolen weapon,
and for the past few hours Slocum figured he was not
the only one on the trail. Not more than three other horses
had crossed the track and then begun following. He
worried that the outlaws might be re-forming, but the gunfire told him that was not the case.

He rode down the center of the meandering valley, heading in the direction of the skirmish. Before he saw the main
battlefield, he caught sight of a blue-uniformed soldier with
a carbine hunkered down behind a tree, intent on someone
ahead.

The dead horse some distance away showed that this
trooper had ridden into a hail of bullets from the Gatling
gun and was lucky to be alive. From the way he fired, he
was no green soldier out on his first patrol. He sighted carefully and squeezed off each round. There was no hint of
rush to his reply. Slocum hoped the others riding with this
soldier were as experienced in combat.

He rode away from the soldier, slowly working his way
forward until he came to a clearing where he got a better

look at the fight. Albert Kimbrell stood in the wagon, turning the crank on the Gatling gun, while two of his cronies worked to remove and replace empty magazines. A third outlaw sat cross-legged in the wagon, frantically loading more magazines from boxes of cartridges. The wagon had been parked in a secure spot, partly protected from attack by low rocks. Being high enough to shoot over the boulders gave Kimbrell an advantage against only three soldiers.

Two of the soldiers were still mounted, further reducing the chance that Kimbrell's position would be taken by a full assault.

Slocum drew his rifle and dismounted. He made certain his paint was out of the line of fire, then began climbing an oak tree with sturdy limbs. Up and up he went until he got to within ten feet of the top. Slocum edged out on a limb and found a tunnel through the leaves for a good shot. He levered a round into the chamber and rested his rifle on the palm of his hand.

The gunfire went on, with the Gatling gun no longer spewing forth as much lead. Slocum watched closely, and decided the owlhoot loading the magazines was falling behind. There was a way to make him fall even further behind.

Finger coming back just as he exhaled, Slocum sent a slug flying the two hundred yards to its target. He had hoped for a killing shot. The man had moved after Slocum fired. The bullet caught him in the arm, causing him to send a box of cartridges skittering around the wagon bed. This caused enough confusion among the outlaws that they stopped firing.

Slocum saw the three soldiers advance, carefully picking their new posts and not risking getting shot. With a little more help, the trio of soldiers might capture Kimbrell and his men.

A second shot found its mark. The outlaw with the empty magazines tumbled over the side of the wagon, taking at least one of the partially loaded columns of bullets with him. Slocum could not hear what Kimbrell said, but he knew how angry the man became.

The Gatling gun opened up on him. Splinters and sap flew from the oak limbs all around. Shredded leaves blew about like a green hailstorm. And then there was nothing more. Slocum wiped sap from his face and smiled.

The Gatling had to be empty now. Kimbrell cranked furiously, but nothing happened. He shoved another of the outlaws, who jumped to the ground and fetched a rifle.

Slocum tried to take out the man on the ground, but the angle was wrong and the rocks got in the way. He saw his bullet kick up a dusty patch along the top of one stone and then go sailing off harmlessly.

This gave the three soldiers the chance to advance again. They moved systematically, firing as they went. Another of Kimbrell's men bit the dust.

Seeing his small gang being reduced, Kimbrell shoved the remaining two forward and barked orders. Slocum could not hear what Kimbrell said, but he guessed. "Don't let them get any closer. Kill them!"

Kimbrell jumped over the side of the wagon and headed into a wooded area. Before he saw Kimbrell come riding out, Slocum was already climbing down from the oak tree. He knew there was a chase ahead of him—and then he would face a cornered rat. For Slocum, that was just fine.

He mounted and kept out of sight of the three soldiers, now closing in on the remaining two outlaws. When he brought down Albert Kimbrell, he would have to return and search the outlaws. Nickson's ring couldn't be lost, not after all he had been through. But if it was, Slocum was determined to take as much satisfaction from running Kimbrell to ground as possible.

He knew the three soldiers were more than capable of capturing or killing the remaining two outlaws. This knowledge gave him added speed going after Kimbrell. His horse had been walking all day. There was no telling what condition Kimbrell's was in. After five minutes of hard pursuit, Slocum saw that the outlaw was flagging. As he rode, Slocum touched the ebony handle of his Colt Navy. It was going to be used soon because he wanted to get close enough to see Kimbrell's face when he shot him down.

Catherine Duggan might have been as crazy as Magee, but she had not deserved what Kimbrell and his henchmen did to her.

Slocum narrowed the gap between them slowly, inexorably. Kimbrell knew he had a pursuer and began firing wildly behind him. Slocum wove from side to side, forcing Kimbrell to fire left-handed at times and at other times to turn almost entirely around in the saddle. With so many six-shooters stuffed in holsters and his belt, it took almost a mile and a half of chase before the outlaw ran out of ammo.

Only when he was sure Kimbrell was in sore need for a loaded six-gun did Slocum close the gap between them. By now, Kimbrell's horse had faltered. Every move he made to attempt to veer away failed, and Slocum finally rode not ten feet away. Reaching down, Slocum got his lariat. He had worked cattle for years and knew how sneaky a calf at branding could be. He spun the rope over his head, getting the loop wider and wider. When he tossed, yanked, and dragged Kimbrell off his horse, it was almost too easy.

The outlaw hit the ground hard and tried to roll. Slocum's paint dug in its heels, kicking up a cloud of choking dust, then began backing when Slocum looped the rope around the saddle horn. He jumped to the ground, pistol out.

"Stop putting up such a fuss," Slocum said. "I've got you."

"Like hell you do!" Although his arms were pinned to his side, Kimbrell came up with a six-shooter in his hand. Slocum fired the instant before Kimbrell. The outlaw jerked and then fell onto his side, dead.

"At least you didn't make me shoot again, like Magee did." Slocum warily approached and kicked the six-gun from Kimbrell's dead hand. Somewhere during the chase, Slocum had miscounted the guns and shots fired at him. Or maybe Kimbrell had a seventh gun hidden away. It no longer mattered. The man who had taken part in fierce, bloody pointless murder had gone to meet his Maker, compliments of John Slocum.

"Let's see what you got on you." Slocum loosened the rope and rolled Kimbrell onto his back. The outlaw had a wad of greenbacks large enough to choke a cow in one pocket and a pocketful of twenty-dollar gold pieces. "You won't need these anymore," Slocum said, transferring the money to his own pockets. It was little enough pay for all he had gone through.

He kept searching, then caught his breath when he felt the outline of the severed finger and ring in the outlaw's vest pocket.

"Don't reckon there's any question whose ring this is," Slocum said, holding ring and finger in the palm of his hand. He had found what he had sought for so long. Now he had to complete his promise to Jerome Nickson.

30

Slocum wiped sweat from his forehead. It had been a long ride down the Arkansas River. Finding Patrick Nickson had not been easy, but Slocum had not expected it to be. An unpaid debt in one town, a saloon keeper who remembered the name, a roustabout who had worked with Nickson, those were the clues Slocum followed almost to Fort Smith, Arkansas.

The younger Nickson had tried his hand at gambling in more than one place and had not been very good. His skills seemed to be working the barges that made their way up and down the Arkansas River all the way to the Mississippi. Other than this, Slocum did not get a good impression of the young man. He was a mean drunk and inclined to fight at the drop of a hat—any hat. He had even been run out of a town near Webber's Falls for public fighting, something Slocum had seldom heard of happening. A marshal would toss a drunk into jail for the night or perhaps levy a fine. It took a powerful lot of public sentiment to be banished from a frontier town.

The town of Braden didn't appear to be as fussy about its citizens. As Slocum rode down the main street, he saw

244

two fights and what might have been a robbery at knife-point. Nobody but him took any notice. He found himself a quiet saloon and went inside. The trail had been long, hot, and uncharacteristically dusty. After weeks of rain, the Oklahoma skies had turned blue and cloudless, letting the merciless sun hammer at him as he rode. Even a small shower would have taken the edge off the heat.

"Beer," he said. He had the money to pay for whiskey or even brandy, but a cool beer to quench his thirst seemed like the medicine he needed most.

"You lookin' fer work?" asked the barkeep.

"Passing through."

"Where to?"

Slocum sipped at the beer. It was better than it had any right to be.

"Looking for a friend."

This caused the bartender to tense a mite. Men looking for other men usually meant to kill them. Unless there was a reward attached to the information, people could lose their tongues mighty fast. Slocum explained before the barkeep walked off.

"Got an inheritance for a friend's son. He was killed out west."

"Them town killers? Heard 'bout that. Hell, the newspapers're still full of stories, and it's been weeks since the last of 'em was kilt."

"Three weeks," Slocum said. "It's been three weeks. I was there at Fort Supply."

"Yup, that's where they kilt the last of them varmints. They really ride into a town and kill everyone?"

"Like the Jayhawkers," Slocum said. He added, "And Quantrill's Raiders."

"Damned soldiers took their time stoppin' 'em, from what I read."

"You know Patrick Nickson? He's the one I'm looking for."

"Nickson? Hell, yeah, ever'one knows that son of a bitch. You mean to kill him?"

"Nope, like I said, I've got a package for him from his pa. That's all."

"Too damn bad. He works as a roustabout down on the docks. Chances are you kin find him there 'bout now. A boat's just come up from the Mississippi."

"Thanks," Slocum said, then drained the rest of his beer. Patrick Nickson not being liked by very many people had finally paid off. He was remembered, when a more likable sort probably would not have been.

Slocum rode down to the docks. As the barkeep had said, a flat-bottomed barge was moored to the docks. Men, both black and white, stripped to the waist, worked to unload the cargo. Slocum left his horse at the foot of the dock and walked out, only to be stopped by a florid man with a gut hanging out over the top of his belt.

"Where you goin'?"

"To talk to Patrick Nickson. You the boss?"

"Nobody talks to any of my men without my say-so."

"Then say so since my business with him won't take five minutes."

"You fixin' to kill him? You wait till the end of his shift. It's damn hard to find workmen."

"I'm not going to kill him. I'm not even going to hit him."

"Too bad," the foreman said with some distaste. "You don't keep him from his work longer 'n five minutes, hear?"

Slocum nodded. He was aware of the man watching him like a hawk as he went to the end of the dock where the bales slowly became a mountain.

"Nickson!" he called. One man jerked around, fists balled and ready to fight. "You Patrick Nickson?"

"Yeah, what of it? I don't know you."

"I was a friend of your father's," Slocum explained.

"Do tell. I'm not payin' his debts neither."

"No debts, but he is dead. He was killed at Cherokee Springs. You hear of the Magee gang and what they did?"

"Ever'one's talkin' about it. My pa got himself killed there?"

"He didn't have much to give you, but he did ask me to give you this."

Patrick Nickson's face softened.

"I never expected to get nuthin' from him. He's really dead?"

"Here," Slocum said, handing Jerome Nickson's son a small wooden box he had picked up to carry the ring.

"Not much, is it?"

"It meant a lot to him," Slocum said, "and he wanted you to have it."

Nickson eagerly opened the box and stared at the West Point ring. He took it out and held it up to the light to get a better look.

"This is it? He wanted me to have his damned ring?" Nickson turned and heaved the ring as hard as he could into the roiling Arkansas River. Slocum couldn't even see where it splashed into the turbulent water. "He always was a cheap son of a bitch." Nickson thrust out his chin belligerently and said, "What you want? A reward?"

Slocum's hand twitched. He could draw and fire before Patrick Nickson could blink.

"No, there's nothing I want." Slocum stepped away, turned, and left. Nickson's foreman bellowed at the young man to get back to work.

Slocum mounted his horse and rode west from Braden until he came to a fork in the road. The right-hand road went back up through the center of Oklahoma, and eventually would lead to Fort Supply and Louisa Magee. By now she would be settled in quarters and Sarah Beth would be married to Isaiah Langmuir. Was Louisa lonely for the man who had killed her husband? Could be. Her send-off had been pretty fine. The left fork angled away down toward Texas, where Slocum had been headed when he rode into Cherokee Springs and made the promise to a dying Jerome Nickson.

Slocum pushed his hat back and studied each road,

considering what lay at the end of each. He pulled his hat back down low on his forehead and picked a road, wondering if he would regret the decision. He doubted it as he rode on.

DON'T MISS A YEAR OF

Slocum Giant
by
Jake Logan

penguin.com

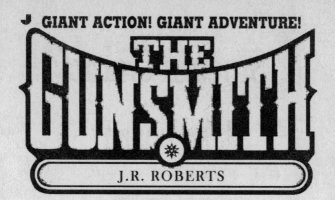

GIANT ACTION! GIANT ADVENTURE!

THE GUNSMITH

J.R. ROBERTS

M228AS0608

LONGARM

GIANT-SIZED ADVENTURE FROM
AVENGING ANGEL LONGARM.

BY TABOR EVANS

2006 Giant Edition:
LONGARM AND THE
OUTLAW EMPRESS

2007 Giant Edition:
LONGARM AND THE
GOLDEN EAGLE SHOOT-OUT

2008 Giant Edition:
LONGARM AND THE
VALLEY OF SKULLS

penguin.com

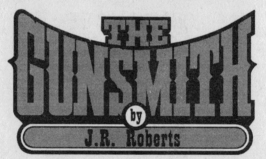